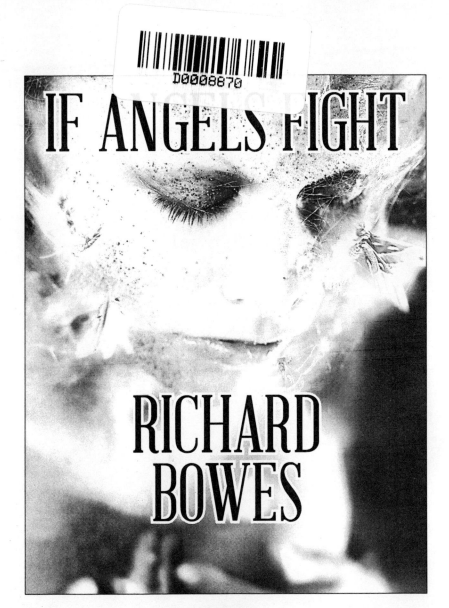

IF ANGELS FIGHT

RICHARD BOWES

FAIRWOOD PRESS
Bonney Lake, WA

IF ANGELS FIGHT

A Fairwood Press Book
October 2013
Copyright © 2013 Richard Bowes

Fairwood Press
21528 104th Street Court East
Bonney Lake, WA 98391
www.fairwoodpress.com

Cover design by
KRISTINE DIKEMAN

Book design by
Patrick Swenson

ISBN: 978-1-933846-40-8
First Fairwood Press Edition: October 2013
Printed in the United States of America

To Paulette and Dennis For So Many Reasons

*My Thanks to the One and Only Kris Dikeman
and also to Patrick Swenson*

CONTENTS

My city is my subject. It's the only place I've ever wanted to live. If I'm somewhere else I think of this place every day. Jeff Ford said New York was like a character in a lot of my stories and that seems right. Several of these stories, "On Death and the Deuce," "There's a Hole in the City," "The Ferryman's Wife," "The Mask of the Rex," were adapted into chapters in my novels. What you read here is each story as it originally appeared.

Part One:
THE STREETS OF NEW YORK

I hadn't written short fiction since I was in college in the early '60s. But in the summer of '89 I started writing spec fiction short stories. "On Death and the Deuce" was the fifth story I wrote and the third one I sold. However it was the first to appear in print (F&SF, May 1992). It was included in a couple of "Best Of" anthologies and reprinted years later in the 'zine, Sybil's Garage *(March, 2007).*

The narrator is Kevin Grierson and over the next five or six years I wrote and published nine more "Kevin Grierson" stories, all but two of them for F&SF. *One novelette, "Streetcar Dreams," won a World Fantasy Award and is included in a couple of my earlier collections. All ten of them became my novel* Minions of the Moon, *which won the Lambda Award and was nominated for the International Horror Guild and the Dublin Impac awards.*

The location for this story is New York City but it's the hard and damaged city of 1974 when I (like Kevin Grierson) was thirty. The dream of being murdered by a doppelganger is one I had. The therapist Leo Dunn is strongly based on Vincent Tracy, who helped me break my drug and drink addictions that year. I wasn't as tough or desperate as Kevin Grierson. But I was, I assure you, every bit as stupid.

ON DEATH AND THE DUCE

In the last days that the Irish ran Hell's Kitchen I lived in that tenement neighborhood between the West Side docks and Times Square. An old lady of no charm whatsoever named McCready and called Mother rented furnished studios in an underheated fleabag on Tenth Avenue. Payment was cash only, by the week or month with anonymity guaranteed whether it was desired or not.

Looking out my window on a February morning, I spotted my Silent Partner heading south toward Forty-Second Street. He was already past me, so it was the clothes that caught my attention first. The camel hair overcoat had been mine. The dark gray pants were from the last good suit I had owned. That morning, I'd awakened from a drinking dream and was still savoring the warm, safe feeling that came with realizing it was all a nightmare and that I was sober. The sight of that figure three floors down filled my mouth with the remembered taste of booze. I tried to spit, but was too dry.

Hustlers called Forty-Second the Deuce. My Silent Partner turned on that corner and I willed him not to notice me. Just before heading east, he looked directly at my window. He wore shades but his face was the one I feared seeing most. It was mine. Seeing that made me too jumpy to stay in the twelve-by-fifteen foot room. Reaching behind the bed, I found the place where the wall and floor didn't join. Inside was my worldly fortune: a slim .25 caliber Beretta and beside it a wad of bills. Extracting six twenties, I stuck the rest in my boots, put on a thick sweater and leather jacket, and went out.

At that hour, nothing much was cooking in Hell's Kitchen. Two junkies went by, bent double by the wind off the Hudson.

Up the block, a super tossed away the belongings of a drag queen who the week before had gotten cut into bite-size chunks. My Silent Partner was not the kind to go for a casual walk in this weather.

Looking the way he had come, I saw the Club 596 sitting like a bunker at the corner of Forty-Third. The iron grating on the front was ajar but no lights were on inside. As I watched, a guy in a postman's uniform squeezed out the door and hurried away. I knew that inside the 596, the Westies, last of the Mick gangs—short, crazed and violent—sat in the dark dispensing favors, collecting debts. I also knew what my Silent Partner had been up to.

But I went to breakfast, put the incident to the back of my mind and prepared for my daily session. The rest of my time was a wasteland, but my late afternoons were taken up with Leo Dunn.

He lived in a big apartment house over in the East Sixties. The outside of his building gleamed white. The lobby was polished marble. Upstairs in his apartment, sunlight poured through windows curtained in gold and hit a glass table covered with pieces of silver and crystal. "Kevin, my friend." Mr. Dunn, tall and white-haired came forward smiling and shook my hand. "How are you? Every time I see you come through this door it gives me the greatest pleasure."

I sat down on the couch and he sat across the coffee table from me. The first thing I thought to say was, "I had a drinking dream last night. The crowd watched like it was an Olympic event as I poured myself a shot and drank it. Then I realized what I'd done and felt like dirt. I woke up and it was as if a rock had been taken off my head."

Amused, Dunn nodded his understanding. But dreams were of no great interest to him. So, after pausing to be sure I was through, he drew a breath and was off. "Kevin, you have made the greatest commitment of your life. You stood up and said, 'Guilty as charged. I am a drunk.'"

Mr. Dunn's treatment for alcoholics was a talking cure: he talked and I listened. He didn't just talk: he harangued, he argued like a lawyer, he gave sermons of fire. Gesturing to a closet door, he told me, "That is the record room where we store the evidence of our mistakes. Any booze hound has tales of people he trusted who screwed him over. But has there ever been anyone you knew that used you as badly and that you went back to as often as you have to booze?"

We had been over this material a hundred times in the last couple of weeks. "You're a bright boy, Kevin, and I wouldn't repeat myself if I hadn't learned that it was necessary. We go back to the record room." Again, he pointed to the door. "We look for evidence of our stupidity."

For ten years my habit and I had traveled from booze through the drug spectrum and back to booze. Then one morning on the apex of a bender, that fine moment when mortality is left behind and the shakes haven't started, I found myself standing at a bar reading a New York Post article. It was about some guy called Dunn who treated drunks.

The crash that followed was gruesome. Three days later, I came to, empty, sweat-soaked and terrified, in a room I didn't remember renting. At first, it seemed that all I owned was the clothes I had been wearing. Gradually, in jacket and jean pockets, stuck in a boot, I discovered the vaguely familiar pistol, the thick roll of bills, and a page torn from the Post. The choice that I saw was clear: either shoot myself or make a call.

My newly sober brain was blank and soft. Mr. Dunn remolded it relentlessly. On the afternoon I am describing he saw my attention wander, clicked a couple of ashtrays together on the table, picked up the gold lighter, and ignited a cigarette with a flourish. "How are you doing, Kevin?"

"OK," I told him. "Before I forget," I said and placed five of the twenties from my stash on the table.

He put them in his pocket without counting and said, "Thank you, Kevin." But when he looked up at me, an old man with pale skin and very blue eyes, he wasn't smiling. "Any news on a job?" He had never questioned me closely, but I knew that my money bothered Mr. Dunn.

Behind him, the light faded over Madison Avenue. "Not yet," I said. "The thing is, I don't need much to get by. Where I'm living is real cheap." At a hundred a week, Leo Dunn was my main expense. He was also what kept me alive. I recognized him as a real lucky kind of habit.

He went back to a familiar theme. "Kevin," he said, looking at the smoke from his cigarette. "For years, your addiction was your Silent Partner. When you decided to stop drinking, that was very bad news for him. He's twisted and corrupt. But he wants to live as much as you do."

Dunn said, "Your Silent Partner had the best racket in the world, skimming off an increasing share of your life, your happiness. He is not just going to give up and go away. He will try treachery, intimidation, flattery to get you back in harness."

He paused for a moment and I said, "I saw him today, across the street. He saw me too. He was wearing clothes that used to belong to me."

"What did he look like, Kevin?" I guess nothing a drunk could say would ever surprise Mr. Dunn.

"Just like me. But at the end of a three week bender."

"What was he doing when you saw him?" This was asked very softly.

"Coming from a mob bar up the street, the 596 Club. He was trying to borrow money from guys who will whack you just because that's how they feel at the moment."

"Kevin," said Mr. Dunn. "Booze is a vicious, mind-altering substance. It gets us at its mercy by poisoning our minds, making us unable to distinguish between what is real and what isn't. Are you saying that you had to borrow money?"

I shook my head. Very carefully he asked, "Do you mean you remembered some aspect of your drinking self?"

"Something like that," I said. But what I felt was a double loss. Not only had my Silent Partner discovered where I lived, but Mr. Dunn didn't believe what I said. My Partner had broken the perfect rapport between us.

At that point, the lobby called to announce the next client. As Leo Dunn showed me to the door, his eyes searched mine. He wasn't smiling. "Kevin, you've done more than I would have thought possible when you first walked in here. But there's what they call a dry drunk, someone who has managed to stop drinking but has not reached the state beyond that. I don't detect involvement in life from you or any real elation. I respect you too much to want to see you as just a dry drunk."

The next client was dressed like a stockbroker. He avoided looking at my street clothes and face. "Leo," he said, a little too loudly and too sincerely, "I'm glad to see you."

And Dunn, having just directed a two hour lecture at me, smiled and was ready to go again.

Outside, it was already dark. On my way across town, I went through Times Square and walked down to the Deuce. It was rush hour. Spanish hustlers in maroon pants, hands jammed in jacket pockets, black hookers in leather mini skirts, stood on corners, all too stoned to know they were freezing to death. Around them, commuters poured down subway stairs and fled for Queens.

Passing the Victoria Hotel, I glanced in at the desk clerk sitting behind bullet-proof glass. I had lived at the Victoria before my final bender. It was where those clothes the Silent Partner was wearing had been abandoned. Without trying to remember all the details, I sensed that it wasn't wise to go inside and inquire about my property.

Back on my block, I looked up at my bleak little window, dark and unwelcoming. Mother's was no place to spend an evening. Turning away, I started walking again, probably ate dinner somewhere maybe saw a movie. Without booze, I couldn't connect with anyone. Mostly, I walked, watched crowds stream out of the Broadway theaters. *A Little Night Music* was playing and *A Moon for the Misbegotten*. Then those rich tourists and nice couples from Westchester hurried into cabs and restaurants and left the streets quite empty.

In Arcade Parade on Broadway, goggle-eyed suit-and-tie johns watched the asses on kids bent over the pinball machines. Down the way, a marquee announced the double bill of COLLEGE-BOUND-BABES and BOUND-TO-PLEASE-GIRLS. Around a corner, a tall guy with a smile like a knife gash chanted, "Got what you need," like a litany.

Glancing up, I realized we were in front of Sanctuary. Built to be a Methodist church, it had gotten famous in the late '60s as a disco. In those days, a huge day-glow Satan had loomed above the former altar, limos idled in front, a team of gorillas worked the door.

Now it was dim and dying, a trap for a particular kind of tourist. Inside, Satan flaked off the wall, figures stood in the twilight willing to sell whatever you wanted. I could remember in a hazy way spending my last money there to buy the Beretta. My trajectory on that final drunk, the arc that connected the pistol, the money, the absence of my Silent Partner, wasn't buried all that deeply inside me. I just didn't want to look.

At some point that night, the rhythm of the street, the cold logic of the Manhattan grid, took me way West past the live sex shows and into the heart of the Kitchen. On long dirty blocks of tenements, I went past small Mick bars with tiny front windows where lines of drinkers sat like marines and guys in back booths gossiped idly about last week's whack.

I walked until my hands and feet were numb and I found my-self over on Death Avenue. That's what the Irish of the Kitchen once called Eleventh because of the train tracks that ran there and killed so many of them. Now the trains were gone, the ships whose freight they hauled were gone, the Irish themselves were fast disappearing. Though not born in the Kitchen I identified with them a lot.

On Death, in a block of darkened warehouses, sat the Emerald Green Tavern. It was on a Saturday morning in the dead of night at the Emerald Green that I had found myself in a moment of utter clarity with a pistol and pocket full of money reading a newspaper article about Leo Dunn. I stood for a while remembering that. Then maybe the cold got to me and I went home. My memory there is vague.

What I will never forget is the sight of a ship outlined in green and red lights. I was staring at it and I was intensely cold. Gradually, I realized I was huddled against a pillar of the raised highway near the Hudson piers. One of the last of the cruise ships was docked there and I thought how good it would be to have the money to sail down to the warm weather.

In fact, it would have been good to have any money at all. My worldly wealth was on me, suede boots and no socks, an overcoat and suit and no underwear. In one pocket was a penny, a dime and a quarter—my wealth. In another was a set of standard keys and the gravity knife I'd had since college.

Then I knew why I had stolen the keys and where I was going to get money. And I recognized the state I was in, the brief, brilliant period of clarity at the end of a bender. My past was a wreck, my future held a terrifying crash. With nothing behind me and nothing to live for, I knew no fear and was a god.

With all mortal uncertainty and weakness gone, I was pure spirit as I headed down familiar streets. A block east of Death and north of the Deuce, I looked up at a lighted window on the third floor. I crossed the street, my overcoat open, oblivious to the cold.

Security at Mother's was based on there being nothing in the building worth taking. Drawing out the keys, I turned the street door lock on my third try and went up the stairs, silently, swiftly. Ancient smells of boiled cabbages and fish, of damp carpet and cigarette smoke and piss, a hundred years of poverty, wafted around me. This was the kind of place where a loser lived, a fool came to rest. Contempt filled me.

Light shone under his door. Finding a key the right shape, I transferred it to my left hand, drew out the knife with my right.

The key went in without a sound. I held my breath and turned it. The lock clicked, the door swung into the miserable room with a bed, a TV on without the sound, a two-burner stove, a table. An all too familiar figure dozed in the only chair shoes off, pants unbuttoned. Sobriety had made him stupid. Not even the opening of the door roused him. The click of the knife in my hand did that.

The eyes focused then widened as the dumb face I had seen in ten thousand morning mirrors registered shock. "I got a little debt I want to collect," I said and moved for him. Rage swept me, a feeling that I had been robbed of everything: my body, my life. "You took that goddamn money. It's mine. My plan. My guts. You couldn't have pulled that scam in a thousand years."

For an instant, the miserable straight-head in front of me froze in horror. Then shoulder muscles tensed, feet shot out as he tried to roll to the side and go for the .25. But he was slow. My knife slashed and the fool put out his hands.

Oh, the terror in those eyes when he saw the blood on his palms and wrists. He fell back, tripping over the chair. The blade went for the stomach, cutting through cloth and into flesh.

Eyes wide, his head hit the wall. The knife in my hand slashed his throat. The light in the eyes went out. The last thing I saw in them was a reflection of his humiliation at dying like that, pants fallen down, jockey shorts filling with dark, red blood. His breath suddenly choked, became a drowning sound. An outstretched hand pointed to the loose board and the money.

"I was just cut down," I told Dunn the next day. "It wasn't even a fight. I left that knife behind when I had to move and the fucking Silent Partner had it and just cut me down." It was hard to get my throat to work.

"It was a dream, Kevin, a drinking dream like the one you told me yesterday. It has no power over your conscious mind. You came home and fell asleep sitting up. Then you had a nightmare. You say you fell off your chair and woke up on the floor. The rest was just a dream."

My eyes burned. "The expression my Silent Partner had on his face is the one I used to see sometimes in the mirror. Moments when it was so far gone I could do anything."

"Nothing else has reached you like this, Kevin."

"Sorry. I couldn't sleep."

"Don't be sorry. This is part of the process. I don't know why, but this has to happen for the treatment to work. I've had detective sergeants bawl like babies, marines laugh until they cried. Until this, you haven't let anything faze you. Our stupid drinker's pride can take many forms."

"I won't be able to sleep as long as I know he's out there."

"Understand, Kevin, that I'm not a psychiatrist. I was educated by the Jesuits a long time ago. Dreams or how you feel about your mother don't mean much to me. But I hear myself say that and spot my own stupid pride at work. If dreams are what you bring me, I'll use them." He paused and I blew my nose. "What does your Silent Partner want, Kevin? You saw through his eyes in your dream."

"He wants to disembowel me!"

"The knife, even the murder, were the means, Kevin. Not the motive. What was he looking for?"

"My money. He knew where I had it."

"You keep money in your room? You don't have a job. But you pay me regularly in fairly crisp twenties and hundreds. It's stolen money, isn't it, Kevin?"

"I guess so. I don't remember."

"Earlier you mentioned that in the dream you went for a gun. Do you own a gun? Is there blood on the money, Kevin? Did you hurt anyone? Do you know?"

"The gun hasn't been fired."

"I assume it's not registered, probably stolen. Get rid of it. Can you return the money?"

"I don't even know who it belonged to."

"You told me that he was in a calm eye when he came after you. That was his opportunity. You described having that same kind of clarity when you decided to leave him. You had the money with you then?"

"The gun too."

"Kevin, let's say that some people's Silent Partners are more real than others. Then, let's say that in a moment of clarity you managed to give yours the slip and walked off with the money the two of you had stolen. Without him holding you back, you succeeded in reaching out for help. The money is the link. It's what still connects you to your drinking past. I don't want any of that money and neither do you. Get rid of it."

"You mean throw it away?"

"The other day you said your Silent Partner was borrowing from the West Side mob. If he's real enough to need money that badly, let him have it. No one, myself above all, ever loses his Silent Partner entirely. But this should give you both some peace."

"What'll I do for money? I won't be able to pay you."

"Do you think after all this time, I don't know which ones aren't going to pay me?" I watched his hands rearrange the crystal ashtrays, the gold lighter, as he said, "Let's look in the Record room where we will find that booze is a vicious mind-altering substance. And we have to be aware at every moment of its schemes." I raised my eyes. Framed in the light from the windows, Dunn smiled at me and said, "Keep just enough to live on for a couple of weeks until you find work. Which you will."

Afterwards, in my room, I took out the pistol and the money, put two hundred back in the wall and placed the rest in a jacket pocket. The Beretta I carefully stuck under my belt at the small of my back. Then I went out.

At first, I walked aimlessly around the Kitchen. My Silent Partner had threatened me. It seemed my choices were to give up the money or to keep the money and give up Mr. Dunn. The first I thought of as surrender, the second meant I'd be back on the booze and drugs. Then a third choice took shape. Payback. I would do to him just what he had tried to do to me.

Searching for him, I followed what I remembered of our route on the last night of our partnership. It had begun at Sanctuary. Passing by, I saw that the disco was no longer dying. It was dead. The doors were padlocked. On the former church steps, a black guy slept with his head on his knees. No sign of my Silent Partner.

But I finally recalled what had happened there. Sanctuary was a hunting ground. Tourists were the game. That last night, I had run into four fraternity assholes in town with seven grand for a midwinter drug buy. Almost dead broke, I talked big about my connections. Before we left together, I bought the Beretta.

Following my trail, I walked by the Victoria. That's where I had taken them first. "Five guys showing up will not be cool," I said and persuaded two of them to wait in my dismal room. "As collateral, you hold everything I own." That amounted to little more than some clothes and a few keepsakes like the knife. With the other two, I left the hotel that last time knowing I wouldn't be back. I recognized my Silent Partner's touch. He had been with me at that point.

Turning into an icy wind off the river, I took the same route that the frat boys and I had taken a few weeks before.

At a doorway on a deserted side street near Ninth Avenue, I halted. I remembered standing in that spot and telling them this was the place. In the tenement hall, I put the pistol at the base of one kid's head and made him beg the other one to give me the money.

Standing in that doorway again, I recalled how the nervous sweat on my hand made it hard to hold on to the .25.

When those terrified kids had handed over the money, I discouraged pursuit by making them throw their shoes into the dark, to take off their coats and lie face down with their hands behind their heads. The one I'd put the pistol on had pissed his pants. He wept and begged me not to shoot.

Remembering that made my stomach turn. Right then my Partner had been calling the shots.

The rest of that night was gone beyond recovery. What happened in those blank hours wasn't important. I knew where the search for my Partner was going to end. Death Avenue, north of the Deuce, had always been a favorite spot for both of us. The deserted warehouses, the empty railroad yards, made it feel like the end of the world.

Approaching the Emerald Green Tavern, I spotted a lone figure leaning on a lamp post watching trailer trucks roll south. Only a lack of funds would have kept a man out on the street on a night like that. Touching the pistol for luck, stepping up behind him, I asked, "Watcha doing?"

Not particularly surprised, not even turning all the way around, he replied, "Oh, living the life." I would never have his nonchalance. His face was hidden by the dark and masked by sunglasses. That was just as well.

The air around him smelled of cheap booze. "We have to talk." I gestured toward the Emerald Green.

As we crossed the street, he told me, "I knew you'd show up. This is where we parted company. When I woke up days later, all I had was these clothes and a couple of keepsakes."

That reminded me of the knife. My Silent Partner knew as soon as that crossed my mind. "Don't worry," he said. "I sold it."

He went through the door first. The Emerald Green was a typical Hell's Kitchen joint with a bar that ran front to back, a few booths, and beer-and-cigarette-soaked air unchanged since the Truman administration. The facilities were the one distinguishing feature of the place. The restrooms lay down a flight of stairs and across a cellar/storage area. You could organize a firing squad down there and the people above wouldn't know.

Or care. The customers that night were several guys with boozers' noses, an old woman with very red hair who said loudly at regular intervals, "Danny? Screw, Danny," and a couple of Spanish guys off some night shift and now immobile at a table. The dead-eyed donkey of a bartender looked right through me and nodded at my Silent Partner. In here, he was the real one. We went to the far end of the bar near the cellar door where we could talk. I ordered a ginger ale. My companion said, "Double Irish."

As we sat, he gave a dry chuckle. "Double Irish is about right for us." At no time did I turn and stare my Silent Partner in the face. But the filmed mirror behind the bar showed that he wore the rumpled jacket over a dirty T-shirt.

The camel hair coat was deeply stained. When the whiskey came, he put it away with a single gesture from counter to mouth. Up and in. I could taste it going down.

It was like living in a drinking dream. I touched the back of my belt and said, "You found out where I live."

"Yeah. Billy at 596 told me you were staying at Mother's. Of course, what he said was that he had seen me going in and out. So I knew." Indoors, my partner smelled ripe. The back of his hand was dirty.

"You owe them money?" The last thing I needed was to get shot for debts he had run up.

"Not even five. My credit's no good," he said. "You left me with nothing. They locked me out of the hotel. Ripping off those kids was something you never could have done by yourself. You needed me." He signaled for a refill. The bartender's eyes shifted my way since I was paying.

I shook my head, not sure I could have him drink again and not do it myself. "I've got most of the money on me. It's yours. So that we don't attract attention, what I want you to do is to get up and go downstairs. After a couple of minutes, I'll join you."

"Pass the money to me under the bar." He didn't trust me.

"There's something else I want you to have." For a long moment he sat absolutely still. The TV was on with the sound off. It seemed to be all beer ads. "When you come back up here," I told him, "You can afford enough doubles to kill yourself." That promise made him rise and push his way through the cellar door.

For a good two minutes, I sipped ginger ale and breathed deeply to calm myself. Then I followed him. Downstairs, there were puddles on the floor. The restroom doors were open. Both were empty. One of the johns was broken and kept flushing. It sounded like an asthmatic trying to breathe.

The cellar was lighted by an overhead bulb above the stairs and another one at the far end of the cellar near the restrooms. Both lights swayed slightly, making it hard to focus. My Silent Partner had reached up and bumped them for just that reason. It was the kind of thing that I would not have thought of. He stood where the light didn't quite hit him.

When I reached the bottom of the stairs, I reached back and drew the .25. He seemed to flicker before me. "Easy does it," he said. "You know how jumpy you are with guns." His tone was taunting, not intimidated.

I realized I could read him as easily as he could me. My Silent Partner wanted me to try to shoot him and find out that I couldn't. Then after I failed, we could both go upstairs, have some drinks and resume our partnership. Carefully, I ejected the clip and stuck it in my pocket. His eyes followed me as I put the empty pistol on the stairs. "You bought this, you get rid of it." I said. "My guess is it's got a bad history."

"You'll never have another friend like me." His voice, my voice, had a whine to it and I knew this was getting to him. I reached into my pocket and took out the money and a piece of worn newspaper. "You thought about what it's going to be like to be broke," he asked. "It's not like you've got any skills."

I'd had thought of it and it scared me. I hesitated.

Then I noticed that the newspaper was the page with the Dunn article. Taking a deep breath, I riffled the money and told my Silent Partner, "Almost six grand. Just about everything I have." I put the cash on the stairs beside the Beretta and turned to go. "So long. It's been real."

"Oh, I'll keep in touch," he said in a whisper. Looking back, I saw nothing but the blur of light in the shadows.

On the stairs, I felt light-footed, like a burden had been laid down. This was relief, maybe even the happiness Mr. Dunn had mentioned. From his perch near the front, the bartender gave me a slightly wary look like maybe I had come in at 2 A.M., drunk ginger ale, and had a conversation with myself. I occurred to me that if that's what happened, the first one to go take a leak was going to get a very nice surprise.

But as I went out into the cold, the bartender's gaze shifted, his hand reached for the pouring bottle, and I heard the cellar door swing open behind me.

The verbal snapshot, the anecdote, the New Yorker "Casual" is a staple of life in this city ("You wouldn't believe what I just saw!").

Recently there's been a newfound interest in very short stories (usually a thousand words or less) referred to as "Flash Fiction." Once this was a popular length for newspaper and magazine fiction and the pieces were called "Short-Shorts." By the late '50s that term was used by people my age for the pants girls wore in summer and boys wore for gym.

Here are three of mine.

EAST SIDE, WEST SIDE

His Only Nose

A few weeks ago I passed a guy on Bleecker Street in Greenwich Village. He was saying in a loud, aggrieved tone of voice to the woman he was with, "I ONLY GOT THIS ONE NOSE." And though I've lived in Manhattan for a long time and heard lots of great mad street cries and wonderful twisted passer-by talk, I still paid enough attention to wonder what led him to mention this.

When I told people about the incident a writer friend suggested that the woman had bopped him in the nose. An interesting premise, but in my quick glance I'd seen no evidence that his nose (a serviceable but common enough medium sized specimen—not a pug, not a wild honker) was bleeding or was in any way not "a virgin."

That's how unbroken noses were described in the South Boston of my childhood, a time and place where it was said that anyone who reached the age of twelve without a broken nose was either a newcomer or a girl.

My friend, Liz, who has known me for decades, was inclined to believe that he came from an alternate world where any individual could have a variety of noses and other body parts. At first I thought this was a nice piece of whimsy on her part and was amused. Then she reminded me of certain experiences we had shared.

The first involved a man with whom the sister of a mutual friend went out, a guy who was fascinated but terrified by electricity. One night, drunk and stoned, he claimed to be from a reality where Con Edison had never moved from very crude Direct Current to Alternating

Current. Thus the New York City of his birth was dangerously lighted and electrical fires were commonplace. The sister soon dropped him and we learned no more.

Another was a bartender with what sounded like a French Canadian accent who worked at a place on Sullivan Street some years ago. He would claim once he'd had a few in him that he came from a world where Napoleon had conquered North America and Noveau York was French speaking.

"You know," my friend said, "that every time there's calamity anywhere in the world: war, poverty, pestilence, man-made or natural disaster, refugees from that location appear in this neighborhood and open ethnic restaurants. It's a law of nature.

"We've got all the old and new trouble spots from Italy to Ethiopia, Vietnam to Afghanistan. I'll bet Libya is next. If all of them end up here why not people from Alternate Realities."

When I mentioned this jokingly to a guy I know slightly, Frankie who's an administrator the University, he told me in a condescending manner that everyone used to say Alternate Reality. But the label is now considered insensitive. The correct term is Diverse Origin Worlds or DOW. And that this was a situation which was just beginning to be better understood.

I mentioned that troubles in places with less fortunate histories than ours always translate into refugees in the neighborhood. Frankie said, "Once you get used to tailors from Xingjian/Uyghur and Italian restaurants with waiters from Bangladesh there should be no surprise at some couple arguing about what nose to wear."

"Why would anyone from a place where people had life sciences so advanced that they could exchange body parts at will, come to live here?" I asked.

"Why did so many people flee Europe when it was the center of culture and technology to come here?" he asked. "Stuff back home forced them to. Everyone keeps quiet about it but I'm told there are DOW support groups to help refugees over the rough passages in their transitions to this world. I think it's kind of interesting!"

Reconsidering the incident that had started all this speculation, I recalled the woman with whom the "one nose" guy was walking. The one she wore was casual but cute and slightly upturned. A fine piece of retrousse nosery if that's what it was—far more stylish than his.

I wondered if she had made some disparaging remark about the one he wore. A thoughtless person might do this, little considering that the nose someone else wears is the only one he owns and thus force him into an embarrassing confession.

Other things happened over the next couple of weeks: a long ago lover came back and visited the city; I got some unexpected freelance work, found a new yoga teacher and a fine gelato shop. I pretty much forgot the man and his nose.

Then one morning, stuck in traffic on Canal Street, I looked out of the taxi and noticed a sign in a third story window. It offered DOW counseling along with assistance on visas and immigration status. Later on that very same day I again passed the man and the woman on Bleecker Street.

I'm 99% positive it was them. But the nose is an important part of one's face and their noses were not the ones I'd previously seen. His was somewhat larger and more commanding. Hers was curved and a bit sensuous. I thought of Anthony and Cleopatra. They looked like satisfied and confident New Yorkers striding down the center of the sidewalk and forcing everyone else to walk around them.

On a nice summer day a bit after that, I sat on a bench in Washington Square Park telling my friend Liz all that I'd found out about noses and Diverse Origins Worlds.

Two extremely thin thirty-something women carrying nicely up-scale shopping bags passed by close enough for us to hear them.

"For June it's clothes for work, weddings and hauntings," said the one.

"Hauntings," said the second one. "You mean at that abandoned place upstate?"

"Uh-huh," said the first.

"But not enough of us are here for a real haunting!"

"Not yet," said the first woman. "But others are trying to get permanent visas."

"The easiest way is to marry a citizen," said the second. At this they both laughed a bit and looked towards the fountain.

Liz and I followed their gaze. Frankie, who first told me about Diverse Origin Worlds, wore a crisp jacket and a bow tie. He grinned and opened his arms to what would surely be his bride.

Whips and Wands

When a question from the past haunts you, rest is impossible until it's tracked down and resolved. Mine involves the last night of Whips and Wands.

Memories that might bother others don't faze me. Gauntlets of girls flay the bare asses of boys who run up long, dark stairs with the flash of photo bulbs as the only light. At the top step stands Mistress Whipwell—aka Babe Jerome—in leather g-string and black boots, mascara-lined eyes framed by a black top hat and gold curls.

What drives me is a front page tabloid photo of Whipwell/Jerome's bloody body in a trash-filled alley. At this late stage of my existence I need to untangle my role in that. It's why I find myself back in New York. But when you've been gone a long while, it's hard to know where to start.

After searching for what seems like years, I get lucky and more. In an exhibition of photos of 1950s Manhattan, there's a shot of half a dozen boys jumping a fence in Madison Square Park. One looks right into the camera and I recognize the eyes. Know Jonny Keagan at any age and you remember them.

Keagan is my key. He grew up in Kips Bay, a working class neighborhood centered on Second Avenue in the East Twenties and Thirties. When Whips and Wands opened there Jon ran the door. I need to find him.

Instinct, a hunch, something overheard, eventually leads me to a book promotion at a big Barnes and Noble on Union Square. At the microphone, a shopworn author doubling as used car salesman and used car reads from a memoir of the legendary late 1960s and early '70s.

A few of the crowd are familiar. But I've been gone so long I'm invisible to them. Then I spot a figure wavering like a ghost or a memory. Jon Keagan, white haired, sits tall on the aisle with a cane across his knees.

He turns his wide, almost unblinking eyes on me and whispers, "I've thought about you lately." Jon stands and gestures toward the exit. As we leave the author's saying, "An abandoned neighborhood contained a secret, dark jewel." And I feel he's talking about Whips and Wands.

It's dusk as we walk uptown and turn on East 26th Street. High rise towers look down on us. It was all five story walkups back when Babe Jerome in guy drag and me passed this way. I was stupid; a would-be actor who rode pay-for-play sex until I hit my late '20s and was old. Babe Jerome was a spoiled brat who showed me S&M was where I could have a few more years of work.

Jon carries his cane like a walking stick. He says, "I'm the neighborhood historian, people always asking about some candy store that burned down fifty years ago. But with ones like you from far away and long ago I feel like a priest, a magician."

The next couple of blocks it seems we're back in the old New York, corner stores and bars, people sitting on stoops. But across Second Avenue where Whips and Wands stood there's nothing I remember.

Jon points to the wall of brick and glass. "When I was a kid Bellevue and all the other hospitals were over on First Avenue with their backs to the river. Everything else was my neighborhood.

"Then one day the hospitals wanted to expand, to house their workers. A bunch of blocks got condemned, houses, stores, Mullins Hall where everybody had wedding parties, graduations. Buildings emptied fast but didn't come down for a year. Landlords made money renting illegally. Whores, junk dealers: no one cared.

"After the army I did door work at clubs—was good at it. Someone said Mullins Hall had a new name and was hiring. This drag with five o'clock shadow, out of her skull on meth, interviewed me."

"Whips and Wands," I say and remember peeling paint, flooded restrooms, manacles and blue lights, glowing death heads in dark halls. "Fairies and Sadists: a little pain, a bit of magic, Mistress Whipwell aka Babe Jerome presiding."

"She starts screaming at me. You tell her the word is I run a door like I got a sixth sense of who to let in and you say I'm hired. She tries to stab you with a scissors."

"I was the second banana, accomplice, sometime top and occasional bottom," I say. "Baby Jerome inherited a chunk of money, spent it getting his girl on. What was left got put into Whips. In two months he'd break even, four months, she'd be rich again and I'd have a bankroll."

We cross Second, walk down the block to where the club stood. It's a playground now. Guys shoot baskets in the dark.

"The place got popular," Jon says, "spoiled kids needing to get spanked. Then came the night I noticed unmarked cop cars all around. Mistress Whipwell and you were fighting. Instinct said to split."

He waits for my story. I drop my eyes and say, "All I remember is waking up with scratches on my face and arms, blood on my hands and no memory of anything but the fight I'd had the night before. Jerome banged my head on a wall. Told me we were through.

"Then I saw the Daily News photo and headline, SHE-MALE IN PAIN PALACE DEATH PLUNGE. That's when I found out about the raid and how she fell six floors head first off the roof. I got out of town. But I wondered . . ."

"If you pushed her?" he asks and I nod.

"You came out the door royally fucked up just before I left. I stuck you in a cab. You don't remember?"

I shake my head.

"Whipwell jumped after the raid started. Maybe that was her release. Like this is yours."

I look into those eyes, realize nothing holds me. He watches me float up over the roofs of Manhattan.

Tears of Laughter, Tears of Grief

There's a little shop way west on Bleecker Street in Greenwich Village. TEARS OF LAUGHTER, TEARS OF GRIEF has been there for years. It advertizes discreetly. *"Trouble expressing yourself emotionally?" "Unable to summon the right response in a timely manner?"*

Which of us has not had those problems? And TOLTOG has the answers. Unable to produce a lingering tear? TOLTOG has handy eye drops! I stop in whenever I pass the shop. It's a boutique, really, small but enticing. And the stock!

Stuff one almost wants to find a use for. Sweat of your brow? Sprays on! Drool with envy? With an oral sponge! Sweating Blood is a simple application.

The whole Blood Sweat and Tears treatment requires a little extra time and effort to apply cream, spray and eye drops. But what a pleasure to take that trouble!

The staff is part of the charm, with their words of comfort (achieved with a gargle solution in several delightful flavors) and, sympathetic smiles (a small oral brace which doesn't interfere with diction in any serious way).

I was reminded of TOLTOG one day not long ago. I'd just started writing a story, a dystopian tale about an orphan boy in a desolate American landscape. His parents have been killed and eaten by Republicans and he is both starving and hungry for revenge.

This, I was afraid, was turning out to be an example of what I call bright flash stories, ones that begin with an image, an idea, an opening sentence, sometimes with all three of those and then linger seductive, unformed and unfinished in back files.

As I fretted about that I got an email informing me that Livonia Failbeck, described as she always was as, "A prominent American fantasy writer," had died suddenly from a stroke.

A surprise and a coincidence, I'd been thinking how Livonia would have taken my story of unutterable wrong, added some little curlicues to flavor the plot, and subtly turned the story into an affirmation rather than an angry cry.

Normally, to write in the short forms is to dance a dance with obscurity. But Livionia's formula had won her attention and awards. Twice in recent years I'd been at conventions because I was on an awards short list. Both times Livy herself hadn't bothered to make an appearance—once because she was elsewhere receiving a more important award. Both times she won. Later she was pleasant about it, shrugging her shoulders at the whims of the fans, the mysteries of the judges' decisions. But being a pleasant winner is easy, losing not so much.

The announcement of the memorial service followed shortly on the death notice. It would be held here in New York City and I'd have to go, wouldn't, in fact, have considered missing it. My problem would be decorum. Could I show the proper regret untinged by sardonic glee?

Very shortly afterwards I felt all had gone well because I was at a spec fiction convention and I was receiving an award—THE GOLDEN GOOSE—given for excellence in short fiction. I remembered that Livonia Failbeck had won this prize seven times.

My story of the orphan boy whose parents had been eaten was the one with which I'd won. Had Ms. Failbeck still been alive this would never have happened. And I stepped up to take the prize, aware that I'd Livonia'd the story with wry verbal doodles and a big, reconciliation for an ending. But I forgave myself.

Apparently I'd forgotten that in fact the trophy WAS a goose— alive and big as me but a loud purple. Later that night after the applause and congratulations, after the victory celebration, we wandered down a hotel corridor. The goose wanted to go back to the bar, got a bit nasty about this. All I wondered was how I was going to get it through airport security and onto the plane.

It was, of course, a dream, possibly brought on by this being the night before the Failbeck Memorial Service. I awoke with a strong sense of disappointment. It was as if the dream was a vision of an alternate life as opposed to the gooseless existence in which I found myself.

There's prophecy and warning in dreams. Often, though, one is reluctant to examine them too closely.

Demeanor is important when you're moving to succeed the old monarch. No one wants to be like Ozzie Nesbitt at the funeral of his legendary rival Norwood Fletcher. Some said Ozzie was drunk. They were being kind.

When Ozzie sprang up, pushed Fletcher's wife (once long ago Ozzie's fiancée) out of the way and kicked the casket repeatedly, he was sober. He kept shouting, "Not much to say now you stupid bastard. Where are all your Hugo Awards now?"

Obviously it was something he needed to express but it did Nesbitt's career no good. All this was in the legendary past. These days, things are handled in a more seemly fashion.

I headed for the little shop on Bleecker. When one is anxious, aware of how important an event could be, there's the temptation to overdo things.

Yes, I've heard those audios of the service in which my sobs compete with the speakers and the music. So demonstrative was my mourning that several people separately asked me when I was planning to rend my garments. And someone I'd thought of as a friend remarked aloud, "What, doesn't TOLTOG have a sackcloth and ashes sachet, dear?"

But I ask myself what Livonia herself would have done. And I don't feel I was that far off her beat. Besides, she's dead and someone will have to win those awards. I take my vision of the Goose to be a portent.

"There's A Hole in the City" got written in the spring of 2005, three and a half years after 9/11. I'd watched the towers fall from a street corner a couple of blocks from my house. The story is as much memoir as fiction. It wasn't just me who needed time to get a bit of distance before writing about that day and what came after. 2005/6 saw the appearance of all manner of stories, novels, films and music influenced by the destruction of the World Trade Center.

I wrote "There's a Hole in the City" for Ellen Datlow's wonderful online Sci-Fiction. *It received immediate attention, won the International Horror Guild and Million Writers awards and made the Nebula and Gaylactic Spectrum short lists. It's been reprinted seven times so far and translated into German and Japanese.*

THERE'S A HOLE IN THE CITY

Wednesday 9/12

On the evening of the day after the towers fell, I was waiting by the barricades on Houston Street and LaGuardia Place for my friend Mags to come up from Soho and have dinner with me. On the skyline, not two miles to the south, the pillars of smoke wavered slightly. But the creepily beautiful weather of September 11 still held and the wind blew in from the northeast. In Greenwich Village the air was crisp and clean with just a touch of fall about it.

I'd spent the last day and a half looking at pictures of burning towers. One of the frustrations of that time was that there was so little most of us could do about anything or for anyone.

Downtown streets were empty of all traffic except emergency vehicles. The West and East Villages from Fourteenth Street to Houston were their own separate zone. Pedestrians needed identification proving they lived or worked there in order to enter.

The barricades consisted of blue wooden police horses and a couple of unmarked vans thrown across LaGuardia Place. Behind them were a couple of cops, a few auxiliary police, and one or two guys in civilian clothes with IDs of some kind pinned to their shirts. All of them looked tired, subdued by events.

At the barricades was a small crowd, ones like me waiting for friends from neighborhoods to the south, ones without proper identification waiting for confirmation so that they could continue on into Soho, people who just wanted to be outside near other people in those days of sunshine and shock. Once in a while, each of us would look up at the columns of smoke that hung in the downtown sky then look away again.

A family approached a middle-aged cop behind the barricade. The group consisted of a man, a woman, a little girl being led by the hand, a child being carried. All were blondish and wore shorts and casual tops. The parents seemed pleasant but serious people in their early thirties, professionals. They could have been tourists. But that day the city was empty of tourists.

The man said something and I heard the cop say loudly, "You want to go where?"

"Down there," the man gestured at the columns. He indicated the children. "We want them to see." It sounded as if he couldn't imagine this appeal not working.

Everyone stared at the family. "No ID no passage," said the cop and turned his back on them. The pleasant expressions on the parents' faces faded. They looked indignant, like a maitre d' had lost their reservations. She led one kid, he carried another as they turned west, probably headed for another check point.

They wanted those little kids to see Ground Zero!" a woman who knew the cop said. "Are they out of their minds?"

"Looters," he replied. "That's my guess." He picked up his walkie-talkie to call the check points ahead of them.

Mags appeared just then, looking a bit frayed. When you've known someone for as long as I've known her, the tendency is not to see the changes, to think you both look about the same as when you were kids.

But kids don't have gray hair and their bodies aren't thick the way bodies get in their late fifties. Their kisses aren't perfunctory. Their conversation doesn't include curt little nods that indicate something is understood.

We walked in the middle of the streets because we could. "Couldn't sleep much last night," I said.

"Because of the quiet," she said. "No planes. I kept listening for them. I haven't been sleeping anyway. I was supposed to be in housing court today. But the courts are shut until further notice."

I said, "Notice how with only the ones who live here allowed in, the South Village is all Italians and hippies?"

"Like 1965 all over again."

She and I had been in contact more in the past few months than we had in a while. Memories of love and indifference that we shared had made close friendship an on and off thing for the last thirty-something years.

Earlier in 2001, at the end of an affair, I'd surrendered a rent stabilized apartment for a cash settlement and bought a tiny co-op in the South Village. Mags lived as she had for years in a run-down building on the fringes of Soho.

So we saw each other again. I write, obviously, but she never read anything I published, which bothered me. On the other hand, she worked off and on for various activist leftist foundations and I was mostly uninterested in that.

Mags was in the midst of classic New York work and housing trouble. Currently she was on unemployment and her landlord wanted to get her out of her apartment so he could co-op her building. The money offer he'd made wasn't bad but she wanted things to stay as they were. It struck me that what was youthful about her was that she had never settled into her life, still stood on the edge.

Lots of the Village restaurants weren't opened. The owners couldn't or wouldn't come into the city. Angelina's On Thompson Street was, though, because Angelina lives just a couple of doors down from her place. She was busy serving tables herself since the waiters couldn't get in from where they lived.

Later, I had reason to try and remember. The place was full but very quiet. People murmured to each other as Mags and I did. Nobody I knew was there. In the background Resphigi's "Ancient Airs and Dances" played

"Like the Blitz," someone said.

"Never the same again," said a person at another table.

"There isn't even any place to volunteer to help," a third person said.

I don't drink anymore. But Mags, as I remember, had a carafe of wine. Phone service had been spotty but we had managed to exchange bits of what we had seen.

"Mrs. Pirelli," I said. "The Italian lady upstairs from me. I told you she had a heart attack watching the smoke and flames on television. Her son worked in the World Trade Center and she was sure he had burned to death.

"Getting an ambulance wasn't possible yesterday morning. But the guys at that little fire barn around the corner were there. Waiting to be called, I guess. They took her to St. Vincent's in the chief's car. Right about then, her son came up the street, his pinstripe suit with a hole burned in the shoulder, soot on his face, wild-eyed. But alive. Today they say she's doing fine."

I waited, spearing clams, twirling linguine. Mags had a deeper and darker story to tell; a dip into the subconscious. Before I'd known her and afterwards, Mags had a few rough brushes with mental disturbance. Back in college where we first met, I envied her that, wished I had something as dramatic to talk about.

"I've been thinking about what happened last night." She'd already told me some of this. "The downstairs bell rang, which scared me. But with phone service being bad, it could have been a friend, someone who needed to talk. I looked out the window. The street was empty, dead like I'd never seen it.

"Nothing but papers blowing down the street. You know how every time you see a scrap of paper now you think it's from the Trade Center? For a minute I thought I saw something move but when I looked again there was nothing.

"I didn't ring the buzzer, but it seemed someone upstairs did because I heard this noise, a rustling in the hall.

"When I went to the door and lifted the spy hole, this figure stood there on the landing. Looking around like she was lost. She wore a dress, long and torn. And a blouse, what I realized was a shirtwaist. Turn-of-the-century clothes. When she turned towards my door, I saw her face. It was bloody, smashed. Like she had taken a big jump or fall. I gasped and then she was gone."

"And you woke up?"

"No, I tried to call you. But the phones were all fucked up. She had fallen but not from a hundred stories. Anyway she wasn't from here and now."

Mags had emptied the carafe. I remember that she'd just ordered a salad and didn't eat that. But Angelina brought a fresh carafe. I told Mags about the family at the barricades.

"There's a hole in the city," said Mags.

That night, after we had parted, I lay in bed watching but not seeing some old movie on TV, avoiding any channel with any kind of news, when the buzzer sounded. I jumped up and went to the view screen. On the empty street downstairs a man, wild-eyed, disheveled, glared directly into the camera.

Phone service was not reliable. Cops were not in evidence in the neighborhood right then. I froze and didn't buzz him in. But, as in Mags building, someone else did. I bolted my door, watched at the spy hole, listened to the footsteps, slow, uncertain. When he came into sight on the second floor landing he looked around and said in a hoarse voice, "Hello? Sorry but I can't find my mom's front door key."

Only then did I unlock the door, open it and ask her exhausted son how Mrs. Pirelli was doing.

"Fine," he said. "Getting great treatment. St. Vincent was geared up for thousands of casualties. Instead . . ." he shrugged. "Anyway, she thanks all of you. Me too."

In fact, I hadn't done much. We said good night and he shuffled on upstairs to where he was crashing in his mother's place.

Thursday 9/13

By September of 2001 I had worked an information desk in the University library for almost thirty years. I live right around the corner from Washington Square and just before 10 A.M. on Thursday, I set out for work. The Moslem-run souvlaki stand across the street was still closed, its owner and workers gone since Tuesday morning. All the little falafel shops in the South Village were shut and dark.

On my way to work I saw a three legged rat running not too quickly down the middle of MacDougal Street. I decided not to think about portents and symbolism.

The big TVs set up in the library atrium still showed the towers falling again and again. But now they also showed workers digging in the flaming wreckage at Ground Zero.

Like the day before, I was the only one in my department who'd made it in. The librarians lived too far away. Even Marco, the student assistant, wasn't around.

Marco lived in a dorm downtown right near the World Trade Center. They'd been evacuated with nothing more than a few books and the clothes they were wearing. Tuesday, he'd been very upset. I'd given him Kleenex, made him take deep breaths, got him to call his mother back in California. I'd even walked him over to the gym where the University was putting up the displaced students.

Thursday morning, all of the computer stations around the information desk were occupied. Students sat furiously typing email and devouring incoming messages but the intensity had slackened since 9/11. The girls no longer sniffed and dabbed at tears as they read. The boys didn't jump up and come back from the restrooms red-eyed and saying they had allergies.

I said good morning and sat down. The kids hadn't spoken much to me in the last few days, had no questions to ask. But all of them from time to time would turn and look to make sure I was still there. If I got up to leave the desk, they'd ask when I was coming back.

Some of the back windows had a downtown view. The pillar of smoke wavered. The wind was changing.

The phone rang. Reception had improved. Most calls went through. When I answered, a voice, tight and tense, blurted out, "Jennie Levine was who I saw. She was nineteen years old in 1911 when the Triangle Shirtwaist Factory burned. She lived in my building with her family ninety years ago. Her spirit found its way home. But the inside of my building has changed so much that she didn't recognize it."

"Hi, Mags," I said. "You want to come up here and have lunch?"

A couple of hours later, we were in a small dining hall normally used by faculty on the west side of the Square. The University, with food on hand and not enough people to eat it, had thrown open its cafeterias and dining halls to anybody with a university identification. We could even bring a friend if we cared to.

Now that I looked, Mags had tension lines around her eyes and hair that could have used some tending. But we were all of us a little ragged in those days of sun and horror. People kept glancing downtown, even if they were inside and not near a window.

The Indian lady who ran the facility greeted us, thanked us for coming. I had a really nice gumbo, fresh avocado salad, a soothing pudding. The place was half empty and conversations again were muted. I told Mags about Mrs. Pirelli's son the night before.

She looked up from her plate, unsmiling, said, "I did not imagine Jennie Levine," and closed that subject.

Afterwards, she and I stood on Washington Place before the University building that had once housed the sweat shop called The Triangle Shirtwaist Factory. At the end of the block, a long convoy of olive green army trucks rolled silently down Broadway.

Mags said, "On the afternoon of March 25, 1911, one hundred and forty-six young women burned to death on this site. Fire broke out in a pile of rags. The door to the roof was locked. The fire ladders couldn't reach the eighth floor. The girls burned."

Her voice tightened as she said, "They jumped and were smashed on the sidewalk. Many of them, most of them, lived right around here. In the renovated tenements we live in now. It's like those planes blew a hole in the city and Jennie Levine returned through it."

"Easy, honey. The University has grief counseling available. I think I'm going. You want me to see if I can get you in?" It sounded idiotic even as I said it. We had walked back to the library.

"There are others," she said. "Kids all blackened and bloated and wearing old fashioned clothes. I woke up early this morning and couldn't go back to sleep. I got up and walked around here and over in the East Village."

"Jesus!" I said.

"Geoffrey has come back too. I know it."

"Mags! Don't!" This was something we hadn't talked about in a long time. Once we were three and Geoffrey was the third. He was younger than either of us by a couple of years at a time of life when that still seemed a major difference.

We called him Lord Geoff because he said we were all a bit better than the world around us. We joked that he was our child. A little family cemented by desire and drugs.

The three of us were all so young, just out school and in the city. Then jealousy and the hard realities of addiction began to tear us apart. Each had to find his or her own survival. Mags and I made it. As it turned out, Geoff wasn't built for the long haul. He was twenty-one. We were all just kids, ignorant and reckless.

As I made excuses in my mind Mags gripped my arm. "He'll want to find us," she said. Chilled, I watched her walk away and wondered how long she had been coming apart and why I hadn't noticed.

Back at work, Marco waited for me. He was part Filipino, a bit of a little wise ass who dressed in downtown black. But that was the week before. Today, he was a woebegone refugee in oversized flip-flops, a magenta sweatshirt and gym shorts, all of which had been made for someone bigger and more buff.

"How's it going?"

"It sucks! My stuff is all downtown where I don't know if I can ever get it. They have these crates in the gym, toothbrushes, bras, Bic razors but never what you need, everything from boxer shorts on out and nothing is ever the right size. I gave my clothes in to be cleaned and they didn't bring them back. Now I look like a clown.

"They have us all sleeping on cots on the basketball courts. I lay there all last night staring up at the ceiling, with a hundred other guys. Some of them snore. One was yelling in his sleep. And I don't want to take a shower with a bunch of guys staring at me."

He told me all this while not looking my way but I understood what he was asking. I expected this was going to be a pain. But, given that I couldn't seem to do much for Mags, I thought maybe it would be a distraction to do what I could for someone else.

"You want to take a shower at my place, crash on my couch?"

"Could I, please?"

So I took a break, brought him around the corner to my apartment, put sheets on the daybed. He was in the shower when I went back to work.

That evening when I got home, he woke up. When I went out to take a walk, he tagged along. We stood at the police barricades at Houston Street and Sixth Avenue and watched the traffic coming up from the World Trade Center site. An ambulance with one side smashed and a squad car with its roof crushed were hauled up Sixth Avenue on the back of a huge flatbed truck. NYPD buses were full of guys returning from Ground Zero, hollow-eyed, filthy.

Crowds of Greenwich Villagers gathered on the sidewalks clapped and cheered, yelled, "We love our firemen! We love our cops!"

The firehouse on Sixth Avenue had taken a lot of casualties when the towers fell. The place was locked and empty. We looked at the flowers and the wreaths on the doors, the signs with faces of the firefighters who hadn't returned and the messages, "To the brave men of these companies who gave their lives defending us."

The plume of smoke downtown rolled in the twilight, buffeted about by shifting winds. The breeze brought with it for the first time the acrid smoke that would be with us for weeks afterwards.

Officials said it was the stench of burning concrete. I believed, as did everyone else, that part of what we breathed was the ashes of the ones who had burned to death that Tuesday.

It started to drizzle. Marco stuck close to me as we walked back.

Hip twenty-year-olds do not normally hang out with guys almost three times their age. This kid was very scared.

Bleecker Street looked semi-abandoned with lots of the stores and restaurants still closed. The ones that were open were mostly empty at nine in the evening.

"If I buy you a six-pack, you promise to drink all of it?" He indicated he would.

At home, Marco asked to use the phone. He called people he knew on campus looking for a spare dorm room and spoke in whispers to a girl named Eloise. In between calls, he worked the computer.

I played a little Lady Day, some Ray Charles, a bit of Haydn, stared at the TV screen. The President had pulled out of his funk and was coming to New York the next day.

In the next room, the phone rang. "No. My name's Marco," I heard him say. "He's letting me stay here." I knew who it was before he came in and whispered, "She asked if I was Lord Geoff."

"Hi, Mags," I said. She was calling from somewhere with walkie-talkies and sirens in the background.

"Those kids I saw in Astor Place?" she said, her voice clear and crazed. "The ones all burned and drowned. They were on the General Slocum when it caught fire."

"The kids you saw in Astor Place all burned and drowned?" I asked. Then I remembered our conversation earlier.

"On June 15, 1904. The biggest disaster in New York City history. Until now. The East Village was once called Little Germany. Tens of thousands of Germans with their own meeting halls, churches, beer gardens.

"They had a Sunday excursion, mainly for the kids, on a steamship, the General Slocum, a floating fire trap. When it burst into flames there were no lifeboats, the crew and the captain panicked. By the time they got to a dock over a thousand were dead. Burned, drowned. When a hole got blown in the city, they came back looking for their homes."

The connection started to dissolve into static.

"Where are you, Mags?"

"Ground Zero. It smells like burning sulfur. Have you seen Geoffrey yet?" she shouted into her phone.

"Geoffrey is dead, Mags. It's all the horror and tension that's doing this to you. There's no hole . . . ."

"Cops and firemen and brokers all smashed and charred are walking around down here." At that point sirens screamed in the background. Men were yelling. The connection faded.

"Mags give me your number. Call me back," I yelled. Then there was nothing but static, followed by a weak dial tone. I hung up and waited for the phone to ring again.

After a while, I realized Marco was standing looking at me, slugging down beer. "She saw those kids? I saw them too. Tuesday night I was too jumpy to even lie down on the fucking cot. I snuck out with my friend Terry. We walked around. The kids were there. In old, historical clothes. Covered with mud and seaweed and their faces all black and gone. It's why I couldn't sleep last night."

"You talk to the counselors?" I asked.

He drained the bottle. "Yeah, but they don't want to hear what I wanted to talk about."

"But with me . . ."

"You're crazy. You understand."

The silence outside was broken by a jet engine. We both flinched. No planes had flown over Manhattan since the ones that had smashed the towers on Tuesday morning.

Then I realized what it was. "The Air Force," I said. "Making sure it's safe for Mr. Bush's visit."

"Who's Mags? Who's Lord Geoff?"

So I told him a bit of what had gone on in that strange lost country, the 1960s, the naïveté that lead to meth and junk. I described the wonder of that unknown land, the three way union. "Our problem, I guess, was that instead of a real ménage, each member was obsessed with only one of the others."

"OK," he said. "You're alive. Mags is alive. What happened to Geoff?"

"When things were breaking up, Geoff got caught in a drug sweep and was being hauled downtown in the back of a police van. He cut his wrists and bled to death in the dark before anyone noticed."

This did for me, what speaking about the dead kids had maybe done for him. Each of us got to about what bothered him without having to think much about what the other said.

Friday 9/14

Friday morning two queens walked by with their little dogs as Marco and I came out the door of my building. One said, "There isn't a fresh croissant in the entire Village. It's like the Siege of Paris. We'll all be reduced to eating rats."

I murmured, "He's getting a little ahead of the story. Maybe first he should think about having an English muffin."

"Or eating his yappy dog," said Marco.

At that moment, the authorities opened the East and West Villages, between Fourteenth and Houston Streets, to outside traffic. All the people whose cars had been stranded since Tuesday began to come into the neighborhood and drive them away. Delivery trucks started to appear on the narrow streets.

In the library, the huge TV screens showed the activity at Ground Zero, the preparations for the President's visit. An elevator door opened and revealed a couple of refugee kids in their surplus gym clothes clasped in a passion clinch.

The computers around my information desk were still fully occupied but the tension level had fallen. There was even a question or two about books and databases. I tried repeatedly to call Mags. All I got was the chilling message on her answering machine.

In a staccato voice, it said, "This is Mags McConnell. There's a hole in the city and I've turned this into a center for information about the victims Jennie Levine and Geoffrey Holbrun. Anyone with information concerning the whereabouts of these two young people, please speak after the beep."

I left a few messages asking her to call. Then I called every half hour or so hoping she'd pick up. I phoned mutual friends. Some were absent or unavailable. A couple were nursing grief of their own. No one had seen her recently.

That evening in the growing dark, lights flickered in Washington Square. Candles were given out; candles were lighted with matches and Bics and wick to wick. Various priests, ministers, rabbis and shamans lead flower-bearing, candlelit congregations down the streets and into the park where they joined the gathering Vigil crowd.

Marco had come by with his friend Terry, a kind of elfin kid who'd also had to stay at the gym. We went to this 9/11 Vigil together. People addressed the crowd, gave impromptu elegies. There were prayers and a few songs. Then by instinct or some plan I hadn't heard about, everyone started to move out of the park and flow in groups through the streets.

We paused at streetlamps that bore signs with pictures of pajama-clad families in suburban rec rooms on Christmas mornings. One face would be circled in red and there would be a message like, "This is James Bolton, husband of Susan, father of Jimmy, Anna and Sue, last seen leaving his home in Far Rockaway at 7:30 A.M. on 9/11." This was followed by the name of the company, the floor of the Trade Center tower where he worked, phone and fax numbers, the email address and the words, "If you have any information about where he is, please contact us."

At each sign someone would leave a lighted candle on a tin plate. Someone else would leave flowers.

The door of the little neighborhood Fire Rescue station was open, the truck and command car were gone. The place was manned by retired firefighters with faces like old Irish and Italian character actors. A big picture of a fireman who had died was hung up beside the door. He was young, maybe thirty. He and his wife, or maybe his girlfriend, smiled in front of a ski lodge. The picture was framed with children's drawings of firemen and fire trucks and fires, with condolences and novena cards.

As we walked and the night progressed, the crowd got stretched out. We'd see clumps of candles ahead of us on the streets. It was on Great Jones Street and the Bowery that suddenly there was just the three of us and no traffic to speak of. When I turned to say maybe we should go home, I saw for a moment, a tall guy staggering down the street with his face purple and his eyes bulging out.

Then he was gone. Either Marco or Terry whispered, "Shit, he killed himself." And none of us said anything more.

At some point in the evening, I had said Terry could spend the night in my apartment. He couldn't take his eyes off Marco, though Marco seemed not to notice. On our way home, way east on Bleecker Street, outside a bar that had been old even when I'd hung out there as a kid, I saw the poster.

It was like a dozen others I'd seen that night. Except it was in old-time black and white and showed three kids with lots of hair and bad attitude: Mags and Geoffrey and me.

Geoff's face was circled and under it was written "This is Geoffrey Holbrun, if you have seen him since Tuesday 9/11 please contact . . ." and Mags had left her name and numbers.

Even in the photo, I looked toward Geoffrey who looked towards Mags who looked towards me. I stared for just a moment before going on but I knew that Marco had noticed.

Saturday 9/15

My tiny apartment was a crowded mess Saturday morning. Every towel I owned was wet, every glass and mug was dirty. It smelled like a zoo. There were pizza crusts in the sink and a bag of beer cans at the front door. The night before, none of us had talked about the ghosts. Marco and Terry had seriously discussed whether they would be drafted or would enlist. The idea of them in the army did not make me feel any safer.

Saturday is a work day for me. Getting ready, I reminded myself that this would soon be over. The University had found all the refugee kids dorm rooms on campus.

Then the bell rang and a young lady with a nose ring and bright red ringlets of hair appeared. Eloise was another refugee, though a much better organized one. She had brought bagels and my guests' laundry. Marco seemed delighted to see her.

That morning all the restaurants and bars, the tattoo shops and massage parlors were opening up. Even the Arab falafel shop owners had risked insults and death threats to ride the subways in from Queens and open their doors for business.

At the library, the huge screens in the lobby were being taken down. A couple of students were borrowing books. One or two even had in-depth reference questions for me. When I finally worked up the courage to call Mags, all I got was the same message as before.

Marco appeared dressed in his own clothes and clearly feeling better. He hugged me. "You were great to take me in."

"It helped me even more," I told him.

He paused then asked, "That was you on that poster last night wasn't it? You and Mags and Geoffrey?" The kid was a bit uncanny.

When I nodded, he said, "thanks for talking about that."

I was in a hurry when I went off duty Saturday evening. A friend had called and invited me to an impromptu "Survivors' Party." In the days of the French Revolution, The Terror, that's what they called the soirees at which people danced and drank all night then went out at dawn to see which of their names were on the list of those to be guillotined.

On Sixth Avenue a bakery that had very special cupcakes with devastating frosting was open again. The Avenue was clogged with honking, creeping traffic. A huge chunk of Lower Manhattan had been declared open that afternoon and people were able to get the cars that had been stranded down there.

The bakery was across the street from a Catholic church. And that afternoon in that place, a wedding was being held. As I came out with my cupcakes, the bride and groom, not real young, not very glamorous, but obviously happy, came out the door and posed on the steps for pictures.

Traffic was at a standstill. People beeped "Here comes the bride," leaned out their windows, applauded and cheered, all of us relieved to find this ordinary, normal thing taking place.

Then I saw her on the other side of Sixth Avenue. Mags was tramping along, staring straight ahead, a poster with a black and white photo hanging from a string around her neck. The crowd in front of the church parted for her. Mourners were sacred at that moment.

I yelled her name and started to cross the street. But the tie-up had eased, traffic started to flow. I tried to keep pace with her on my side of the street. I wanted to invite her to the party. The hosts knew her from way back. But the sidewalks on both sides were crowded. When I did get across Sixth, she was gone.

Aftermath

That night I came home from the party and found the place completely cleaned up with a thank you note on the fridge signed by all three kids. And I felt relieved but also lost.

The Survivor party was on the Lower East Side. On my way back,

I had gone by the East Village, walked up to Tenth Street between B and C. People were out and about. Bars were doing business. But there was still almost no vehicle traffic and the block was very quiet.

The building where we three had lived in increasing squalor and tension thirty-five years before was refinished, gentrified. I stood across the street looking. Maybe I willed his appearance.

Geoff was there in the corner of my eye, his face dead white, staring up, unblinking, at the light in what had been our windows. I turned toward him and he disappeared. I looked aside and he was there again, so lost and alone, the arms of his jacket soaked in blood.

And I remembered us sitting around with the syringes and all of us making a pledge in blood to stick together as long as we lived. To which Geoff added, "And even after." And I remembered how I had looked at him staring at Mags and knew she was looking at me. Three sides of a triangle.

The next day, Sunday, I went down to Mags' building, wanting very badly to talk to her. I rang the bell again and again. There was no response. I rang the super's apartment.

She was a neighborhood lady, a lesbian around my age. I asked her about Mags.

"She disappeared. Last time anybody saw her was Sunday 9/9. People in the building checked to make sure everyone was OK. No sign of her. I put a tape across her keyhole Wednesday. It's still there."

"I saw her just yesterday."

"Yeah?" She looked skeptical. "Well there's a World Trade Center list of potentially missing persons and her name's on it. You need to talk to them."

This sounded to me like the landlord trying to get rid of her. For the next week, I called Mags a couple of times a day. At some point the answering machine stopped coming on. I checked out her building regularly. No sign of her. I asked Angelina if she remembered the two of us having dinner in her place on Wednesday 9/12.

"I was too busy, staying busy so I wouldn't scream. I remember you and I guess you were with somebody. But no, honey, I don't remember."

Then I asked Marco if he remembered the phone call. And he did but was much too involved by then with Terry and Eloise to be really interested.

Around that time, I saw the couple who had wanted to take their kids down to Ground Zero. They were walking up Sixth Avenue, the kids cranky and tired, the parents looking disappointed. Like the amusement park had turned out to be a rip-off.

Life closed in around me. A short story collection of mine was being published at that very inopportune moment and I needed to do some publicity work. I began seeing an old lover who'd come back to New York as a consultant for a company that had lost its offices and a big chunk of its staff when the north tower fell.

Mrs. Pirelli did not come home from the hospital, but went to live with her son in Connecticut. I made it a point to go by each of the Arab shops and listen to the owners say how awful they felt about what had happened and smile when they showed me pictures of their kids in Yankee caps and shirts.

It was the next weekend that I saw Mags again. The University had gotten permission for the students to go back to the downtown dorms and get their stuff out. Marco, Terry and Eloise came by the library and asked me to go with them. So I volunteered.

Around noon on Sunday 9/23 a couple of dozen kids and I piled into a University bus driven by Roger, a Jamaican guy who has worked for the University for as long as I have.

"The day before 9/11 these kids didn't much want old farts keeping them company," Roger had said to me. "Then they all wanted their daddy." He led a convoy of jitneys and vans down the FDR drive, then through quiet Sunday streets and then past trucks and construction vehicles.

We stopped at a police checkpoint. A cop looked inside and waved us through.

At the dorm, another cop told the kids they had an hour to get what they could and get out. "Be ready to leave at a moment's notice if we tell you to," he said.

Roger and I as the senior members stayed with the vehicles. The air was filthy. Our eyes watered. A few hundred feet up the street, a cloud of smoke still hovered over the ruins of the World Trade Center. Piles of rubble smoldered. Between the pit and us, was a line of fire trucks and police cars with cherry tops flashing. Behind us the kids hurried out of the dorm carrying boxes. I made them write their names on their boxes and noted in which van the boxes got stowed. I was surprised, touched even, at the number of stuffed animals that were being rescued.

"Over the years we've done some weird things to earn our pensions," I said to Roger.

"Like volunteering to come to the gates of hell?"

As he said that flames sprouted from the rubble. Police and firefighters shouted and began to fall back. A fire department chemical tanker turned around and the crew began unwinding hoses.

Among the uniforms, I saw a civilian, a middle-aged woman in a sweater and jeans and carrying a sign. Mags walked towards the flames. I wanted to run to her. I wanted to shout, "Stop her." Then I realized that none of the cops and firefighters seemed aware of her even as she walked right past them.

As she did, I saw another figure, thin, pale, in a suede jacket and bell bottom pants. He held out his bloody hands and together they walked through the smoke and flames into the hole in the city.

"Was that them?" Marco had been standing beside me.

I turned to him. Terry was back by the bus watching Marco's every move. Eloise was gazing at Terry.

"Be smarter than we were," I said.

And Marco said, "Sure," with all the confidence in the world.

When I was very young my parents and all their friends were theater people, actors. I spent the best parts of my great, misspent college career hanging around the drama department. I liked the slippery ways actors found their way into a part, saw kids who found a role that was a perfect fit and never quite got free of it. I was fascinated by the love/hate of the typecast actors for the parts that engulfed them.

Now I live on the corner of MacDougal and Bleecker Streets and many a morning I've come out my door to find a film being shot. The best moments are the ones when it's supposed to be 1950 or 1930 and the last six or eight decades have been papered over. New York IS theater. The stage, the screen are just manifestations.

By the time I was invited to contribute to Ellen Datlow's Urban Fantasy anthology Naked City, *I had been typecast: in my case as a slithery, noir type, and "On the Slide" was a natural vehicle.*

ON THE SLIDE

Sean Quinlan caught the 6:30 wake up call almost before his cell phone began its first ring. He murmured, "Thanks," glanced at Adrianne La Farice who wore only a soft, lovely smile and barely stirred in her sleep, thrust the phone aside, slipped from the bed in the pearly morning light, and padded quietly out of the room.

He wasn't awake so much as in a place where the line between work and dreams had been erased. In the ample living room he flicked on the DVD player, keeping the sound way down. In the kitchen he started the coffee. Back in the living room he sat in his shorts on the arm of the couch and watched the opening scene in an episode of the old *Naked City* TV show.

Grainy black and white detectives in suits and hats chased a gunman over the roofs of early 1960's New York. Sun through the apartment windows made the gray figures look like ghosts, and Quinlan liked that effect.

The gunman turned to fire and the detectives ducked behind a chimney. An actor playing a uniformed cop fell, shot. The fugitive fled down a fire escape with the two detectives firing after him.

Quinlan turned up the sound half a notch to catch the voice of the old character actor who played the hard-bitten police lieutenant in the series. "Wounded in the hunt, with the law on his trail, the fugitive returns to his final lair, his first home, the old neighborhood." The trumpets playing the city-at-dawn theme music which mixed nicely with early rush hour street noise from Downtown Manhattan fifty years later.

The episode was set in a neighborhood of five story tenements that Quinlan didn't quite recognize. It had probably been torn down and turned into high-rises. When coffee smells spread, he stood and discovered Adrianne in a floor length robe, with her eyes barely open, leaning in the doorway and watching him. Her smile was gone.

"More detectives," she mumbled. "You never stop working, do you, Sean."

"My granddad and his friends used to make fun of what they called '24 hour a day cops'—guys who were always on duty," he said. "Now it's like I've become one. Can I offer you some of your own coffee?"

"Yes please." She made her way to the bathroom saying, "When we were kids, I remember guys backing off from confronting you because they just *knew* you were the law."

Adrianne La Farice had been Adie Jacobson when they were in their early twenties and she waited tables while he took care of the door at Club Red Light over in the Meat Packing District back in the now legendary early-nineties.

She returned saying, "I don't need to be up this early. I don't need to be up at all. With business the way it is, I could spend the day in bed and I think I will." She uttered some variation on that every morning and never followed through.

His divorce had left him broke. Adie's divorce from Henry La Farice, the designer, was much more successful, leaving her with this renovated condo and a partnership in a prosperous real estate business. Sadly, like everything else in New York, that was now in the tank.

Over the last several years they'd made it their pleasant habit to get together like this each time he'd been in New York on a job. And it was in Quinlan's mind to see if they could turn this into something more permanent.

When he brought Adie the coffee and half a bialy, she was sitting up in bed reading email on her laptop. "No apartment in Manhattan's going to be sold today. Everybody who owns one remembers when it was worth two million dollars. Anyone who wants one will offer a quarter of that and then either can't get financing or can't explain where they got the cash."

Quinlan took a jacket and slacks out of the corner of the closet that he'd been assigned, got socks and underwear from the rolling suitcase in which he'd brought them.

In the bathroom he stared through the steam at the serviceable face he was shaving, the short hair with almost no gray. "The family face, anonymous and perfect for stakeout work," his grandfather "Black Jack" Quinlan had said. Jack Quinlan had made detective lieutenant on the job. He'd died almost thirty years back when Sean was barely thirteen. He thought about the old man almost every day.

Sean looked in the mirror and smiled just a bit. Lately he'd had occasion to notice that the Quinlan face was also perfect for a man on the run. He put on a jacket and shirt but no tie because suddenly there wasn't time. On the way to the bedroom he picked up the brown snap brim that he'd been wearing for practice and put it on his head with just enough tilt.

When he kissed her Adie said, "Brazil! I've got a Brazilian with money interested in a penthouse and with that trade agreement he doesn't even have to explain where he got the cash."

Then she looked up and said, "You are beyond retro, Mister. You disappear and I'll start believing in Sliders."

"People talk about Sliders. Have you ever known one?"

"It's escapism not reality. I think they took the name from some old TV show nobody watched. I know a woman who described her teenage son as a perfect 1969 hippie. He had the clothes and the hair; his room was papered with old posters and he hardly ever left it. One morning he disappeared and she thinks he slid back there, claims she found notes from him written on old yellow paper and telling her he was okay. Of course she's also delusional enough to think the Dow will hit 16,000 some fine day."

Turning to go he said, "Remember the Peggy Hughes party tonight."

Adie nodded and pointed to a set of handcuffs attached to one of the brass rods on the headboard. "Can you hide those before you go? The cleaning lady's coming today."

Outside on Rivington Street, it was still early enough that Quinlan got a cab with no problem. This Lower East Side drug pit of his youth had gotten gentrified and hip beyond measure. But times like this, on mornings with bright, merciless sun shining on empty shop windows, it had started to look a bit shabby again.

As the cab rolled across Houston Street into the East Village, he noticed people setting up folding tables on the widened sidewalks, opening for business in the big informal flea market that had grown up there.

Portable dressing rooms lined Avenue B. On Tenth Street police barricades blocked traffic onto that side street. Miss Rheingold posters and ads for Pall Malls covered over the Mexican restaurant and reflexology parlor signs. Extras were ready to stand on the corner in greaser haircuts or lean out of first floor windows in housecoats and hairnets. Down the block, lights brighter than the sun illuminated a tenement.

Getting out of the cab Quinlan was spotted by a couple of the film crew. "Morning officer," one said and they all laughed.

For their amusement and his own he did an imitation of the old cop he'd heard on TV. "This is my once and future city. My life consists of long periods of waiting and brief, flashes of action and violence. My name's Sean Quinlan. And when I can get the work, I'm an actor."

Big parts of Quinlan's life were in a condition he didn't want to think about. But he had a good part in a medium-sized film. Nothing else would matter for the next few hours.

At 9:22 one day in the spring of 1960, New York Police Detective Pete McDevitt climbs out of an unmarked Buick, flicks his half smoked cigarette away, and steps into East Tenth Street. His suit is gray and his shirt is blue to match his eyes. His tie is blood red and his hat is tilted back a tad to give full value to his face. Detective Pat Roark exits from the driver's side wearing brown with a white shirt and blue tie as befits a steady back up man and faithful partner.

McDevitt was played by Zach Terry, star of *Like '60*, a Hollywood production currently shooting exteriors on the streets of NYC. Detective Roark was Sean Quinlan's role. As a featured player it was his duty to exit on the far side of the car and step smoothly into his proper place one pace behind and two feet to the left of the star.

Pete McDevitt keeps his eyes fastened on an upper floor of the tenement opposite. But Pat Roark gives a quick scan over his shoulder, to see if anyone is watching them.

Quinlan planted that gesture in rehearsal and put it in each of the takes, wanting it there to emphasize that his character was the competent by-the-book cop. No one has commented one way or the other.

What he kept in his mind was a street full of guys and women setting out dressed for work, kids going to school on a spring day over fifty years before. He blocked out what he actually saw, the trucks, the crew, the commissary table, the lights and the crowd of gawkers.

Sean Quinlan felt a bit dizzy, like he was about to fall or maybe fly and wondered if this was how the start of a Slide felt. He had created a background for his character. Roark and McDevitt were supposed to pick up Jimmy Nails, a two bit thug suspected of having ambitions above his station, for questioning. Roark was a ten year veteran of the force, a guy with a wife and two kids who was talking about moving to the suburbs. He would not be bouncing on his toes on an ordinary morning on a routine assignment.

A sound crew moved with them just out of camera range as the two cops continued a conversation that the audience would just have heard them have in the car. That scene got filmed in California a couple of weeks back.

"Definitely it's spring, Pat my boy," says McDevitt and comes to a halt. Roark's expression is mildly amused, a bit bored until he follows the other's gaze.

Without looking, Quinlan knew Terry was wearing the trademark same half bemused, half aroused little grin he had used at least once in every episode of *Angel House*.

Then Roark sees what McDevitt sees and his jaw drops just a bit. They hold the pose.

"Cut!" said Mitchell Graham, the director. "I think we may have it." Crew members moved; traffic began to flow. Zach Terry looked Sean Quinlan up and down for a moment before the two of them stepped apart.

The actors had worked together once a couple of years before when Quinlan appeared in an episode of *Angel House*. That's the HBO series featuring a law office whose partners are angels but not necessarily good ones—an amusing show Quinlan thought, once you accepted the premise. Terry was one of the stars.

Quinlan had played a quirky hit man who didn't happen to be guilty of the killing with which he'd been charged. Their two scenes together had gone well and Quinlan hoped the look just then didn't mean some kind of tension.

On the way back to his dressing room he passed a girl, maybe twenty, in peddle pushers, teased hair and pumps. She smiled and he turned to watch her walk away.

A production assistant saw him look and said, "That kid has all the moves. This location is a magnet for Sliders. They think if they dress in period and hang around sites like this they'll wake up in 1960. One told me that the trick was NOT to think about Sliding back while you did all that."

The kid had a nice ass but not nice enough to make his head spin like it did. In his dressing room Quinlan did relaxation exercises, sipped ice tea, sat silently for a few minutes, and finally listened to his calls. Arroyo, the lawyer was first.

"Sean. I assume everything you wanted to keep is already out of the condo. As of today it's repossessed. Second, my colleague who's handling your case up in San Bernardino says there's no word from the DA's office. We don't know if an indictment is coming down. But as we discussed, an indictment is just their way of getting you to testify. I'm wondering if you got my bill."

Quinlan had gotten the bill. The condo was one more casualty of his divorce and bankruptcy. When he could have sold, he couldn't bring himself to do it. When he had to sell there were no buyers.

Everyone had consoled him about the divorce like he'd suffered a death in the family or been laid off from work. Monica Celeste had the better career, was a major presence on daytime cable. Quinlan told himself that if the situation had been reversed he wouldn't have dumped her. But all that was in the past.

The San Bernardino matter was current. A runaway grand jury led by a self-righteous young DA was investigating collection agency practices. Some debtors apparently testified that a few years before Quinlan had led them to believe he was a cop. So far nothing had gotten out to the media.

That time just after the divorce was still a jumble in his mind. One thing he was sure of was that testifying meant implicating his former employers, which would be very unwise. Another thing about which he was positive was that lawyers had eaten up his *Like '60* pay.

Adie was at the office and in full business mode when she left a message. "For the Peggy Hughes thing, we can meet at Ormolu at eight. I mentioned that to a prospective client and he knew all about it. So we may meet him there."

The last call was a voice from deep in a disreputable past. Rollins said, "You asked around about me. Here I am. I know where to find you." Quinlan was a bit amused.

When they knocked on his door to say he was due on the set,

Quinlan thought about his character for a few moments. Roark had the usual problems trying to raise a family on a cop's salary. His wife and he had disagreements. But she was a cop's wife and understood what that meant. A steady guy was Roark, a good partner.

Detectives McDevitt and Roark hold the same poses as at the end of the previous scene. The audience has just watched a sequence shot two weeks before on a sound stage in California. It shows what the two cops are watching—a nude woman standing behind gauze curtains.

The viewers see a reverse strip as she hooks her bra, pulls up her panties, draws on nylons, wriggles into a slip, a blouse and a skirt. She bends slowly to put on her shoes.

Suddenly McDevitt shakes himself awake. "Decoy!" he says. "She's letting him get away." The pair of them run for the front door of the building.

Locations had found an untouched and ungentrified tenement. Props had filled the dented cans in front with in-period trash, a partly crushed Wheaties box, a broken coke bottle, a striped pillow leaking feathers.

A little old lady with a wheeled shopping cart gets in their way. The stoop is worn and paint is peeling on the railing. As they run up the steps the front door opens.

And there stands Laura Chante, the first time the audience gets a good look at her. Laura is the girlfriend of a very wrong guy, hard but soft, bad but good. She wears high heels, a black sheath skirt and a jacket open to reveal a pale, shimmering blouse. A scarf with a streak of scarlet covers most of her blond hair. "You boys looking for someone?" she asks with an innocent expression.

Laura was played by the young London actress Moira Tell. Her posture, her accent, her attitude were impeccable.

Peggy McHugh still had a sassy smile. Back in the 1950s and '60s she had made a career playing bright young girl friends and wise cracking best pals of too sweet heroines. She was the young detective's fiancée in the *Naked City* TV series.

At eighty she played tough old broads with a regular role on *As the World Turns* and a girlfriend thirty years her junior. In a nod to nostalgia she'd been cast as Detective Pete McDevitt's hip, utterly unsentimental grandmother in this movie.

It was her birthday and Mitchell Graham, the director, along with the movie's producers threw a little party for her at Ormolu's on Union Square and invited the press.

Ms. Hughes had already knocked back a Jameson's on the rocks and was swirling champagne in her glass when Quinlan came up and hugged her.

"How are you doing, you old witch?" he asked.

"Sean! Thought I'd see more of you on this shoot. How's your mother? Still living in New Mexico with what's his name?"

Peggy McHugh and Quinlan's mother, the former Julie Morris, had been pals back when his mother was acting, back when she married his father, Detective Jim Quinlan.

"Arizona. Lou Hagan is the current husband. Nice guy—retired broker. She's fine. Sends her love."

"Your mother was gorgeous. She and your father when they met were more like a movie than any movie I've been in." And having taken the conversation to a place where Quinlan didn't want to go, Peggy caught sight of someone else and said, "Bella! So wonderful of you to come!"

Quinlan stepped away, went to the bar, sipped a scotch, and looked around the room. Ormolu's tin ceiling had been polished to a fine shine, the wood paneling looked rich as chocolate. The place had been a dump twenty years before when it was a rock club called Ladders. Long before that it had been an Italian wedding hall.

Sean's parents were quite a story, the young actress and the young cop who got himself quite dirty trying to keep her in style. Jim Quinlan shot himself when the shit came down. Sean had been three when that happened and found it out in bits and pieces.

Once when he was small his grandfather had explained how it was growing up in the Irish New York of the '20s and '30s. "Kids who got in trouble, which was most of us, got let off with a warning if we had cops in the family. Those without a relative on the force got a criminal record. Simple justice and nothing less."

Out of nowhere Quinlan asked about the father whom he barely remembered and knew almost nothing. "Did my dad get into trouble?"

He never forgot the grief on the old man's face as he said, "Your father got more than a couple of warnings."

Adie was across the room talking intently to a thin man wearing thousands of dollars worth of suit and a long, dark pony tail.

Where Quinlan was standing he could hear Mitchell Graham say, "Sometimes acting is beside the point and it's the physical presence you want. Someone walks on camera unannounced and the audience knows he's a killer."

Quinlan shifted slightly and saw that the director was talking to Moira Tell and a reporter. "In America, real Mafiosi go to jail, get involved in the prison drama group, get out and go into business playing Mafiosi on stage and screen. When Friedkin shot *Sorcerer* down in Latin America he hired a couple of Sing Sing School of Drama graduates to play the thugs. The two stopped off on the way down there and helped pull a robbery. This delayed them and held up the shooting. When they showed up Roy Scheider, the star, said, 'I was told we were waiting for actors—these are just gangsters.' Supposedly, the two were deeply hurt that their artistic bone fides were being questioned."

Moira Tell laughed and moved toward the bar. On her way she noticed Quinlan. "You are very good," she told him.

"Sing Sing School of Drama."

"Oh, he was *not* talking about you. Graham admires what you're doing, the presence you bring. He believes all that nonsense about inner emotion American versus exterior detail English acting."

"You were great this afternoon."

"It's wonderful to visit a past that has nothing to do with me at all."

From across the room they heard Peggy McHugh in full voice speaking to a cable interviewer, "Back when the economy was first going down the toilet, someone asked me if I'd like to go back sixty years. I thought they meant would I like to be young again. Instead they just meant me going just as I was. 'Before heart bypasses, before air conditioning?' I asked them 'You're out of your mind,' I said. Sweetheart, we lived like dogs back then."

Adie said as they were leaving a bit later, "The one I was talking to is the Brazilian from this morning. He wants to buy a penthouse. He's loaded." Somehow money had not really come up in all the years they'd known each other.

*

The ferry boat called The Queen of Union City *disembarks passengers onto a Hudson River pier in the West Twenties. A woman wearing a veiled hat leads a small boy in an Eton cap and a girl in a straw boater by their hands, a tall man in a three piece suit and a topcoat follows them. An old, slat sided truck piled with crates of live chickens rolls onto the pier past a large sign reading "Erie Lackawanna Ferry Company."*

Under that in smaller letters is, "Departures from Manhattan on the hour and the half hour. 4 a.m. to 8 p.m."

Detectives Pete McDevitt and Pat Roark stand under a clock that says 2:25 poised, alert and ready to step out from behind the make-shift ferry shed. Then McDevitt says, "Now," and moves to his right. Roark at the same moment moves to his left.

Roark served a year in Korea. Firemen are navy; cops are army. Quinlan knows this. The next line is his:

"Ok Nails, freeze."

"Cut!"

The truck with the chickens went into reverse and parked next to a mint condition 1955 Oldsmobile and an old fashioned ambulance the size and shape of a station wagon.

Before the first take Mitchell Graham had said, "Sean, you're so perfectly in period that I feel like I should film you in black and white."

As McDevitt that day Zach Terry wore his hat at the same great angle as Quinlan. Graham noticed that. After the first take he told Quinlan, "It's distracting to have both of you with your hats alike. Could you straighten yours?"

The game was called protecting the star. Sean knew that game. McDevitt's hat was an important prop today. He shifted his own fedora.

"Perfect," said the director.

A featured player yields gracefully in the hope that a director will remember when casting in the future. Quinlan wondered how many movies Graham would direct after this one. He wondered what his own career would look like if an indictment came down in California.

Crews were setting up for the next scene, which would be shot in front of an old three story building just across from the piers. For the movie a sign had been erected on the front that read, "Murphy's Fine Food and Drink. Rooms by the Day or Week."

Once this had actually been a waterfront tavern with rooms rented to sailors on the upper floors. For a while after the waterfront shut down it had been a notorious gay bar called The Wrong Box.

Carter Boyce, the actor playing Jimmy Nails, was in costume and taking a practice walk toward the ferry shed. Carter Boyce was a nice guy who happened to have a mug two feet wide with bad news written all over it.

In the next scene, Jimmy Nails was supposed to have just come down the wooden exterior stairs that led from the second floor of Murphy's. He had an overcoat on his arm and carried a satchel.

The scene of Nails on those stairs had been completed the day before through the miracle of second unit work.

Detectives McDevitt and Roark stand exactly where they were at the end of the last shot. In the background as they start to move towards Murphy's, the Oldsmobile and the chicken truck roll off the dock in one direction, a red Studebaker station wagon goes by in the other.

Twenty feet away from them Jimmy Nails drops his luggage and overcoat and swings a double barrel shotgun their way. McDevitt acting instinctively whips off his fedora and flings it at Nails' face in one gesture. Jimmy, his eyes rolling like a trapped beast, is a creature of instinct and empties a barrel at the hat. Roark's gun jumps into his hand and he fires three times. Jimmy Nails goes down firing the second barrel into the ground.

The hat flying through the air and getting blasted into felt confetti was being shot that same week by a special effects outfit in California.

"Thanks," Roark says.

"That hat cost me seven bucks at Rothman's," says his partner, his buddy.

"Cut. Let's put Zach and Sean about a foot further apart," said Graham. "And Sean, slower on the reaction. Let the hat surprise you as much as it does Carter. Sean, are you with us?"

Quinlan nodded. For a moment he'd felt like the back draft of the antique vehicles was pulling him away from this time and place.

Over several takes the vintage Studebaker blew a tire and the wind and the sun played hell with Mr. Terry's hair. Half a dozen people surrounded him, spraying his chestnut locks.

"Exposure to the elements . . ."

"It's not, of course, but the light makes it look thin."

". . . lighting adjustment . . ."

This Quinlan knew was also about protecting the star as was the scene they kept enacting. McDevitt needed to save Roark's life to mitigate, for the audience, the fact that his misjudgment was going to cost Roark his life.

As they prepared for what turned out to be the last take, Quinlan couldn't stop thinking, each time he looked at Zach Terry, that this was the bastard who was going to get him killed.

At some point during the last couple of takes, Sean Quinlan became aware of a figure from his disreputable past. Rollins stood across the street dark and sharp in a navy blue suede jacket and soft leather shoes and watched everything that went on.

When they were finished with *Like '60* for the day, he and Rollins went down the avenue to what had been a nouveau chic diner and now seemed to be slipping into just being a diner with a liquor license.

"We had some rare adventures, you and I," Rollins remarked when they settled into a back booth, "a pair of theater students out looking for adventure."

"And not caring where they found it."

"Always on the right side of the law, though."

"Not as I remember. There was the time we unloaded the Quaalude those crazy guys from NYU manufactured in their chemistry lab."

"We weren't caught. That's being on the right side of the law as far as I'm concerned. Glad you got in touch. I've been following your career. Sorry about the divorce. Monica Celeste must be loaded."

Quinlan shrugged. "I see you're still the Well Dressed Passerby," he said. "That routine keeps working for you?"

"In any large city there are always the lost, the confused, and the lonely that need an assist from a passing stranger." Rollins gave a charming smile. "Actually, though, I've gone legit. I'm in the tourist business—tours of various old New Yorks. You heard about that?

"We have people taking daytrips to 1890s New York. Out in Brooklyn in a couple of spots you can walk down a street and almost think it's a hundred and twenty-five years ago. Any decade you can think of, people want to see the remains."

Rollins smiled. "It's an amazing confluence, you being back in town and making this movie. *Like '60,* is on the cusp of the hottest boom in this tired town. Your movie is going to be porno for the ones who go for '50s New York. That ferryboat sliding up to the dock and that truckload of chickens and you and your pal in those hats and padded shoulder suits will make them cum in their Dacron/rayon pants."

Sean gave a grin. "In tough times people want to go elsewhere," Rollins said. "With every corner of the planet going down the drain, the places they favor are in the past. Some lunatics even want to go back to the Great Depression. Like this one isn't bad enough for them. But I don't ask questions, I just set up the tours. Who would have guessed that a master's degree in History from Columbia would stand me in such good stead?"

"Especially since you never went there."

Rollins shrugged. "What makes it all weird and twisted and thus makes it my kind of enterprise is that some of the clients believe that if they can find a place with enough artifacts that evoke a certain time; they'll get a jolt and wind up there.

"Most of them want to go back to the seventies, the sixties, the fifties. They figure things would be comfortable enough. I.D. requirements were still loose back then. Sliders know enough about those times that they could make a nice living betting on the World Series and buying Xerox stock. One said that if he could get back to 1950 he'd have almost sixty years before stuff got really screwy."

"You've heard them talk all this out? Ever help any of them do it?"

"None of my clients and no one else I've ever known has actually managed the Slide. They've all heard about someone going back in time. They know someone who found a message from someone who disappeared saying he's living like a king in 1946. Psychiatrists say it's delusional. People can't deal with bad times."

"You believe the shrinks know what they're talking about?"

"They diagnosed me as a sociopath back when I was in high school. It sounded good and I went with it. If you're looking for a guide to the Slide you're out of luck. If you want a job leading 1950s nostalgia tours I'd be happy to hire you."

"Thanks, but I have other plans." Quinlan rose and put a ten down on the table. "Nice talking to you Rollo."

For a moment Rollins looked hurt. Then he said, "Sorry to break your heart, Quinlan. It's nice that you figured if anyone in New York knew how to Slide it would be me. You've been in and out of the city over the years without ever trying to get in contact so I wondered what you wanted. Somehow I didn't think of this. Either you got stupid out in California or you got very desperate."

In the early morning light, stepping carefully along a tenement fire escape just off Tenth Avenue in Hell's Kitchen, Detective Roark edges forward revolver in hand. Up ahead is Figs Figueroa's window. In another moment his partner will knock on the door of the apartment and Figueroa will be on the move. Roark curses the stupidity that led him into this. Backup is on its way and they could have waited. But the Lieutenant is not happy with the way they'd bobbled Jimmy Nails' arrest the other morning or the way they'd then made him too dead to talk. McDevitt thinks the two of them need some redemption.

As Roark inches forward, the window right behind him opens. He drops to a crouch, revolver at the ready, turns and sees the terrified face of an old woman about to hang a basket of wet laundry on her wash line. When Roark turns back, Figueroa stands on the fire escape with an automatic leveled on him.

"Cut."

On the roof just above Quinlan were the assistant director, the script girl, the camera man, and the director himself. "We need this one more time," said Graham. "Just do what you've done before." He looked closely at Quinlan and said, "Get this man some coffee."

It was late in the morning and Quinlan had already gone up this fire escape six times. He guessed this particular building got cast for the part because of this fire escape, which was as black and labyrinthine as the stairways of a Piranesi prison. People fussed with his clothes and his makeup. He'd lain awake all night next to Adie, who slept soundly. Somebody brought him coffee.

This scene was his best moment in *Like '60*. By coincidence, it and the one they'd shoot immediately afterwards were his last ones in the film. His work in New York was over.

If someone asked him what *Like '60* was about, Quinlan would have said it was the story of a cop who was an ordinary guy wanting the ordinary things and living in a simpler and not very enlightened time. This man is pulled by circumstance and human weakness into a situation where his life is on the line.

Again he climbs the stairs and inches forward. Again the window opens and, revolver at the ready, he stares into the terrified face and looks up too late to see his killer.

This morning, it seemed as if Rollins was right about the Slide being a delusion. Quinlan felt no distant hum of past times. His stomach was tight, his shoulders tense.

In his dressing room he looked at his messages. Adie had called from her office to say she had a meeting with a client and would have to miss the wrap party. This morning she had asked him—gently, indirectly, not like he was being evicted yet, if everything was okay for him back in L.A. She hadn't mentioned the Brazilian, but he was an invisible presence.

As Quinlan sat absorbing this, Arroyo, the lawyer, called. "My associate in San Bernardino says the grand jury will hand down indictments in an intimidation/extortion scheme this afternoon at around 6 pm New York time. You're accused of impersonating a law officer. One alleged victim says you showed him a badge, threatened to run him in on false charges if he didn't come up with his payment."

"That's a lie." Sean said that automatically but the only memory the accusation evoked was an appearance he'd made as a rogue cop on *NYPD Blue* many years before in which he flashed a shield.

"Sean, they're not interested in you. They want the ones who hired you."

"Speaking those names means I'll be dead or in witness protection," he said. "I'll get back to you."

Quinlan remembered when he turned thirteen and decided that instead of becoming a cop, which was all he'd wanted up until then, he was going to be an actor. His grandfather had said, "Tough luck kid, you drew your father's face and your mother's brains."

He jumped when a woman from props knocked on the door and came in to put him into a bloody shirt.

Pat Roark lies sprawled face up in the alley with the gun still clasped in his lifeless hand, his hat beside his head, his dead eyes staring at the sky.

The scene was shot from above. The camera looked down as a dozen extras, kids carrying school books, women in curlers and house dresses, guys in work clothes, idlers and honest citizens suddenly converged from all directions to see the dead man who had fallen from the sky.

The computer imaging of Roark falling backwards off the fire escape and slamming into the asphalt had been completed before he left Los Angeles.

"What was he doing up there?" a woman with a Spanish accent wanted to know.

"He's a cop," said a wise-ass kid, "see that police special."

As the sirens wail and echo off the alley walls, Pete McDevitt runs down the fire escape, yelling, "Pat! Jesus, no!" His voice breaks in a sob.

Quinlan couldn't tell if he used the dippy smile. The shot of Pat Roark dead in the alley would be used repeatedly in the film as a motive for Zach Terry's Peter McDevitt in his quest for the killer and the ones behind the killer who, it turned out reached all the way to the Commissioner's office.

The old stage actor Denny Wallace, whose father was a Polish Jew and whose mother was a French ballet dancer, played Lieutenant O'Grady.

Standing over the corpse, he delivers Roark's epitaph. "He was worth twenty of you. I'll have your badge and your gun for this, boyo."

Quinlan heard applause on the set, which meant this was probably the last take. There was comfort in lying dead in an alleyway killed in the line of duty in a time when that meant something. This was the part of his life that actually made sense.

The applause faded and died. Smell was the first thing he noticed, tobacco smoke and garbage and exhaust. Sirens sounded on the avenue. Quinlan focused his eyes on a kid with bat wing ears, a crewcut and jeans so stiff that could stand up by themselves. A bunch of scruffy street rats stared down at him.

"It's a cop!"

"How'd he get here?" The city accents were thick enough to cut.

He closed his hand on his prop gun and they all stepped back. "You been shot mister. You need a doctor?" Quinlan remembered the prop blood on his shirt front. No one, he noticed, talked about calling the cops.

"He's a fuckin' actor. Look at the make up," said an old lady with way too much lipstick peering into the alley.

All Sean wondered as he got up was how long it would take Graham and the rest to notice he was gone. He dusted himself off, buttoned his jacket to hide the dye on his shirt front, and wiped his face clean with a pocket handkerchief.

It was a five story city and the sun shone directly from across the Hudson. Everyone got out of his way as he walked down the alley. He stuffed the gun in his pocket.

"Anyone follows me," he gestured to it. He doubted that anyone in Hell's Kitchen was going to call the police. But he moved quickly, got on Tenth Avenue and started walking.

Cars and clothes gave only a hint of the year. A corner newsstand had a big display of papers dated May 19, 1957.

His father would be about half his age and still in the army in Germany. His mother would not have moved here from Buffalo. His grandfather and grandmother lived up on Fordham Road in the Bronx. The avenue was lined with pawn shops. The gun was a fake but he figured it would be worth a buck or two.

Black Jack Quinlan and he would be about the same age. If he was here. He had to be here. Once he explained things, once he showed this face, Sean Quinlan couldn't imagine them denying this fugitive a welcome.

Alternate Worlds floating in the Time Stream have been an interest (obsession?) of mine. *Warchild*, my first novel and the first piece of speculative fiction that I wrote, begins in New York but has all Time as its setting.

Part Two:

ACROSS WORLDS AND TIME

The Time Stream is the back story for my novelette, "The Ferryman's Wife." The setting is suburban Westchester in the mid-1950s.

A favorite short story author of mine, John Cheever, was known in his lifetime largely as a New Yorker writer and chronicler of the social mores of the mid-20th century American suburb. An article on Mad Men, *the TV series set in 1960s Madison Avenue, mentioned that the producer has Cheever's* Collected Stories *on his bookshelf as a reference tool. Recent biographies reveal that Cheever himself was more complicated socially and sexually than was generally known at the time (more like a* Mad Man *character, in fact).*

His style, normally naturalistic in The New Yorker *manner, could unexpectedly shift into magic: a suburban evening might evoke nymphs and gods. Some Cheever stories, "Torch Song," "The Enormous Radio," "The Swimmer," are overtly fantastic. Death is a lady in Manhattan; a radio broadcasts the private lives of the residents of an apartment house, a young man on a whim swims across his suburb by going from one backyard pool to the next. In the course of a day he travels into the neighborhood's decline and his own old age.*

Around 2000, I began writing Alternate World/Time Stream stories. For one of the first I used a Cheever setting. This was my first story to be on a Nebula short list.

THE FERRYMAN'S WIFE

1.

At 7:40 on the first warm day of April, on a Tuesday, that least remarkable of days, the platform at Grove Hill train station was all but deserted. Cars soon arrived, a Country Squire first, a Desoto V8 next, then a flood of fins and chrome. Commuters disembarked.

As 7:49 approached, Oldsmobiles jockeyed with Pontiacs; sunlight gleamed on waxed finishes. A few women got out of autos and waited on the platform. But mostly it was husbands who gave goodbye kisses to wives with hair still in curlers and babies with zwieback-stuffed mouths.

For in that year, 1956, the great nation of the West was reinventing itself, changing from a land, part urban and part rural, into something not seen in the world before.

Linda Martin sat behind the wheel of the blue and white Chevy Bel Air and savored her favorite moment of the day. She rolled down her window as Roy slid of out the passenger seat beside her, passed before the car making goo-goo eyes at six-year-old Sally in the back seat.

He doffed his narrow brimmed hat, ducked his head to the open window. His mouth tasted of Pepsodent, coffee, eggs and bacon, and a single on-the-way-to-the-train Chesterfield. "Keep Lady Olivia amused," he murmured.

"She'd be happier if you did that," Linda whispered in his ear.

"Nah, no aristocrats for me. I'm a damn commissar. Comes the Revolution they all get shot.

Linda giggled but glanced in the rearview mirror. She could just hear their daughter's voice, loud and clear, asking in public, "Mommy, why is daddy a commissar?" But Sally was watching intently for the appearance of the commuter train.

With the ghost of a wink, Roy stuck his hat on at the perfect angle and joined the marching husbands. Linda admired his easy way among the topcoated men. They were joined by old Mrs. Egan who liked to visit her specialists in the city and by Minnie Delahunt who, for reasons much speculated about, had kept her job in the fashion business even after getting married.

The train was out of sight as Linda turned on the radio for news. Driving out of the parking lot, she still felt Roy's parting touch and, holding that memory, was with him as he walked through a rocking car, greeting a man in horn rims whom they both knew through the PTA.

Roy found a seat, opened his briefcase. Unlike the rest of the passengers, Roy could see in the dark and differentiate one set of footsteps from the dozens behind him on a crowded city street. And unlike almost anyone else in that time and place, he was aware of his wife's contact. And he could deflect it, which he did with a little smile.

Linda smiled too as she steered into traffic. An announcer on the car radio said, "A perfect blend." Maybe he was pitching coffee or a new miracle fabric. But to Linda it described the life Roy and she had made in this time and place. Because a road crew was repairing the usual route, she detoured down Main Street.

"Mommy?" asked a voice with a keen edge. In the air was that precarious moment when a thought becomes an idea.

And Linda, her attention focused on the back seat, saw in the mirror the slight quiver of a six-year-old's pigtails, the growing light in the eyes which were Roy's eyes. "Yes, hon?"

"How long is Auntie Olives going to stay?" The idea took form.

"A little while. Why?"

"Because last week Timothy brought his rabbit to school and nobody else has one and everyone got to touch her."

"And you wondered?" Linda felt the idea become a plan.

"No one else has an aunt from England. And she could sing."

The plan was broached.

Much of Linda's concentration was focused on Sally. Most of the rest was devoted to negotiating traffic on the two blocks of shops that constituted downtown Grove Hill. So she only glanced at a delivery truck making a left turn beside Stillwell's Grocery.

Just a black, closed truck driving down a shadowed alley, but it caught her attention. The driver's face, seen for a moment in profile was so ordinary as to escape the memory. The phrase "hard to pick out of a police line up" occurred to her.

Driver and vehicle evoked dark deeds when the whole point of a village like Grove Hill was never to suggest anything even remotely like that.

The voice from the back seat said, "Can she, Mommy? Huh?"

And Linda heard herself say, "You have to ask Auntie Olives, honey." She realized that she too was calling their guest that.

Driver and vehicle were out of sight and contact. Alone, she would have cut back immediately. As it was, she drove to the Pathfinder Elementary School. Half distracted, she agreed that Sally could ask their house guest to be that week's Show and Tell.

When Linda returned to Main Street ten minutes later, there was no sign of the delivery truck either behind Stillwell's nor anywhere else. In the gray stone and white clapboard stores of Grove Hill's Main Street, she made quick purchases of a quart of milk, light bulbs, a pack of cigarettes. In each place she made casual mention of a truck that she said had cut her off. Her discreet probe produced the information that there had been no deliveries that morning.

Roy, long gone down the tracks to New York City, would not be accessible until evening. She reached for Sally. Right hand on left side. Not like Perry Gibson next to her who had it wrong.

Saying the magic words, ". . . one nation invisible . . ."

Linda considered the slippery path from proper precaution through solipsism to paranoia as she got back in the Chevy. Still, instead of heading directly home, she drove onto the Parkway and off again. East Radley was the town next to Grove Hill. It lacked a commuter station and was considered a bit dusty and decayed.

A place on the corner where she turned was owned by an old Italian couple who had a small vineyard out back, a statue of the Virgin Mary in the front yard. The neighborhood was mostly large, older houses. As she had been taught since she was eleven, Linda did not reach out.

Abruptly, she felt the touch. Like a sudden ripple on the water, swirling leaves, a shooting star seen at the corner of an eye. Dearest? Mrs. Wood was home.

She tried to keep her memories of the truck, the driver, the people she questioned, as clear as they had been when she first saw them. Mrs. Wood accepted her offering.

Linda Martin pulled up in front of a tall shingled, Queen Anne house. It had an old-fashioned conservatory attached. No car sat in the driveway and the blinds were drawn. A slide and some see-saws could be seen out back. The voices of children were heard. But the back yard was big and overgrown and the voices sounded far away.

Aware of neighbors and casual curiosity, Linda scribbled a note, an actual one about needing a sitter for that Thursday. She walked up to the front porch as if that was why she had come.

Bending to slip the paper under the door, she caught the images of the truck, the driver, the store keepers on Main Street. All had been rearranged and examined. Clumsiness too is a strategy. Just that and no more. She had turned to go when Mrs. Wood touched her again. Your guest. Linda caught the image of a woman, wild haired, naked. It took Linda a moment to realize what the woman was doing. Her passage is in your hands.

Linda remained bending. "Sally is safe?"

She saw another face then, black and white. Beautiful. Mrs. Wood smiled as if that hardly needed asking.

It was well after nine by the time Linda parked the car in her driveway. That's when she heard the voice. A soprano clean as a child's trilled up the years from a place where being a ruined woman was an identity and a full time occupation.

> *I leaned my back up against some oak,*
> *Thinking that he was a trusty tree.*
> *But first he bended, then he broke,*
> *And so did my false love to me.*

Think of the song as compensation, Linda told herself as she opened the door and saw a petticoat—her petticoat from Bendel's!— draped over the hall table. Slips had been taken out of drawers and dropped on the floor without even being tried on. Linda followed the trail of undergarments down to the rec room. This world did not hold enough chemise and lingerie to satisfy the guest. Linda had come to regard it as like being around a magic animal, one which sang wondrously but shed everywhere.

Olivia Wexford sat in a green silk, floor-length robe, her skin like fine porcelain. She brushed her auburn hair with long strokes. It was something she had, with great reluctance, just learned to do for herself. Still, the repeated gesture was elegant each time. She looked up as Linda entered, with an unguarded expression of cold speculation.

She wonders, Linda thought to herself, where I've been for the last hour when I should have been here entertaining her. In her slacks, blouse, and French-bobbed brunet haircut, Linda was cute and knew it. But here she felt dowdy, almost sexless. The TV was on with the sound off. Captain Kangaroo and Mr. Greenjeans skipped around a table. Mr. Greenjeans, a proper second banana, was poker-faced, but the Captain mugged each time he passed the camera.

The guest gave a surpassingly raucous laugh. "Amusing rustics," she said. Her eyes sparkled, her face was animated. If one could ignore the background of pine paneling, the local florist's calendar on the wall, she could have stepped out of a painting by Gainsborough or Romney, "Lady Olivia Wexford at her toilette."

Hated and feared back home, unable to boil water, resentful of having to dress herself, disturbed and aroused that men could see her bare ankles, wherever Olivia was it would always be 1759.

Idly, out of habit, Linda brushed her guest's mind. And was stopped abruptly by an image of a silk fan in pink and pearl. On the fan, half dressed and agape, Bacchus and Ariadne encountered each other for the first time. With a slight nod, Linda backed off. Lady Wexford had a powerful protector.

Aware of what had just happened, suddenly reflective, Olivia sipped chocolate out of a doll-size china cup. "HE knew my life up and down, how I had lived it and what I'd do next," she said. "HE promised me all of Time but little did I guess that I would see it as a fugitive in flight."

She had fallen hard not for an ordinary lord, goodness help them all, some ass in a powdered wig and silk stockings. No, her particular daemon lover was a power of a kind that made Linda wary. It was not well to know more than a god wanted you to.

"In the last place where the Rangers had me, shock was a favorite word," said Olivia. "It referred to glassy eyed ex-soldiers, hysterical young women with skirts above their knees. And to me."

Fresh from the ruins of her own world, Lady Olivia had stayed in a private nursing home just outside London in a certain 1920. This particular sanitarium was secretly controlled by the organization known, where they were known, as the Time Rangers.

"Scarcely could I concentrate my mind enough to wonder why I was there much less what was to be done to me. Here, I have begun to unravel various mysteries."

Linda saw the image of the fan snap shut, replaced by what looked like a Watteau painting. Light shone through trees, moss grew like velvet, a white body reclined, privacy protected by long auburn hair and chains. They were graceful chains but secure all the same. Lady Olivia Wexford was staked out in the woods. "Bait," she said, "is what I will be, a playing piece in the games of the Rangers and the Gods."

Linda thought to herself, 'After what you and your lover boy did you're lucky not to have been burned at the stake.' Aloud she said, "Let's finish getting you dressed. Make up first."

Olivia's nose wrinkled. "In that last London where I stayed, girls who had not been kissed, much less deflowered, wore whores' paint."

"Nonetheless. We must honor local custom."

"Let us," Olivia said as she rose, and Linda noted how she barely overcame the instinct to issue orders. "Let us, go into the city."

"Not today. I didn't arrange for a babysitter." Linda thought of the black truck. Instinctively, she reached out.

Through Sally's eyes, a mile away, she saw a blackboard and on it the letter H written as big as a six-year-old.

"We're going to the supermarket," she said. Lids rolled over the guest's wide blue eyes. Life with Sally had prepared Linda for these moments, so she added, "And on the way, we can have a driving lesson."

Lady Wexford's eyes opened at this and she allowed herself to be guided upstairs. A bit longer afterwards than Linda would have thought possible, Olivia had helped to dress herself in a velvet jacket and a pair of Linda's toreador pants under a flared skirt. She had put on flat pumps and was standing at the front door.

"Lord Riot, was what HE was called and after a summer of HIS rule the city lay in smoldering ruins. All burned, the palaces and churches, the docks and the slums. And the populace, gentry and commoners were gone to whatever place HE had led them. But in that other London where I just stayed, it was 1920 and while all else was changed, the palaces and churches still stood and nobody had ever heard of the summer of Lord Riot."

'Damn right,' Linda thought. 'The Rangers spent a lot of effort making sure your particular London never got heard of again.'

She opened the front door and Olivia stepped out. Linda noticed the other woman's slight shudder as she entered an alien world.

In the driveway, Lady Wexford touched the hood and roof of the Chevy as if she were acquainting herself with a new horse. While they drove, she listened intently to Linda's explanation of the ignition, the steering wheel, the clutch, the gas pedal.

At the supermarket she was at once coy and haughty, dizzy in what seemed to her to be public nudity. Linda was aware of the assistant manager at the meat counter, an Italian kid, appraising them. Olivia noticed also. Linda couldn't see the glance that was thrown, but the young man took a step back, face flushed, eyes wide open.

'Amusing rustics,' Linda thought. 'That's what we are for her.'

"Duz, Palmolive, Ivory," Olivia said. "A cornucopia, a soap for every purpose. But every place looks like every other. Your house is the mirror duplicate of one at the corner of your street. The house across the road from yours looks exactly like one three doors down. You tell me this isn't the same store we were in on Friday last?"

"Not even the same town. That was an A&P in Larchmont, remember? This is a Safeway. In the Leather Stocking Shopping Center in Grove Hill." Then she repeated something she had said before to other refugees fleeing Upstream or Down. "These suburbs sprang out of nowhere. No one knows anyone else." She added, "Here you are my English cousin, Olivia Smithfield. A bit odd, a bit exotic. But a recognizable commodity. Here everyone is a bit of an Anglophile. This is where you learn to blend."

Lady Olivia's eyes narrowed. Blending in was not why she had been born and raised. In the checkout line, she fumbled with a wallet and bills. The lesson for today was paying for purchases. In her prior life she had never touched so much as a penny. "Foolish colonial monies!" she said, but smiled as she did, amusing the cashier and winning an approving nod from Linda.

It was well after noon by the time they had wheeled the cart out to the Chevy, loaded the groceries into the trunk, and sat in a booth at the back of a mostly empty luncheonette.

"You said that you were raised in this time." Lady Wexford's expression indicated that she found the idea fascinating and appalling.

The oldest student trick, Linda knew. Get the teachers to talk about their VERY favorite subject. Themselves. Still, her cover story came in layers, so she peeled one off and said, "I'm a Ranger's wife. We go where he's assigned. I'm happy that we're where I can help him.

"Yet you are not a Ranger."

"No. My mother was. A station chief like Roy. 1950s North America was her assignment. More or less the same one he has. Keeping the peace, managing the Time Stream. Jake Stockley was her husband. He was a Ranger field operative, kind of low level. Not a bad guy at all. Lovable. But he wasn't my father. My dad was dead before I could remember him. My mother had remarried."

Olivia listened intently. Linda found herself surprised by how much she wanted to talk.

"The first time we hit 1960, I wasn't even two and didn't know the difference between that and 1950. All I understood was we were in a new house. Outside Chicago. Mom and Jake were real estate agents. A nice cover. It fooled me.

"By my second 1959, I was eleven. I thought Tony Curtis was dreamy and had a major crush on Danny Larogga in my sixth grade class because I thought he looked like Tony Curtis. I was lobbying for a poodle skirt and training bra in exchange for having to wear braces on my teeth. Couldn't have been more typical if I'd been trying.

"Mom had been dropping hints for a long while. And the evidence was all around me, the number of strange 'friends' who stayed with us, the way Jake traveled on business all the time, the fact that Mom read the papers, watched the news constantly but was never surprised by anything. So I knew, but I didn't want to find out." Linda looked inquiringly at Lady Olivia, who nodded her understanding.

"At that point, Mom took me aside and explained that she and Ranger Stockley and I were going to move. Bad enough. But, instead of it being to an identical ranch house in another town, we were going where I could get to see them build the ranch houses. Where Tony Curtis was still waiting tables and Danny Larogga was being toilet trained.

"The name of our new home was 1950. The Korean War. Harry

Truman. Ancient history. We, it turned out, had reached the end of Mom's Beat. As Jake put it later, 'Weird, huh kid, whores and cops have beats.'

Linda caught Olivia's look, distant, speculative. She had said too much. "Want to get behind the wheel?" she asked.

As they got in the car, she reached out and was aware of blue. Bouncing in the air. The whole class had been given balloons. Sally's was blue. The bus was here and she was taking her blue balloon home.

A few minutes later, Linda and Olivia were in the Chevy. Lady Wexford marveled as she headed for the parking lot exit, "As if I had in hand a team of a thousand horses!" In her enthusiasm, she stepped down on the break. The car bucked and stalled.

A trailer truck with Wonder Bread logos was pulling into the lot. Gears ground, what sounded like a steam whistle blared. From his high seat, the trucker yelled, "Drive it or park it, lady!"

As he did, Linda saw a black delivery van the same or the twin of the one that morning speed by on the access road. Instantly, she took a deep breath and said. "Get out of the seat!" The van had already disappeared. It was between her and Pathfinder Elementary School.

Lady Olivia obeyed instantly. Ignoring the horn and the yelling, they changed places. Linda had orders to protect her guest. But she had a higher priority. She drove in the same direction as the truck. Olivia sat silent beside her. As they approached the school, Linda began to circle. She reached out:

Blue bounced beside her. Holding onto blue. Red across the aisle jumped back and forth. Green spun out of control. BANG! Green disappeared. Perry Gibson cried. Other kids laughed.

On a quiet street, Linda caught sight of the yellow bus making its slow, easy way toward a cluster of women and carriages and pre-schoolers. She looked around, saw nothing and so made no move for the .32 caliber automatic concealed under the driver's seat.

"It's Sally, isn't it?" Linda had forgotten about Olivia. "You have sensed a threat." Linda nodded, circled the block. Found nothing. Pulled into a wider arc around the bus. "I would aid you however I can."

The air was full of balloons and she was holding onto the blue balloon. All around were yellow balloons and red. But only one blue balloon. Perry, sticky with tears, grabbed for it, and her elbow went out and stopped him.

Linda approached her house cautiously. She drove up the next street, looked at the back of her place and saw nothing. She pulled into her driveway as the yellow bus turned the corner. While it pulled to the curb, she checked the house and garage doors. No sign of forced entry.

"How long have you had the ability you just showed?" Olivia asked.

Linda knew this woman had studied her all the while her attention had been focused on her daughter. She cut the truth to fit the moment. "Before Sally? Randomly. And only with those I could actually see. With her? As you observed."

She and Olivia walked out to the sidewalk. The balloon came toward them. "Mommy, I told them that Auntie Olives was from England and she'd sing." Linda saw Olivia blink and realized that she too had caught Sally's memory of standing before her class announcing what she was bringing to Show and Tell.

"Honey." Linda pretended this hadn't happened. "I said you had to ask her first. What if she doesn't want to?"

Linda turned and found the Lady looking at Sally with a mixture of tenderness and regret. Olivia had a daughter. A child born and taken from her. Two hundred years ago. A few months before.

"I will, my dear Sally," said Olivia. "I'll sing and I'll tell a story." A thought seemed to amuse her. "I'll tell you all about the Ferryman and the Wolf."

Roy, Linda and Olivia had been invited to a dinner party that evening at the Stanleys'. George and Alice Stanley were celebrating their wedding anniversary. They lived two doors down on the block behind Roy and Linda Martin. Cindy, a rare teenager in this neighborhood of young couples and small children, had agreed to babysit with Sally.

When Roy got home, Linda told him about the truck. They agreed not to change their plans. But, as if on a whim, Roy went out the back door carrying a bottle of champagne. No fence or hedge separated their yard from the Hackers who lived directly behind them. He let the women go first, hung back. Scouting the ground, Linda knew, in the off chance he had to come back from the party in a big hurry.

In her black party sheath, she watched Olivia sweep before her in full skirt. Frank and Marge Hacker, on their way to the party paused and awaited them. "How do you like America?" Frank asked Olivia.

"Your driving is exhilarating!"

"Different side of the road than in England."

"Your provincial rules are an endless plague!"

Frank was dazzled; Marge was plainly annoyed. Linda caught a glimpse through their eyes, of Olivia and herself. And of Roy behind them. He scuffed at something with his shoe.

Alice and George Stanley had gotten married shortly before he was sent over to England with the Army Air Corps. Wartime now seemed to them distant and romantic.

At dinner, Linda's attention rode on a dream taking place in Sally's bedroom a few hundred feet away. It involved a class of bad dogs who would not listen to their teacher.

Then she heard George Stanley ask Olivia, "Were you in London during the Blitz?" Lady Wexford paused. Conversation stopped. Olivia said, with just a slight tremor, "Awful. Terrible. The city destroyed. Nothing but rubble." Everyone made consoling noises.

After dinner, Marge Hacker remarked to Linda Martin, "You seem so far away." She followed Linda's gaze and saw Roy amid a group of men who were discussing the old Joe DiMaggio and the new Willie Mays. Roy was silent. He looked at Olivia, who was looking back. Several of the women, in phone conversations the next day, pinned Linda's distance to the fine rapport that had sprung up between her English relative and her handsome husband.

"But you picked up nothing from the driver," Roy said that night when he and Linda were in bed. Slightly drunk and needing sleep, he was reviewing her account of the delivery truck driver. "Clumsy," he said. "Our Upstream friends use their human agents a lot more adroitly."

"Unless they want them to be seen." Linda lowered her voice, though Olivia was asleep down the hall. "Any word on how much longer our guest will be with us?"

"Another week, possibly two. Then she gets moved up closer to the Front. I don't know what the game is." He sounded wistful. In the

Time Wars, 1956 was a rear area, far away from the action. "I thought you found her interesting."

"Mrs. Wood showed me something today." Linda felt him tense at the mention of Mrs. Wood. But she said, "Olivia was a wild-haired, pregnant Bacchae. She sat on a pile of rubble, naked except for a silk wristlet. She carried a head. Its mouth was open. Like it was still indignant at having been separated from its body.

"We in the Main Stream know the head's former owner as the one who became King George III," Linda said. "In that particular 1759, Lady Olivia Wexford helped tear it off his shoulders, impetuous minx that she is."

"I say, no Boston tea party for Georgie that time around," Roy murmured in a silly ass voice and sank under deep waters. Even in sleep, Linda was deflected from his thoughts. What she felt when trying to touch them reminded her of the static between stations on the radio dial.

She remained awake in the midst of the quiet streets, the slumbering neighborhood. Then she saw a face, round and flushed, youthful but with deep, ancient eyes under white powdered hair. Olivia dreamed of her former lover. Linda automatically looked away.

Lord Riot was what the London mobs called him. He had an abundance of names along the Time Stream. Linda thought of him as Dionysius. But Riot was as good as anything else.

Lord Riot had swept up a large part of the population of Olivia's England, joined it to hordes from a dozen similar places, hurled the frenzied mass Upstream, and pushed the frontier back a few years. The Gods were going down hard.

They have ruled the back of our minds, the willing places in our hearts for a thousand generations. But their reign will last only as long as human thought and emotion. A couple of centuries Upstream is a Frontier. On the other side, beings move and communicate. But we would call them machines and they will call us meat.

Jake Stockley, Linda's stepfather, had tried to explain to her the alliances of the Rangers and the Gods. She was twelve and first asking questions. "Politics, makes strange bedfellows, kid," he said. "Somewhere up the chain of command this game makes sense." But even he didn't seem convinced.

In that game, Olivia was a prize. It seemed to Linda that using Riot was like trying to harness a cyclone or ride a tidal wave, that Lady Wexford was dangerous to be near.

On the night air, she heard a cry, saw an image sharp as a Blade: an infant, swaddled, wrapped in rabbit fur, seen one last time. Lady Olivia dreamed of her baby being taken away from her. Ancient eyes stared out at Linda. Lord Riot claimed his child.

2.

Nice towns like Grove Hill exist outside every city in the nation. Pass through there on the train today and you'll find that the stores on Main Street have become antique shops and boutiques. The trees that survive are bigger. The parking lot is larger. ATVs have replaced the station wagons and many women await the 7:49.

But much looks the same as on a Thursday morning almost fifty years ago when Linda drove the Chevy to the station. Olivia and Sally rode in the back seat. Today was Show and Tell.

Roy sat beside her smoking his fifth cigarette of the morning. The day before, he and Linda had argued at any moment when they were alone. In the morning it had been about how Sally was being brought up. "I don't want you leaving her with the God damn witch." When he was that angry, tiny cracks appeared in his twentieth century American accent. "Mrs. Wood!" He managed to say the name as if it was a euphemism for shit.

Wednesday evening, the argument had been about Ranger procedures. "How much longer will we be saddled with her Ladyship?" Linda snapped.

At home, in front of Sally and their guest, small domestic difficulties produced monumental silences. By Thursday, they hardly spoke. Silent tension seemed almost natural to Linda, raised in a household with a secret mission in the heyday of the Cold War. Roy, used to active combat, found it maddening.

"Can I see you sing tonight?" Sally asked, Olivia.

That evening, a concert version of Handel's Acis and Galatea was being given at Carnegie Hall. Olivia had seen it two hundred and five years before and had her heart set on seeing it again. They were, she, Roy and Linda, going into the city.

"Foolish girl," Olivia said. "Professional singers," a slight disdain in her tone, "will entertain us."

A day or two before, Linda would have made a note to explain to their guest that in this brave new world, professional singers were the aristocracy. That, as they spoke, a new king swiveled toward Memphis waiting to be crowned.

But this was no innocent herded Upstream, dazed by all she saw around her. Lady Wexford needed no help from anybody.

"And you will get to stay with Dorrie whom you love," said Olivia. "And with Mrs. Wood," she added and suddenly asked, "What is your Mrs. Wood like?"

Before Linda could interrupt, Sally frowned and replied, "She's a TV."

As they parked, Roy said, "Train's here," jumped out of the car like he was escaping, and came around for his kisses and hugs. Perfunctory for Linda, fervent in the case of his daughter. "See you ladies this evening," he said. Sally had eyes only for him as he bounded onto the platform, mingled with the crowd, and boarded the 7:49.

Linda felt Roy on the train. He nodded to a pair of vets who were comparing Ike and MacArthur, slid into the seat behind them, and buried himself in work. More than that she couldn't know.

His fellow commuters had learned all that men needed to find out about Roy from chance remarks exchanged in line at the hardware store, leaning against a fence at a backyard barbecue.

He was from the West Coast, had flown with the Air Force in Korea, had his own small import/export company, and traveled a lot.

They rode the train together. But once in the city, all went their separate ways. They joked with Roy about how much time he spent out of his office. When Frank Hacker or George Stanley remembered that they were supposed to invite him to play golf that weekend, or solicit a contribution to the Fresh Air Fund, they would get his secretary, a formidable lady with a slight and unplacable accent. Roy usually wouldn't return their calls until the end of the day.

Even catching him as they left the train at Grand Central wasn't possible. They might notice him, attaché case in hand, newspaper under his arm, walking through a now crowded car as they pulled out of Pelham Manor. Asked, he'd mentioned getting off at 125th street to see a man at Columbia University who translated his business correspondence with Iran.

Because he was so adept, but mainly because none of them could envision such a thing, no one ever saw Roy walk into Time. That usually happened in the confusion of their imminent arrival in the city. With a brisk step or two and the help of the train's motion, he would stride away from 1956. Sometimes he went up towards '59 for liaison with a neighboring Station Chief. Or back toward '50, a recurrent trouble spot where tensions were always near a boiling point.

That morning while Olivia, unaccompanied, sang Froggy Went A'Courting to an audience of enraptured six-year-olds and their teacher, Linda wondered if she knew any more about her husband than did the men on the train.

When Olivia began the story of the Ferryman and the Wolf, Linda half listened.

Once there was a ferryman who lived with his wife in a little house on a river bank. When his son was born, the father asked the river to be the boy's godfather. In answer, a stout tree branch floated ashore. The father carved it into a pole for his son.

Linda began to pay attention. Rangers were recruited as children. She recognized a tale of the Stream, worn smooth by passage up and down the human ages.

The boy grew up to be a ferryman also. He carried passengers from one side of the river to the other. The river was very wide and each day he could only make three trips one way and three trips the other. His boat was small and on each trip he could carry only one load beside himself.

The story was a riddle, a challenge. As she listened, Linda wondered if Lady Wexford told this more out of boredom than contempt, or the other way around.

One day a farmer asked him to carry a prize cabbage as big as a small child across the river where the king's own cook would give him a silver coin for it. The Ferryman agreed. But before he could start out, a shepherd appeared with a hungry lamb and asked the Ferryman to take her across the river to a field of clover. As payment the Ferryman could have her wool, which was soft as silk.

The Ferryman agreed, but he noticed how the lamb looked at the cabbage and knew he must never leave them alone together. He was about to take the cabbage across, when a wolf appeared with a sack on its shoulder and said, "Kind sir, I must cross the river. Carry me and I will give you what is inside this sack."

In this story of choice and chance, Linda noticed, only the wolf and the ferryman spoke. Only they were acting on their own behalf. Cabbage and lamb were just baggage.

The wolf looked longingly at the lamb, anxious to be left alone with her. The ferryman did not think long, but he did think hard. He put the lamb in the boat. Since he knew the wolf would never eat a cabbage, he left those two together. He carried the lamb across the river and on the way he sang:

> *Oh river deep and river wide*
> *Bring me swift to the other side*

The ferryman left the lamb. Returned. Picked up the cabbage and carried it across. As he did, he sang:

> *Oh, river wide and river deep*
> *I pray you safe my cargo keep*

The lamb was happy to see the cabbage. But the ferryman picked her up and took her back with him. When he got to the other bank, it was growing late. The wolf was overjoyed to see the lamb. But the ferryman told him to get in the boat. The wolf was very hungry, but he obeyed. As they went, the ferryman sang:

> *Oh river brave and river swift*
> *Please send a tide my hopes to lift*

The ferryman carried the wolf across and told him to guard the cabbage. The wolf agreed, thinking that when the ferryman returned with the lamb it would be dark and he would snatch his prey.

By the time the ferryman reached the lamb it was almost night and too late to make another trip. But he put the little beast aboard his boat, and as he poled his way across he sang:

> *Oh river swift and river brave*
> *Grant me now a favoring wave*

And in the last moments of light, Godfather River reached up and bore the tiny craft from one side to the other faster than the eye can blink. The wolf was pacing back and forth on the other side.

As the sun fell and the boat put in to shore, the wolf leaped. But the ferryman took his stout pole and whacked him over the head so hard that the wolf dropped his sack and ran away.

The king's cook was so delighted with the giant cabbage that he gave the ferryman a bag of coins. And the lamb when he brought her to pasture yielded wool as soft as silk.

Over the heads of the children, Linda watched Lady Olivia look at Sally. The wolf and the lamb, she thought to herself. And the cabbage, she added, including herself.

So the ferryman brought home the coins and the wool and the sack to his wife and daughter. His wife opened the sack. And what was inside? Oh, wine and sweets and a jeweled hen who laid a gold egg every morning and could tell your fortune. But The Ferryman's Wife is a tale for another time.

A story of desire, distortion of Time and even the hint of an oracle. With a happy ending. Real life would not be so nice. Linda was certain of one thing. Olivia and Sally would never be left alone together.

Dinner that evening was under the perpetual Christmas ornaments of the Russian Tea Room. The waiters, old and disdainful, each with an account of aristocratic privileges lost along with the Czar, were deferential around Roy. As if they instinctively detected a greater, scarier fraud than their own.

Over blini, caviar and vodka, Linda watched her husband lean forward and tell Olivia, "This place is a sentimental favorite of mine because of how my wife and I met."

The Englishwoman wore black and silver. A cameo at her throat showed an ivory profile set against rich blue. The blue caught the color of her eyes. "You mean to say you met in Russia. Two . . . Americans." She still hesitated on the word. She was amused, curious. Linda watched her.

"Not quite. In Budyatichi," said Roy. "A miserable town of shacks and mud, far enough into Poland for the population to be surprised when the Red Cavalry Army showed up." Roy's eyes grew somewhat misty. He had already put away two double martinis.

"Vladimir Khelemskya was my cover, a junior officer on General

Budyonny's staff. A glorified dispatch rider. But I was twenty and this was my first independent Ranger assignment."

Linda shook her head. He refused to see this.

"A dashing young subaltern!" Olivia's expression was the same as that of the children hearing the story that morning. "When was this?"

"On a September in a 1920," he said. "Always a dangerous passage in Eastern Europe. Things go badly that year but can get worse. The Russian Revolution must succeed but not triumph. In Budyatichi was an International Nursing Station where I had been told there would be allies with information of use to a Ranger. And who did I find?"

Linda looked at him furiously. He never hesitated.

"You were there?" Olivia, all surprise, asked Linda. "So far from home."

"A summer job, after sophomore year in college." Linda tried to sound bored. "Other kids were camp counselors, bummed around France. Because of my family connections, I ended up in a hot, dusty hell hole. People lived in filth and terror. No radio, No car. No shampoo. My supervisor was away that afternoon."

"So much for a Ranger undercover to do," Roy said. "False orders to deliver. Supplies to misdirect. Seeds of doubt to sew. Downstream college girls to seduce. Especially ones who thought they were going to give me orders." He laughed.

A man talks nostalgically about his youth, Linda knew, when his current life has hit a wall. She remembered that morning they met: the scent of wood smoke and the first hint of autumn, the jingle of spur and slap of holster as he slung himself off his horse, his white teeth and blond mustache.

Once, when she was very young, Linda had been promised that she would know every mind but one. That first morning, she had reached out to touch his and almost jumped when she found she couldn't.

They had told her that far Upstream there was an implant that blocked telepathy. Just as they had warned her about Upstream boys supplemented in all kinds of ways that Mother Nature never intended. They had, in fact, told her just enough so that she had to see for herself.

"I was there," said Lady Olivia brightly, interjecting herself into a sudden silence. "In that very year you two were in Poland. At Hendom House outside London," she said. "I remembered the place from my childhood. My mother's sister, the Duchess of Dorset, lived there. I'd seen it burn. But in that 1920, it still stood and had become a kind of hospital."

Hendom House in 1920 on the Main Stream was a private hospital. The Rangers found it convenient to stash various casualties of their own among the trauma victims of the First World War. Linda knew that while recovering from her time with Lord Riot, Olivia Wexford had precipitated several fights and an actual duel between inmates.

Olivia arose. How well she knew the moment to leave a couple to talk about her. And to quarrel. Roy watched her elegant passage, the patron struck numb by the sight of her.

Linda tried to decide when these two had first rutted. Recently. That she knew. Tuesday morning, she decided. Roy had doubled back in Time, returned shortly after they had left for the train. He and Olivia then screwed amid the petticoats. Evidence of that, a stray footprint perhaps, was what he had compulsively scuffed away on Tuesday evening.

Roy took out his silver cigarette case, opened it and offered it to her. She shook her head. "You're talking too much." She said, "Upstream they can and will tell her whatever they want. Here we will maintain security."

"My impression, was." He drew on his Chesterfield, looked at her from under his lids, suddenly not from this Place or Time. "My impression was, that you two exchanged girlish confidences."

"How much longer is she supposed to be here?"

"Current plans are that I'm to take her Upstream sometime next week."

"I want it sooner. I want it immediately."

"Yes, ma'am. I will do my best, ma'am. A Ranger always obeys. OK?" He stared at her. Right through her.

So, Linda thought, the Ferryman was bored with his job and wife. When the wolf turned out to be a vibrant creature with whom he shared a lot in common, nature took its course. They both felt tenderness for the lamb. Cried, perhaps, as they ate the stew. But both found it easy to ignore the cabbage. Only the lamb loved the cabbage.

She had made the classic mistake of anthropologists and time travelers, Linda realized, gotten too close to the locals and fallen into their pattern. She had become the numb suburban housewife.

Olivia, on her return, tried one of Roy's Chesterfields. "As a girl I'd half imagined having my secret snuff box when I was old and double chinned," she said. "Then, in that London where I stayed, everyone had these and thought them wonderful and wicked. I thought them disgusting." She inhaled, coughed, but inhaled again.

"I smoke a few a day," Roy told her. "Otherwise, I'd be remembered as the guy who doesn't smoke."

"And honor could not countenance that," said Lady Olivia.

They had been together again that afternoon, Linda knew. While she drove Sally over to stay with Dorrie. Roy could easily return to the house unnoticed. Rangers had their ways.

The only question was, which of the two had thought of sending the black truck to distract her.

"Can Auntie Olives come and see Mrs. Wood and Dorrie?" Sally had asked on the car ride that afternoon.

"I don't think she'll have time, honey," was Linda's answer.

3.

On Saturdays there was no 7:49. The nearest thing to it was an 8:03. No other trains stopped at Grove Hill for half an hour before or after. So it wasn't strange that a small knot of people had accumulated on the station platform. Most were locals with early appointments in the city. A few were strangers.

The man who sat in the Buick sedan reading the *Herald Tribune*, his tennis racket cases beside him, had doubtless driven over from another town to catch this particular train. The black woman plainly was returning to Harlem after serving at a party and sleeping over. The man in overalls carrying a tool case was somehow connected to the railway.

Today, Lady Wexford was being taken Upstream. Closer to the front. Closer to the point in Time where humanity, of which she was so astounding and complicated an example, ceased to exist.

Pulling up at the station, Linda took in the Ranger deployment. She also spotted George and Alice Stanley standing beside a couple of suitcases. Alice, she remembered, was going up to Rhode Island to be with a sister who had just had a baby girl.

Roy saw them at the same moment and cursed under his breath. A jump in the Stream would already be difficult with a novice like Olivia. George and Alice would want to talk. The other Rangers would have to act as a buffer.

A few days before, Linda would have felt a pang of sympathy. Even now, shared memories and a child, an immense secret and a common assignment, had a hold. She was about to say something.

Then Olivia, in the back seat, sang almost under her breath:

> *When lovely woman stoops to folly*
> *And finds too late that men betray*
> *What charm can sooth her melancholy*
> *What care can wash her guilt away?*

It's not her fall that she's been singing about, Linda realized. It's mine. She drove the Chevy right up to the station. They all got out and Roy went to the trunk for Olivia's luggage. The man in the Buick gathered up his tennis rackets.

The train came into view. The Stanleys and the other passengers looked that way while the maid and the railway man watched them and everything else.

Linda and Olivia kissed. "It saddens my heart not to see Sally again," the Englishwoman said. "Please give her this from me."

The wristlet was a beautiful thing, silk roses and tiny pearls. And familiar. Linda remembered seeing Olivia Wexford wearing nothing else. She noticed that the design was a bit off kilter. Was that spot, perhaps, royal blood?

Linda took the memento and stuck it in a pocket of her slacks. "I'll save it for when she's old enough to understand."

For the last couple of days Linda had not brought Sally back from Dorrie's. Not even to say goodbye. Roy had the suitcases. He and Olivia had fucked in the rec room earlier that morning while Linda was out on errands. They hardly bothered to hide it.

"We caught the truck driver," Linda said. "This morning." She had both of their attention. "He was waiting when I left the house. I let him follow me. Mrs. Wood and I took what he knew."

She watched their reactions. "It wasn't much. He thought he was the look-out man in a kidnapping. That a rich grandfather would give a million dollars to ransom Sally."

Roy's eyes flashed with fury. Because Sally had been threatened. Because someone had tried to do this to HIS daughter. Because Linda was always right.

"The driver?" he asked.

"Done," Linda said and he nodded. She'd wanted this to be none of his doing. But she'd had to make sure.

She couldn't read Olivia's face. Brushing the other's mind, she caught a glimpse of a silk screen. On it, in the softest of colors, a nymph, covered by a flimsy drapery, glanced back at a pursuing Bacchus. And Linda, even in anger, could not violate what was reserved to a God.

The train pulled into the station. Linda caught Olivia in an embrace, turned her away from Roy and whispered, "You mentioned The Tale of the Ferryman's Wife. Well we're in that story now and she is a bitch with a long memory. If anything happens to Sally. No matter what, no matter when, I'll find you and tear out your breath."

"The wolf loves only the lamb," Lady Wexford murmured, took a step backward, turned and went up to the platform between the man with the tennis rackets and Roy who carried her bags. Neither she nor Roy looked back.

Linda drove away from the station and watched the train depart in her rear view mirror. From then on, whenever she thought of Roy on the September morning when they met, she would also remember him hauling Lady Wexford's luggage Upstream.

Roy would be back this evening and Sally would be there. He and Linda would wind up this operation quickly and go their separate ways. If he'd given even a hint of having sent that truck and driver to distract her, he would never have been allowed near their daughter again.

She drove not home but over to East Radley. On the way, she passed the spot where the crumpled black truck had run full speed into a concrete and steel overpass support. The body had been removed. The county police were waving traffic around the accident scene.

A few hours before, the man at the wheel, following Linda intently, had reached the outer fringe of Mrs. Wood's awareness. The goddess revealed herself to him as he sped off the exit. Stunned and agape, he spiraled out of control. As he did, Linda laid open the vicious, stupid mind. He knew very little. Still it was too much. The truck crumpled, but he was already dead. Linda drove home to her husband and her guest.

On her second trip, she noticed flowers and Spring greenery adorning the statue of the Virgin in the Italians' yard on the corner. She parked before the tall gray house with the swings and slide in the back yard.

"He always wanted action. He hated it here," Linda said a while later. She sat in the kitchen drinking tea. The house was quiet. The other children, the ordinary children, were at home that day. Sally was back in the conservatory with Mrs. Wood. Dorrie listened, endlessly patient and kind.

"He once told me that riding herd on the Cold War, making sure that Ike gets two full terms and Krushev comes to power, is like near beer when you're used to iced vodka. It could be a tabloid headline: TIME WARS BREAK UP MARRIAGE!" Linda started to laugh, but instead began to cry.

Dorrie was the perfect avatar. She was like a well. Linda wondered if she could ever learn to be like her. "My mother didn't bring me to the Goddess until I was almost twelve," Linda said. "Mrs. Wood looked to me like the most amazing black and silver movie publicity shot ever made. A face beautiful but impossible to pin down. Tony Curtis and Debbie Reynolds and everyone else all rolled into one. She touched me and I was Hers. It was that simple."

That's how it went for a while, Dorrie refilling the tea cup, nodding at a familiar tale, Linda alternating giggles and tears.

"That first day I met Roy. After we got intimately acquainted, I asked Mrs. Wood how long he'd be faithful. She said, 'As long as he can be. And to no one as faithful as you.' Because I was young that sounded like more than enough."

Eventually, Linda breathed more calmly and all was silent in the kitchen. Then the door to the conservatory slammed open and Sally called, "Mommy! Mrs. Wood told my fortune!"

As her daughter came tripping down the hall, Linda caught the image. Gray and magic as TV, it showed Sally older. Seven at least. Wearing a robe of stars. Perhaps a school play. Maybe something more. The question was where and when?

"Can I have my cookie now?" Sally burst into the room, hugged Linda, then remembered and asked Dorrie, "Please?"

Dorrie smiled and drew the cloth off a still warm figure with a frosting dress and raisin eyes. She and Linda exchanged glances. The older woman nodded. Linda rose and went down the hall.

She remembered that her mother had waited too long to tell her the truth. About the Rangers. About the Time Stream. Linda had cried. Threatened to run away. Her mother had also delayed bringing her to Mrs. Wood until then.

Until today Linda had been able to see no reason for that. With puberty, her gift was apparent. The alliance of necessity between Rangers and Oracle was a long standing one. Shrines of the Goddess were within easy reach of any Ranger operative.

Now she knew more than she wanted to about alliances made Upstream. She had learned that the Gods could give the Rangers Lady Olivia. And, in return, the Rangers could give Lady Olivia Roy. She understood too her own mother's reluctance. Mrs. Wood had opened Linda's mind that first day and it had never again been entirely her own.

On that first occasion, Mrs. Wood had promised, You will know every mind but one. Ah, but the Oracle was deep. Or just slippery. Seven years after that, almost to the day, Linda had encountered Roy and imagined that his mind was that one. In the seven years that followed Linda encountered others whose thoughts she could not catch. Only now, thinking about it, did she realize that the one mind was her own.

At the conservatory door, Linda bowed slightly before the Presence then stepped forward into the warmth and sunlight. Here, where Chance and the Seasons merged, she would learn the nature of her new assignment.

4.

They talked for a time in Grove Hill about Roy and Linda Martin. Even in a nation founded on rootlessness, the speed with which they disappeared was remarkable. The Stanleys, George and Alice, often described their Saturday morning train trip with Roy and the exotic house guest.

"I knew," she would say, "just by the way they avoided us."

"At Grand Central," he would add. "No sign of them."

Olivia was never seen again. Roy returned but not for long. He was busy winding up his affairs. When pressed, he talked about taking over an uncle's business in Seattle. Linda said something about going to stay with her family.

Divorce would, in a few years, be as common as babies were right then. But Roy and Linda Martin's marriage was the first this circle had seen collapse. Marge Hacker, who lived right in back of them, described the distance she observed. "Not a smile. Not a touch. They talk to each other through the kid."

Time passed and neighbors moved away from Grove Hill. But when Marge Hacker and Alice Stanley met by chance at a church rummage sale in Rye ten years later, it was the Martins they talked about. Rather than discuss their own marital woes, they recalled how quickly the house had been sold, how abruptly little Sally was taken out of school.

A decade further Upstream, as the protean nation of the West continued to change and transform itself, George Stanley and Frank Hacker met for lunch. Both were on their second marriages. George said, "Tried to get in touch with Roy once or twice, to maybe ask him about that British bimbo."

And Frank smiled at his memory of Lady Olivia on an April evening and of a time and place gone by as fast as a lighted window seen at night from a speeding train.

One might think that in a genre devoted to the unknown and the unimaginable, surrealism and literary experimentation would be common modes. Not so. For a brief time (what's been called the New Wave of the 1960s, early '70s), Spec Fiction found a place, even a prominent place for experiment and the inexplicably strange.

The New Wave passed fairly quickly; old ways and formats reasserted themselves. Things never returned to the stories-for-eleven-year-old-boys-of-all-ages that dominated the pulp magazines of the '40s and '50s, but there was no ready market for artistic innovation.

So it remained until the rise of the 'zines in the late 1990s. Kelly Link/Gavin Grant's Lady Churchill's Rosebud Wristlet *was the first. The off-beat was the staple fare and the TOC was impressive. For a while after that it seemed as if every young writer also edited and published, often irregularly, a small, quirky magazine devoted to the odd angles of storytelling.*

Like butterflies these 'zines appeared, wonderful in their color and variety, then mostly they were gone. LCRW survives and I was happy to discover recently that so does my own personal favorite, John Klima's Electric Velocipede.

It was John and EV who published two stories by Mark Rich and me, including "Jacket Jackson." I don't collaborate much in my writing. But I prize the stories Mark Rich (poet, short story writer, critic) and I wrote together. Especially this one about a kid poet with a great old car loose in the US of the mid-'60s and in worlds and times beyond ours.

On my own I might have created some aspects of Chris Brown/ Deware/Jackson. But not all aspects by any means and certainly not the poems. Like magic Mark produced them whenever we decided one was necessary (and even once or twice when I just wanted to see another one).

A lot of the American West seen in the story is Mark's. Creating the Maxee was fun for us both.

What did I contribute?

Mainly the feel of driving at eighteen blasted out of your head at the wheel of your car and waking up barefoot and cuffed to the outside of a holding cell because of the benevolence of suburban county cops.

From each according to his abilities . . .

JACKET JACKSON

Richard Bowes and Mark Rich

I close my eyes and draw in
blue distances of smoky air
the coiling strands
of a City of No Time
City of Castoff Futures
　　　—Jacket Jackson

1.

In a year of promise deep in the heart of the 20th century, Chris Brown hit the road. He was nineteen. His draft board had lost touch with him. His mother and step-father were just divorced, and he had flunked out of college back east. Driving a blue, beat-up 1954 Dodge Royale ragtop, Chris was as free as any American.

The man at the last gas stop on 66 had a boozed-up grin and see-nothing eyes.

No one sees anything, Chris thought. I walk in a dead land with an invisible city carried in the air over my head, and no one sees.

Chris wrote poetry.

The tank topped out at two dollars and thirty-five cents' worth of gas.

As he pulled away with sixty-seven cents in change, he caught a flash of silver—something barreling down an ebony causeway . . .

2.

In Maxee, City of Lost History, a bike and rider swept along the otherwise deserted Esplanade of Silk Serpents. The hands and head of the biker were shiny aluminum. Blue liquid dribbled from its mouth. It wore jeans and boots. A leather jacket, unzipped, flapped in the wind.

"Ah, but this is bracing to observe," said the Clockmaster to Tomkin of the Tomkins, his Flux-Agent. They stood in Maxee, City of a Dozen Suns, looking down from the terrace of the Pitch of Dreams. "Desperate fun." His voice rang like chimes. "Jackson's remarkable jacket has a new friend. All metal, and on a motorcycle."

One sun rose while another set. Orange light bounced off the aluminum torso as the bike roared across Tangle Tongue Bridge, past the Graveyard of Unbearable Children and the centuries-wide Patio of Platitudes. The biker hung a left at the Tobacco Gardens.

"Remember the Summer of the Raggle Taggle Girl?" the Flux-Agent said, lips pursed in amusement. "We had ground Seth Jackson to dust. All but destroyed the memory of his existence. Yet he returned. A bit of him, anyway. That Girl. She dashed in here wearing Jackson's jacket and left us with those Gardens."

"Then I found her near the Hissing Stairs," said the Clockmaster. "Creating something that involved an absinthe fountain and a carousel. The tinkle of the music was at the edge of my ear when I drilled the Raggle Taggle Girl full of the darts of Time."

"Always deadly, that arm of yours," said Tomkin of the Tomkins.

"Yet the jacket crawled off her back, and got away to some obscure solipse in the Outer Possibilities. Only to return with this chrome manikin."

As the motorcycle roared past the Tobacco Gardens, the cigar trees all glowed at their tips and puffed clouds of welcome.

The Flux-Agent heard the Clockmaster tick a bit faster at that. Saw his lips twitch.

On a terrace elsewhere in Maxee City of Dreaming Spires, a small rubber ball bounced on the marble floor, once, twice, and went over the edge.

Far below them, Jackson's jacket said, "Hard right. Go for the Barrows."

Metal hands steered the bike toward a long marble ramp. On a terrace five levels down, red flashed on the couch where Pauline of the fiery hair stretched and turned in her mechanical boredom.

When the cycle hit the ramp, thousands of tiny metal jacks, the kind kids grab at between ball-bounces, went scattering across the road. Piles of them broke and sprayed like gravel beneath the tires. They clicked and clattered, catching in the spokes. They rattled against the engine. The motorcycle coughed and skidded.

It smashed through a railing.

As it fell, the aluminum driver raised its hands from the handles. The jacket slipped off its arms and billowed open in the air. All akimbo, it floated within sight of the balcony where Pauline now stood at the railing, her eyes bright, her hair twining around her shoulders.

She reached for the jacket.

Like a bullet, the rubber ball ricocheted off a wall. It smacked into the jacket and drove it spinning away from Pauline's outstretched arms. The jacket fell, turning over and over, growing smaller as it fell out of Maxee, City in the Pink Smoke Clouds.

Seth Jackson was dead. The jacket knew this. The Clockmaster, Prince Of Stasis, had pressed him into the dust that was ground ever finer by Maxee's turning and writhing foundation.

Still, the aroma of those trees . . .

It remembered the factory workroom somewhere in a backwash town near the West End of Humankind, where the liquid fire first flowed from Jackson's veins into the jacket-shaped webwork of carbon and steel, circuitry and leather. Life coursed into its fabric. It rippled, at its edges, just outside time.

Jackson had draped the jacket over a stool, then leaned back against a table, lighting a cigar. He stared at his creation. The jacket would stay shining and dark despite the dulling of months. Its fabric would ripple and turn after the hammering of years. Its shape would hold without tattering against the gales of the centuries it swept through.

Carbon and steel, circuitry and leather, and love and . . .

Jackson disliked a certain Prince of Stasis.

As the jacket fell, it called out to the dust of its creator.

"Where now?" it said.

"Find him . . ."

"There?" said the Jacket, seeing a sunbaked, hardened place

within a cracked and broken stretch of time. "Listen; there must have been a million jackasses through the centuries who have breathed out one or two of the bubbles that expanded to become Maxee, City of Null Time. What makes you think I can find someone who's any more important than anyone else?"

The jacket fell tumbling into the turbulence of the post-Bomb years, toward the backbone of a continent with not much more than gas engines crossing it.

At first the distant dust being ground beneath the turning city stayed silent.

Then, with leathery sensors the thin sharpness of glass, the jacket caught the words:

"This is where the dream is born, in the cracks of this torn-apart version of the world. Here are ones in whom the vision of Maxee, the City Out of Time, is deeply rooted.

"And here there is one to tear Maxee from the hands of the one who . . ."

3.

In the middle of the day under a hot Nebraska sun, on the old wooden bench behind the diner, Chris wrote carefully in the ledger, with his No. 2 Eagle. The ledger had to be as old as the town was, with leather library binding and green-edged paper. Cost almost nothing at the secondhand store.

Three weeks dishwashing at Jake's, with his Dodge Royale slowly rusting back at the lot. Seemed a hell of a lot longer than three weeks.

He closed his eyes. He must not see. Must not think. Blank. Blank. Not think. He closed his eyes. Opened them. He started writing.

> *Red is the color of the sky*
> *above a dozen sunsets. Red*
> *when I close my eyes to her hair.*
> *Red is red. Red is the glassy eye*
> *burning the forest of my head.*
> *The timeking laughs upon his chair:*
> *the manikin falls from on high*

onto the fossil riverbed
leaving red chrome everywhere
and a scattering of metal leaves.

Chris stared at the words. The image of a red-haired woman edged into his mind and out of it.

"Maxee, Number Twenty-Five," he wrote at the top of the ledger page.

"What you doing, jackass?" said Weed, the cook.

"Numbering your good points."

"Didn't know you could count that high."

"All the way to two."

Weed counted to two, with one finger up from each hand. "Count of three, I'll kick your ass, Chrissy."

"Get the hell out of here, Weed," said old Jay, standing in the door.

"I'll kick his ass someday," Weed said. "I'll kick his ass."

"Kicking your own if you do," said Jay.

Later the sun cooled down enough, and enough time had passed, to let Chris think again.

Out of this town, he thought.

Out, but with the vision of the city carried with him, greater than even these twenty-five pages in an old ledger.

Still, they were good pages, so he took them with him.

4.

"You want the jacket because it's so much better than you," said Tomkin of the Tomkins, Flux-Agent of the Clockmaster, Golden Peregrine to the Far Lands. He stood in his amber robe. Blue laurel twisted around his helmet's beak, feathered crest, and glassy eyes. "The last creation of your precious Seth Jackson."

"It is not better than me. But it is very good."

Red Pauline's dark dress mirrored lights of Maxee that extended far below and far above the black platform on which she and Tomkin of the Tomkins stood, in that rare moment when none of the suns of Maxee shone.

"And you," she said, "want it because it has something on you."

"It is something I want on me. It probably has something on everyone. But I would have something on poor, dead Jackson, wouldn't I, if I had it on me?"

Red Pauline laughed.

"There must have been a good occasion," said Tomkin of the Tomkins, "to have generated such a laugh for you to recall now, in your cold years, for social purposes. How nice of you to revive it for me, out of your circuits."

"How nice of you to unveil your unceasing cynicism. I appreciate nakedness in men."

"Exactly the nakedness I would expect a machine to appreciate."

She laughed again.

He smiled. "You realize you are engaging in crime," he said, "encouraging the jacket to change things this way."

"You and the Clockmaster destroyed Seth, and now have exiled his last creation from the Brightness to the Years of Shadow."

"Where it will die, too," said Tomkin of the Tomkins, maintaining his smile. "Eventually. Already it is weaker."

"You force my hand," she said, "by rigging the Contingencies and tampering with the Time Streams from the Beginning of the Brightness, to hold Maxee, the Protean City, to its unchanging pattern."

"You have been listening to that Simmoo's wild surmises. The Clockmaster is capable. But not of that. He will find stopping you well within the range of the possible, however. The flow of the Streams is now quite steady, and any disruptive action against Maxee, City Out of Time, will be caught."

"I am interested in actions for Maxee. But for a Maxee the Clockmaster will not let come into being."

"As you will."

The stage winked out of existence, leaving the figures hovering for a moment between the twisting spires of Maxee . . .

A humming of bees between radiant flowers . . .

The roar of a distant elevator between stars . . .

Then they, too, of the burning hair and of the watchful helmet, winked away.

5.

Chris carried an empty gas can down a twilit road a hundred miles from anywhere.

He saw his dream rising briefly against the sky, down another darkening road, and so turned that way.

How long since he left the Dodge by the road?

Every kid nineteen years old should be free as the breeze.

So he had thought with a full tank of gas.

Breeze, and sand, and stone . . .

And wind and the roar of a distant elevator between frozen stars.

Chris abruptly dropped the can and doubled over. He thought he would lose his lunch. The road spun below him, then above him, then below him again. A shimmering vastness passed before his eyes. He saw clearly. He had such moments.

"Seth Jackson sent me," it said.

Just the wind.

"I cannot quite reach you," it said.

Yet, after a time, it did.

The thing sent by Jackson fitted itself around the kid's shoulders as he lay face-down, dry-mouthed and empty-headed on the cold sand in that Arizona night. A scorpion regarded him from a pile of black stones.

"You are too simply blood and nerve," said the thing that had flapped out of the violet darkness. "Those spineless jelly things of Maxee: they are closer to me than you—but even they I cannot quite fit around, not as I should." The thickness of the jacket pressed around Christopher. "But we will try this. We will do this, and we will succeed."

"Maxee," said the hollowed-out boy, seizing on the syllables. He felt fingers in his head.

"It is a where, and it is a when." The words crept along behind the fingers. "The shadows, the lights, the waterfall of a million miles. The chiming thoughts of a century of bell-headed children."

The tendrils of voice pulled away from the boy's mind, and left in their place a vision of a city so immense it wrapped around the sky. The vision was, Christopher knew, an ideal, a fairy painting made as a collage from all the dim pictures in his mind.

After a moment he remembered to breathe again. He found himself remembering a box of crayons he had when he was five. He drew pictures in his head, and tore them up.

"And it is a nowhere, and a nowhen. It is a future, but not the Future," said the thing on his back. "I'll show you."

"I've seen it," said Christopher. "It's real, isn't it? It's beautiful."

"You'll see it in more than just your mind."

The thing from the future rose off the boy's shoulders and spread itself as a gauze of black tissue against the stars. It searched and found what it wanted, on another dark highway: two minds with a touch of Maxee, Citadel of the Ice of Time, playing around their edges. It called them.

Hours later, two figures appeared over the rise of hard earth and stones.

One voice, a woman's, said, "There!"

The figures saw a shadow standing among the shadows as they walked near.

"We heard there was a boy here, in a leather jacket," said a man's voice. "The boy who sees."

The shadow vanished.

They saw in its place a form splayed unconscious on the sands. Radiant above the boy they saw the spirals of the City of Nets, turning through the stillness of a future with no past.

When the jacket told them of Maxee, they recognized their own dreams.

When it told them into what hands Maxee had fallen, they wept.

"Save the boy, and save Maxee," said the jacket to them.

They picked Christopher up and carried him away. Not to the City, but to a city, east and into the dawn.

6.

"Did you know," said Simmoo, the One True Historian, in a break from his One True History Class, while sitting with his one true student, "there was only the one person who had a chance to stop what was going to happen."

"So I've been guessing," she said. "Had to have been Seth."

"Jackson, builder of the first glass bridge across Time. Had no clue what he was getting into, or what sort of chance he was offering the one who would call himself the Clockmaster."

"They say he died."

"Killed, actually. Most of him was killed, at least. Part of him fled back in Time."

She frowned. "Rumor is that he's back, though."

"Where did you learn that?"

"Just on the grapevine."

"Maxee, the One True City, has no grapevines," he said, smiling. "No people, thus no grapevines. QED."

"Yet there are," she said, pleased to have information Simmoo did not. "I saw two large people, and several small. What clothes they wore were no more than bright colors, and they gazed about with wild surmise." She used the phrase to see Simmoo's eyebrow twitch. "They waved color brochures at me. Asked where they could see the Overall Waterfall. I told them it didn't exist."

"Not yet," Simmoo said thoughtfully.

7.

The Outer Possibilities, especially those in the second half of the 20th century, abounded in cults. Mayan temples, pyramids, odd crop patterns, runes and riddles all attracted adherents. Lenin and Lindbergh, by the time of Bill and Alice Deware, were bygones. "Helter Skelter" and lemonade parties in the jungle were yet to be. Houses rose in rows, made of ticky-tacky. The City of Perfumed Sidewalks lay just beyond them, and just beyond the edge of many minds, touching, teasing, and tempting.

Bill ran a construction business. Alice sold real estate. Everywhere they looked they saw bits of Maxee, without knowing it. Their large, ranch-style house stood on an acre of land, with a carport on the side and a swimming pool in back. Bill's boy from a former marriage had come to stay with them while he enrolled in the local community college.

They explained Chris that way.

Neighbors thought this quiet kid, Christopher, might have been in a little trouble wherever he had been before.

Not particularly tough, but not particularly friendly in his leather jacket. The kid drove around in his old ragtop and stuck to himself, and it was like the car drove him, one of the neighbors said. The car and the jacket. Always together.

One evening Christopher found himself on a sidewalk near school staring at a meaningless sign propped in a window.

The letters finally fell into place. Three names, he saw. The middle one was Chris Deware—his name at present.

"Beat Poetry Jam," it said underneath.

The jacket took him inside. Smoke in a gray smudge against the ceiling. The warm voice of the bartender. A woman sipping a fizzing drink. Five or six tables of students hunched toward each other, and a few older sorts looking around. Sometimes they glanced at Christopher.

"An impromptu," Christopher said when it was his turn on the small, four-by-four stage shoved against the wall opposite the bar. Paper posters for literary events and art openings covered the wall in haphazard patches, the corner of an old Moxie sign appearing in one spot.

Christopher closed his eyes, then opened them again. He saw words as geese curving through the sky before circling down to the river below. They came down. Christopher opened his mouth. He spoke with each syllable falling from his lips with even weight. Even the stops for breath or phrasing fell into a shuffling time that made cool drinks warm in their glasses.

He said,

"A Poem for Somewhere"
"And the crow falls from the sky saying the city's name
At the base of the towers of the Congress of Sighs.
The uncounted, unspoken wishes for order at all times
Meet in a rushing of insect-wings, and in the blind eyes
on the helmet of Flux the Deceiver. They fall into
slumber as my words make spires of encircled silver strands."

When he was done, finger-snapping and a smattering of applause stirred the smoky air like the wings of bats.

"Whiskey on the counter calls," whispered the jacket to him. "It is a melodious song." It took him to the far end of the bar. The kid carried an I.D. for Christopher J. Deware. His fake draft card made him twenty-one.

"There is no Congress of Sighs," said the jacket.

"There is now," said Christopher.

"How do you know of the Flux-Agent?"

"Beats me. I also know he was called by another name."

"Tomkin of The Tomkins," said the jacket, "Friend of the great Seth Jackson. Or former friend. Betrayed my creator. How did you know?"

Christopher shrugged.

"Let it pass," said the jacket.

It whistled. The boy's hand raised the empty glass toward the bartender.

When he drained it, the jacket whispered. "Time we found the road. And that you met the lovely one named Blue Maria."

Christopher nodded.

8.

"I don't think I will even respond to Red Pauline's provocation," said the Clockmaster. "Her punishment is to long in vain for her precious jacket. She sits in the yearning fires of her own desolate hell."

"We know how she clings to the memory of Jackson," said the Flux-Agent. "But she could be swayed. She might be induced to become devoted instead to you."

"She's gone too far from the girl I knew." The Clockmaster regarded the turning spokes of light panning across Maxee, the City of the Time Helix, and sipped his water. "Another immortal entity might give way to feelings for a childhood sweetheart who has chosen to make herself a machine. But I am devoted to trying to make Time work in an orderly manner. There it is. I am an old-fashioned entity, dedicated to old things and old ways."

"And to stopping the jacket and the ones with whom it returns."

"They are opposed to old things and old ways," said the Clockmaster. "Especially my old ways."

At that moment, a blue Dodge Royale with its top down came barreling over the Lake of Tears by way of the Bridge of Scant Regard. The green lenses of the Frog Observatory reflected the light of two rising suns.

The eyes of Clockmaster and Flux-Agent met, as the thought

struck them both at once that nothing like the Frog Observatory had ever before stood in that place.

Before they could react, the car vanished.

Their gazes shifted to an eighty-story Art Deco folly, topped with anchorages for spaceships. The light of various suns glowed pink on the silver spires and minarets of the new and eternal Congress of Sighs. Sun-tinted doves settled across the wide expanse of scale-like tiles.

A voice arose, somewhere, in a sigh that was not theirs.

9.

In the kitchen, Alice stirred the pot of beef stew heating on the range.

"You had him out late last night," she said. "Got to keep up his strength."

The jacket hung on the back of a chair.

"Yes," it said. "But that strength of his must be exercised."

Sounds of a shower running, of water splashing and a voice complaining, almost crying, came from the bathroom.

"It hurts, Bill."

"Sure, it hurts."

"We saw Maxee. The City Of Diamond Knives. Oh, man. My mouth hurts."

"Don't talk, then."

"It's wonderful," Alice said, "being a part of this. Saving Maxee, the City Of Unraveled Time. And in the end we can visit and see its wonders. Really, I can't wait."

"Of course," the jacket murmured to her, while thinking such a visit akin to flying pigs and sulfur tasting of honey: possible, but purposeless.

The splashing ceased. Bill's voice came again, gently coaxing.

"It's crazy," said Alice. She looked away and smiled. "He's all gooey about the kid. And, you know, he's the one who didn't want to have children."

"Sentimentality," said the jacket, tightly.

Bill Deware led a towel-wrapped Christopher into the kitchen. The kid moaned as the jacket was placed over his shoulders. His lips were stained blue. Bill helped him into his seat.

"I need him to drive again tonight," said the jacket.

Christopher's hand holding the fork shivered. Bill took it. He guided the fork to the bowl, speared a gravy-soaked carrot, and brought it up.

Christopher averted his face. "It hurts." His voice was faint and hoarse. "That Blue Maria burned my mouth. Please. Let me sleep."

The jacket rose, with the kid inside it, and walked him down the hall. Christopher fell face-down on the bed.

"Sir," said Bill respectfully, looking in from the hallway. "That stuff he's taking. Makes him sick. Could he ease up?"

"Blue Maria was given to us by the great Seth Jackson to ease our path back to Maxee. He created it before he created me. Long before he made and populated these Outer Possibilities. Long before the Bridges of Glass."

"It's hard on him."

"I believe Christopher is the chosen instrument."

Bill nodded, and rubbed his forehead. "Right," he said, quietly. "It's our fight. To save Maxee." The jacket had said these words many times.

"He's a strong kid."

"He's a strong kid," repeated Bill.

"Maybe too strong," the jacket said. "Driving back here we missed a tree by inches, before I finally got the boy's foot down on the brakes. He fought me. He could have been killed."

"What would we do then?" Bill asked.

"Find someone more willing," Alice said, from behind Bill.

The jacket said nothing, floating at the edge of Christopher's dulled mind, probing. This boy had found turns on the Time Lanes the jacket had never seen before. Yet it could dig through these mental layers and find only the tangled thoughts of youth, speared through with strangely vivid poetry.

Christopher, asleep, his sweating forehead pressed to the pillow, dreamed of playing with brick-shaped blocks. He placed brick atop tiny brick. Then he stepped back, to see what he had built. Structures ornate and aimless rose from the floor, in an untidy mess of a miniature city.

In his hand he found a small metal figure. A man with a clock for a hat. Very carefully, he bent down and placed it atop a pedestal at the center of his miniature city.

Now the walls of the room went away. He stood on the grassy

hill, in a park. Great feathered trees swaying beneath floating globes of light caught his eye. When he looked back at what he had built, it had changed. The buildings grew toward the sky. The man on the pedestal loomed, an enormous giant. The clock on his hat shone. Crowds of tiny figures walked on his shoulders.

The giant waved his arms, and what seemed like white, glistening bullets flew through the air and bit into the grass, churning up clots of turf and cutting Christopher in two.

He woke up face-down on a drenched pillow.

"Come on, kid, up and at it," said the jacket, tugging at Christopher's limp form.

"My head's still crapped out from yesterday," Christopher said. He shut his eyes, asleep again.

The hill and the lights and the city and the metal man were gone. All was dark in this place now except for the shining in Christopher's own hands.

The swirling stuff of stars coalesced in his palms. This he mashed together with his palms, then with his fingers, until it became firm. He pressed it into the shape of a glowing block. He put down the block, only to find the space between his hands aglow again.

The pile of blocks grew through the long ages of night.

At some point, when the bridge was nearly built, he realized his mouth no longer hurt.

10.

The lights dimmed. The helix spun more swiftly. "The jacket has a way with the time streams," said the Clockmaster. "They keep opening onto Maxee, when it's riding them."

He stared at the images appearing on the back of his Flux-Agent's hand. The '54 Dodge, with its rag top down, sat parked beside a road. Chris took a drag from a small bottle, stuck a blue pill in his mouth, and pulled his leather jacket tightly around him.

"It's that boy and that wonderful car," said Tomkin of the Tomkins, looking at the image. "Couldn't they find themselves in some dark corner of the Possibilities?"

"The time is not right," said the Clockmaster. "No time is ever right."

"I'm sorry."

"Beautiful, in its way, that pink hairbrush on the grass by the road," said the Clockmaster, pointing. "Meaningless details are the stuff of Time."

"But you cannot tend to them all."

"I cannot attend to any of them. I maintain the illusion that I tend to a few, for the sake of appearances. The Helix turns, and I dream that I tug and shape it here and there. I shine lights where necessary. And that, really, is all. I am like someone who nudges gently at the reigning stasis."

"O, Demiurge."

"Sweet of you to call me that, but not true."

Tomkin of the Tomkins then sang an old, old song, making the Clockmaster frown, then smile, his eyes looking far into the distance.

11.

Once and sometime, the jacket raised armies of wanderers who bore it aloft as their standard, and flashed fangs of steel at the slave beings pushing the Great Wheel, turning Maxee on its endless rotations and grinding Time and its victims to ashes of forgetfulness.

Once and sometime again, it rode the back of a champion with flaming hands, who leaped from a bridge of glass to dig burning fingertips into the Obelisk of Oblivion at the heart of Maxee, City of Gestalt and Zeitgeist, City of the Lost, City of Loneliness, City of Forever and Never, City With No End.

Those assaults came to nothing. A flash, a slap, a puff of wind, and the jacket found itself in some 1949, in some weary Massachusetts warehouse with distraught pigeons fluttering between rafters, with the steed it rode toward victory now become more or less a pumpkin, and with the armed hordes it raised out of deep, dusty regions of the past reduced now to a scattering of mice and rats.

Never had the jacket entered Maxee, City of Infinite Chance, as it did with Christopher Deware at the wheel of the blue Dodge. Never before had it seen the bright red Cyrillic lettering on the dome of the Helium Exchange. Never before had it seen the Ballroom Of The Reluctant Elephants rise from the dry bed of the Lake of Desuetude.

Yet on the edge of triumph it felt stabs of intense longing for those lone, lost crusades.

Now the city shimmered in the presence of the one who had reimagined it. The liquid in the capsule burned Christopher's smiling mouth. Where Christopher turned his gaze, glowing esplanades rippled along the river banks.

A figure rose above the buildings. On the front of the Clockmaster's slouch hat appeared the face of Big Ben. Out of his ears and along his shoulders moved the same mechanical procession of princes, priests, and populace that emerges twice a day from the great, high clock of the Cathedral of Ghent. Seconds sprayed from the Clockmaster's long right arm. Hours pumped from the short left one.

"Don't be alarmed," the jacket said sharply. "It's an illusion. He's not as big as a whale. Nor as tall as many castles."

The Clockmaster raised both hands. Seconds and minutes rattled off the hood of the car. Hours and days smashed the trunk. The blue Dodge hung a sharp right and passed through the Arctic Portals that sprang into being to greet its rusting grille. The shrapnel of hours and the scattered buckshot of seconds embedded themselves in the diamond surface of ice, where they would become the Memorials to Time Once Frozen, in Maxee, City of Stillness, when it was no longer still and dead.

The Clockmaster seen in the rearview mirror, reminded Chris of an amusement park ride.

The Dodge thundered down a winding marble slope. On a terrace just over the edge of the ramp, Christopher saw a flash of red hair. The jacket quivered on his back. A name appeared in Christopher's mind as he felt the heat the passion course quickly through him: Red Pauline.

A figure in an amber robe and feathered helmet appeared beside her.

He raised his Flux staff and called out. He wished to talk.

"I'm glad someone the hell wants to talk," said Christopher, hitting the brakes.

Then he yelled. The jacket forced his hands off the steering wheel. The Dodge left the marble road and spun in the air. Maxee spiraled.

Christopher yelled again and bit viciously on what remained of the Blue Maria, trying to get his hands back on the wheel.

Then it was night. Headlights blazed and horns blared. Under a quarter moon, the Dodge touched down on asphalt, drove diagonally across a highway and jumped an embankment as Chris and the jacket struggled for control.

12.

Iron doors clanged in the distance. A static-filled radio echoed down a hall.

Christopher rolled his head back. His eyes opened a slit to a smear of fluorescent lights.

"Watch him." Hands held him up, went through his pockets. "Kleenex. Stick of gum. Sixty-five, no, sixty-seven cents. Keys for the Dodge. House keys. Wallet. Two dollars. State College I.D. for Christopher J. Deware. Driver's license for same. Birthdates June 3, 1945. Draft card, 2S, says he's exactly two years older. Wrist watch looks like it got smashed just now. High school ring."

"Christopher Deware? Chris? CHRISTOPHER! You hear me?"

"Look at his eyes. Nobody home in there. He spends the night." Hands unbuckled his belt, whipped it through the loops and off him. "One brown leather belt. Hold your pants up, stupid bastard. Shoes off. Pair of black loafers."

"Hold him. Going to fall."

"Lock him down."

Christopher found himself moving barefoot. His head lolled. Through silted eyes, he saw a metal door open. Someone whistled and said, "Ohhh, my," when they saw him.

"Lou, this one's too fucked up to take care of himself. Mr. and Mrs. Deware won't like finding out their baby choked to death on his own vomit while getting gang raped."

"Cuff him outside the cage, then. Get that jacket off him."

"Fancy leather. Never felt anything like it. Like butter."

Christopher felt it slipping away. His eyes opened all the way. He twisted. "Down boy." Slammed against the bars. The pain was like an echo. He fell. The jacket came off. The light went out of his eyes. His tongue lolled out of mouth. Blue liquid dribbled on his chin. "What's that stuff?"

Chris saw the jacket fall, end over end, past steel walkways, past halls of glass and stone, blown like a leaf out of Maxee, the Spiral City.

Beyond the jacket, he saw the one who had thrown the jacket free. The figure bent over the Bridge of Unspoken Remorse. Chris knew the figure's name. Seth Jackson.

Then he saw the Clockmaster rise behind the creator of the jacket.

And everyone, the bailiffs, the prisoners, paused and listened to the sound of bells that tinkled like ice in a thousand big, big, highball glasses.

13.

Bright metal fish gathered in the air, their shadows blocking the light from the double suns high in the noonday sky.

In that twilight, a red-haired figure stood on a walkway overlooking the Charm Chasm. She stared down at the spinning turbines that powered Maxee, the Artificial City, and at the long lines of husklike dead souls, who provided the fuel to power the turbines.

Chimes tinkled. A glass swan floated up. Its side opened, to release Tomkin of the Tomkins.

"You have heard," he said.

"About the Clockmaster," said Red Pauline. "Rooted to the spot where that young man last saw him."

Her voice had a rare warmth.

"And all is changed. On my way here, I was stopped by a crowd—what they call a family. Of people! They asked me where all the tourists were. I told them there were none. None at all. Never can be. Maxee grows out of the stillness of all Time."

He paused. A tinkling filled the air.

"At least that was my understanding," he said.

"He will return, you know," said Red Pauline.

"We must be ready, then."

"I already am." Her distant smile was like the faint swell of a wave.

14.

Chris awoke to the smell of ammonia and a bailiff poking his shoulder.

"Rise and shine, son. Parents here."

A radio blared early morning news. "Campaigning in Wichita yesterday, President Johnson promised a new small farmer initiative. His opponent, Senator Goldwater, decried what he described as Big Government. In local news, several people reported a bright object the size of a car in the sky last night. The Air Force National Guard reports no unusual incidents."

An old black man washed the floor. Chris tried to move an arm. The bailiff unlocked the cuff from the bar.

Chris's eyes focused for a moment. "That jacket . . ."

He stopped trying to speak. His voice was slurred and hoarse.

The bailiff nodded and said, "Don't worry. On your feet." He held the open cuff and pulled the kid along to the restroom. Chris held up his pants with his free hand.

Ordinary-enough looking, Chris sensed the bailiff thinking, but headed down a very wrong road.

Down a very wrong glass bridge, Chris added.

The Dewares, Bill and Alice, both wore car coats and expressions of anxious concern. Bill was writing a check at the front desk.

When the room steadied again, Chris found the cuffs off. He had his shoes and belt in one hand, and his valuables in a manila envelope in the other.

Alice turned. "Honey! You OK? We were so worried." She embraced him. "Oh, you're cold! Where's your jacket?"

"Right here." The bailiff came out of the office, reading the label. "'Made in Maxee, the Well Upholstered City.' Never seen anything like this."

"Peru," Bill said. "Picked it up on a business trip."

He tried to get Chris to put the jacket on. Chris shrugged him off. He was seeing clearly, all of the sudden.

"We need to have a talk, son," said Bill.

The bailiff, with a chuckle born of having heard many such talks, saw them out the door.

The Deware's Country Squire station wagon sat parked beside the ragtop.

Chris, the jacket held in one hand, put his face back to absorb the warm sun, then looked around. No one else stood in the lot.

"I saw it," he said, his voice still unsteady and hoarse. "I saw Maxee, City of Steel Lace. Saw it. And then," he said, almost laughing, "I played it like a piano."

"Oh, shit, Bill," said Alice. "His eyes."

"What the hell happened, sir?" Bill asked the jacket.

The reply was no more than a distant tinkling.

"Honey, what's happened to the jacket?" said Alice.

"Thing tried to kill me," said Chris. "It wants to control me, but I don't trust it. Especially now."

"It must have had reasons for whatever it did," said Alice. "It's saving the City. So are you. The jacket said so. It wouldn't hurt you."

Chris carried the jacket by the collar, and tugged the car door open. "I need to shave and shower, and get my stuff."

"What do you mean?" said Alice.

"I'm leaving. Taking the jacket back home. For good, this time," Chris said. "Before it kills me or I rip it apart."

"To Maxee!" She wailed. "But we've never even seen it!"

Chris reached into his jeans pocket, drew out three blue capsules, handed one to each of them and kept one. He finally smiled, seeing how the Dewares' eyes glistened.

"One bite and you're on the road to Maxee, City of a Million Busted Metaphors." He said, "Just ignore the part where the inside of your mouth tries to climb onto the top of your head."

15.

On the approach to Maxee, City of Cosmic Brain Waves, Chris drove slowly, keeping his mind blank.

Nothing around the car changed. He wanted it that way, this time.

"You did what Seth Jackson wanted," he said to the jacket. "Your job's over. This way's best."

The only sound then from the jacket was the faint humming of an ancient skip-rope song.

Chris stood by the blue ragtop, at the outskirts of the City Without End and waited.

They came as metal fish, swimming slowly above the pavement. One was huge and green. The second, red. The third, tiny and silver, hovering behind the other two. The three floated where the Crystal Road met the Boulevard of Ancient Dances, an intersection Chris had created on his last visit.

In the distance, looming above a Day-Glo minaret, the

Clockmaster stood faced in another direction, motionless save for the ant-like priests and soldiers marching up and down his shoulders.

"I am Tomkin of the Tomkins, former Flux-Agent of Maxee," said the green fish. "And this is Red Pauline, a local agitator. And now I see," the fish said, turning so one bulbous eye could gaze backwards, "We also have Simmoo, the Last Teacher. He would insist on coming. 'An eye on the present is an eye on the future,' he is always saying. Hello, Simmoo."

The fish to the rear folded inwards, and became a slender man with hair white to one side, golden to the other.

At the transformation, a sigh escaped the green fish. The scales of its sides trembled and then became panes of glass, and then air, leaving Tomkin of the Tomkins standing in the street.

Laughter escaped the fish that shrank into the bright splash of hair atop the head of Red Pauline.

"Chris Brown," said Chris.

"Pleased to meet you," said Simmoo, staring intently.

"Chris," said Tomkin of the Tomkins. "I have much for which to thank you. Having the jacket will complete me. It embodies what Jackson knew, and what he denied the Clockmaster." Tomkin of the Tomkins smiled and held out his hand. "Please. I do appreciate it. You are so kind in coming."

"It is for her," Chris said. "Not you."

"Alas, she can do nothing with that jacket. She is a creature merely of the city, thus of mine, as new Clockmaster."

"This intersection needs a traffic signal," Chris said. Tomkin of the Tompkins stood rooted in place and began to flash green then yellow, then red then yellow.

Beside the door of the '54 Dodge, Pauline kissed Chris: fire on ice.

"Hello," she said then to the jacket. "I think we need to take up your sleeves a little."

The skip-rope song changed to a single oboe note of quiet despair.

Simmoo laughed and followed them back into Maxee.

Then Chris stood alone beside his ragtop, blinded by the vision of beauty wrapped in flame from the edges of the sky. One sun rose while another set. Blue Maria bitterness was in his mouth.

A fast U-turn, and away.

In moments, the Dodge rolled down an early-morning street full of mid-Twentieth Century ranch houses. Its driver was a young man in a really beat up car with no home to go to.

He was happy.

And chilled. Reaching into the duffel bag stuffed with notebooks and clothes, he drew out an old denim jacket.

Before he reached the highway, he remembered the sight of the Clockmaster rising above the buildings of Maxee, the Terminal City.

Before that could fade like a dream, Chris stopped and wrote a few lines.

16.

In a Western city, some years later, a young editor named Will Clark listened to the clang and honking of metal works and traffic coming in a window. Stupid-ass place for a bookshop and publishing house, Will had thought a hundred times. He planned to think it a hundred times more.

Will liked it here.

"That crazy kid publishing those City Bright things out East, you know him? Real name's Chris something. But calls himself Jacket Jackson, right?" said Will, settling in the chair in front of Marty Stein's desk.

"Sure," said the publisher.

"Look at this."

Stein looked at what seemed to be and then did not seem to be a hand-written manuscript.

"What the hell is this, and where the hell from?"

"Supposed to be like a tourist guide to that city, Maxee, the kid writes about. Someone I know introduced me to this couple, the Dewares. Seemed nice and straight, at first.

"Then they started talking about a leather jacket that was like a god and that now some lady in Maxee has dyed it red to match her hair. Said they were Jacket Jackson's adoptive parents, which is crazy. But they had this picture, mug shot actually, from some DWI bust. Could be of him when he was real young. The I.D. says 'Christopher Deware.'

"Anyway, they'd been grooving to Maxee for years. Before the kid began publishing or anything. Finally got up courage to go there themselves."

"To a make-believe city?"

"Right. That's what they said. And then they said this is the tourist guide everybody carries there. I just laughed, then I read it. Wingy as all hell, but really well done. Holds your attention, too."

"Same stuff as what that kid's writing, you say."

"Right."

"But nothing he's published?"

"Nope. Checked."

"They want royalties?"

"Not really. Don't even claim to have written it. Someone in Maxee did, according to them. They just want the world to know. I can't say it's bad work. Might go somewhere."

"What are you thinking? Getting in touch with him?"

"Him? Why?" Will Clark picked at his fingernails for a while. "I see it this way. We do a run. Sell some copies. Then when someone asks, you say, 'Oh, heck, you know, now that we have this published, people are telling us this stuff has something to do with that kid who's getting famous out east.'"

"Got you."

In a few months it sold enough to pay for the lease for the shop, a year in advance.

A New York house, the one that picked it up from the agent who dropped the lawsuit and then looked the other way as Stein finished selling out his run, saw the book through thirty printings.

Some years on, when neither were kids anymore, Will Clark had a chance to meet Chris 'Jacket' Jackson, who was on a reading tour across the West and was in the city for two nights.

The first night and day's readings were bookstore events. Jackson was a cult writer, so cultists turned out, hanging on every reference to Maxee, the City Of Hornet-Nest Hearts. The second night Jackson read in a local art bar.

"I wrote this for a woman who kissed me once, many years ago. Haven't seen her since," he said, introducing a recent poem.

> *"I came back broken from the guerre*
> *and all I wanted is a red-headed woman*
> *said Apollonaire*

while worms danced upon the stair.
Her tin-tin-tintinnabulation's
swirled whichever way they chose to go
said Edgar Poe.
Now where the clock-hands point will rise
into endless skies a night that will not fall
says no one at all. "

"When he finished he said, "Maybe she and I will meet again. In Maxee, City of Retirees." He looked a little surprised the line got a laugh.

Will Clark stepped up to the bar afterwards and introduced himself.

"Good to meet you," Jackson said. "Call me Chris. Only part of my original name that's still good."

Jackson had a beer and a bourbon in front of him and was puffing on a cigar. This guy's leaned on a lot of rails, Will thought

Later, while leaning on the third or maybe fourth brass rail of the night, Chris blew a fat smoke ring and said to Will, "You met the Dewares. My 'foster parents.' I never knew my real father. All my mother ever told me was he smoked cigars and liked to tinker around. They hitched up in the war."

Will was not sure what to say.

"My guess is that his name was Seth Jackson and that he designed the sentient leather jacket. The one that took me to Maxee. Like in the poems. Maybe we'll meet up when I go there. I hear it's real easy, now, to go."

Jackson's eyes looked glassily at Will.

"I think they're great poems." Will regarded his beer uneasily. "As poems, you know."

"You think I'm crazy." Jackson finished off his beer and ordered a bourbon. "You're entitled."

He drank and smoked for a while, then said, "You know, with all the dancing stairs and singing fleas I put into Maxee, not to mention all those goddamned tourists, the thing I remember best is a hairbrush beside the road."

Will listened.

"I got out of this car, an old ragtop that the jacket and I had almost managed to wreck, and there it was in the grass. Why the hell should there be a hairbrush there? In a perfect world, no one would lose a hairbrush. To me it means hope. A space between the cracks."

"Sure," said Will.

"So now," said Jackson, "if I see a hairbrush by the road, I say, thank goodness for a little goddamned glitch in the inexorable wheel of fate."

Poor guy, Will thought, after he got back home and before he passed out. Haunted by the early works that had made him famous, and not able to separate reality from imagination anymore. The poor fucker called himself Jacket Jackson and believed his own stories. Not that he was alone in that. Someone was even building a monument to him in the desert somewhere.

Will fell asleep thinking of that, and dreamed about a place that glittered and twirled through the falling leaves of a torn-apart book of poems.

". . . because of the poetry, we have the movies, the books, the music that celebrate Maxee, City of A Thousand Cuts. The city we see beneath us as we stroll around the brim of the Clockmaster's hat is there because of him. All who walk these streets still read his words with their feet, and ears, and eyes."

—*City Too Bright: Simmoo's Guide to Maxee,*
City of Satisfied Tourists (Tenth Edition)

"The Mask of the Rex" was the story I'd written just before 9/11 happened. I don't recall that I changed anything in the story. It was sold to The Magazine of Fantasy & Science Fiction *later that year. It was the cover story in May of 2002—one of the strongest issues of any magazine or anthology I've ever been in. Jeff Ford's magnificent short story "Creation" got nominated for every award and won the World Fantasy Award. "Mask" got a Nebula nomination but didn't win.*

Write spec fiction and eventually you'll use everything you know along with everything you've imagined or dreamed. By the time I started writing "Mask" I'd already come to the understanding that my Time Travel/Alternate Worlds novel From the Files of the Time Rangers *would feature ancient gods, mainly Greco/Roman. The deities' squabbles carry them, their servants and their pawns all the way into the 21st century.*

For this I re-read the old classics: everything from the Iliad *and* Odyssey *to Livy and Thucydides and the* Letters *of the Younger Pliny. In English translation even Virgil's "Aeneid," which in its original Latin had been high school torture, was bearable, and "Caesar's Commentaries" read like action adventure.*

My guidebook was Betty Radice's Who's Who in the Ancient World. *Spritely and entertaining, it mixes biographical information with examples of visual art and modern adaptations. In Radice's book I found an entry about the temple of Diana at Aricia on the shore of Lake Nemi and its priest, the Rex, an escaped slave. Radice quotes from Macaulay's "Lays of Ancient Rome:"*

"The trees in whose dim shadow
The ghastly priest doth reign
The priest who slew the slayer
And shall himself be slain"

In Radice and Robert Graves I became reacquainted with the pagan sensitivity to place, the idea that certain locations are sacred. Through the generosity of my sister Lee Bowes, I enjoyed summer vacations on Maine's Mt Desert Island back in the '70s and early '80s.

Thinking about it in the days after the towers fell, this place of crystal light and air seemed the perfect spot for a pagan shrine and for the home of an American political dynasty favored by the gods.

THE MASK OF THE REX

1.

The last days of summer have always been a sweet season on the Maine coast. There's still warmth in the sun, the cricket's song is mellow, and the vacationers are mostly gone. Nowhere is that time more golden than on Mount Airey Island.

Late one afternoon in September of 1954, Julia Garde Macauley drove north through the white shingled coastal towns. In the wake of a terrible loss, she felt abandoned by the gods and had made this journey to confront them.

Then, as she crossed Wenlock Sound Bridge, which connects the island with the world, she had a vision. In a fast montage a man, his face familiar yet changed, stood on crutches in a cottage doorway, plunged into an excited crowd of kids, spoke defiantly on the stairs of a plane.

The images flickered like a TV with a bad picture and Julia thought she saw her husband. When it was over, she realized who it had been. And understood even better the questions she had come to ask.

The village of Penoquot Landing on Mount Airey was all carefully preserved clapboard and widow's walks. Now, after the season, few yachts were still in evidence. Fishing boats and lobster trawlers had full use of the wharves.

Baxter's Grande Hotel on Front Street was in hibernation until next summer. In Baxter's parlors and pavilions over the decades, the legends of this resort and Julia's own family had been woven.

Driving through the gathering dusk, she could almost hear drawl-

ing voices discussing her recent loss in same way they did everything
having to do with Mount Airey and the rest of the world.

"Great public commotion about that fly-boy she married."

"The day their wedding was announced marked the end of High
Society."

"In a single engine plane in bad weather. As if he never got over
the war."

"Or knew he didn't belong where he was."

Robert Macauley, thirty-four years old, had been the junior senator from New York for a little more than a year and a half.

Beyond the village, Julia turned onto the road her grandfather
and Rockefeller had planned and had built. "Olympia Drive, where
spectacular views of the mighty Atlantic and piney mainland compete
for our attention with the palaces of the great," rhapsodized a writer
of the prior century. "Like a necklace of diamonds bestowed upon
this island."

The mansions were largely shut until next year. Some hadn't
been opened at all that summer. The Sears estate had just been sold to
the Carmelites as a home for retired nuns.

Where the road swept between the mountain and the sea, Julia
turned onto a long driveway and stopped at the locked gates. Atop a
rise stood Joyous Garde, all Doric columns and marble terraces. Built
at the dawn of America's century, its hundred rooms overlooked the
ocean, "One of the crown jewels of Olympia Drive."

Joyous Garde had been closed and was, in any case, not planned for
convenience or comfort. Julia was expected. She beeped and waited.

Welcoming lights were on in Old Cottage just inside the gates.
Itself a substantial affair, the Cottage was on a human scale. Henry
and Martha Eder were the permanent caretakers of the estate and
lived here year round. Henry emerged with a ring of keys and nodded
to Julia.

Just then, she caught flickering images of this driveway and what
looked at first like a hostile, milling mob.

A familiar voice intoned. "Beyond these wrought iron gates and
granite pillars, the most famous private entryway in the United States,
and possibly the world, the Macauley family and friends gather in
moments of trial and tragedy."

Julia recognized the speaker as Walter Cronkite and realized that
what she saw was the press waiting for a story.

Then the gates clanged open. The grainy vision was gone. As Julia rolled through, she glanced up at Mt. Airey. It rose behind Joyous Garde covered with dark pines and bright foliage. Martha Eder came out to greet her and Julia found herself lulled by the old woman's Down East voice.

Julia had brought very little luggage. When it was stowed inside, she stood on the front porch of Old Cottage and felt she had come home. The place was wooden-shingled and hung with vines and honeysuckle. Her great-grandfather George Lowell Stoneham had built it seventy-five years before. It remained as a guest house and gate house and as an example of a fleeting New England simplicity.

2.

George Lowell Stoneham was always referred to as one of the discoverers of Mt. Airey. The Island, of course, had been found many times. By seals and gulls and migratory birds, by native hunters, by Hudson and Champlain and Scotch-Irish fishermen. But not until after the Civil War was it found by just the right people: wealthy and respectable Bostonians.

Gentlemen, such as the painter Brooks Carr looking for proper subjects or the Harvard naturalist George Lowell Stoneham trying to loose memories of Antietem, came up the coast by steamer, stayed in the little hotels built for salesmen and schooner captains. They roamed north until they hit Mt. Airey.

At first, a few took rooms above Baxter's General Provisions And Boarding House in Penoquot Landing. They painted, explored, captured bugs in specimen bottles. They told their friends, the nicely wealthy of Boston, about it. Brooks Carr rented a house in the village one summer and brought his young family.

To Professor Stoneham went the honor of being the first of these founders to build on the island. In 1875, he bought (after hard bargaining) a chunk of land on the seaward side of Mt. Airey and constructed a cabin in a grove of giant white pine that overlooked Mirror Lake.

In the following decades, others also built: plain cabins and studios at first, then cottages. In those days, men and boys swam naked and out of sight at Bachelors' Point on the north end of the island.

The women, in sweeping summer hats and dresses that reached to the ground, stopped for tea and scones at Baxter's, which now offered a shady patio in fine weather. There, they gossiped about the Saltonstall boy who had married the Pierce girl then moved to France, and about George Stoneham's daughter Helen and a certain New York financier.

This filet of land in this cream of a season did not long escape the notice of the truly wealthy. From New York they came, and Philadelphia. They acquired large chunks of property. The structures they caused to rise were still called studios and cottages. But they were mansions on substantial estates. By the 1890s, those who could have been anywhere in the world chose to come in August to Mount Airy.

Trails and bridle paths were blazed through the forests and up the slopes of the mountain. In 1892, John D. Rockefeller and Simon Garde constructed a paved road, Olympia Drive, around the twenty-five mile perimeter of the island.

Hiking parties into the hills, to the quiet glens at the heart of the island, always seemed to find themselves at Mirror Lake with its utterly smooth surface and unfathomable depths. The only work of man visible from the shore, and that just barely, was Stoneham Cabin atop a sheer granite cliff.

Julia Garde Macauley didn't know what caused her great-grandfather to build on that exact spot. But she knew it wasn't whim or happenstance. The old tintypes showed a tall man with a beard like a wizard's and eyes that had gazed on Pickett's Charge.

Maybe the decision was like the one Professor Stoneham himself described in his magisterial *Wasps of the Eastern United States*. "In the magic silence of a summer's afternoon, the mud wasp builds her nest. Instinct, honed through the eons, guides her choice."

Perhaps, though, it was something more. A glimpse. A sign. Julia knew for certain that once drawn to the grove, George Stoneham had discovered that it contained one of the twelve portals to an ancient shrine. And that the priest, or the Rex , as the priest was called, was an old soldier, Lucius, a Roman centurion who worshipped Lord Apollo.

Lucius had been captured and enslaved during Crassus' invasion of Parthia in the century before Christ. He escaped with the help of his god, who then led him to one of the portals of the shrine. The reigning priest at that time was a devoted follower of Dionysius. Lucius found and killed the man, put on the silver mask, and became Rex in his place.

Shortly after he built the cabin, George Lowell Stoneham built a cottage for his family at the foot of the mountain. But he spent much time up in the grove. After the death of his wife, he even stayed there, snow-bound, for several winters researching, he said, insect hibernation.

In warmer seasons, ladies in the comfortable new parlors at Baxter's Hotel alluded to the professor's loneliness. Conversation over brandy in the clubrooms of the recently built Bachelor's Point Aquaphiliacs Society, dwelt on the "fog of war" that sometimes befell a hero.

There was some truth in all that. But what only Stoneham's daughter Helen knew was that beyond the locked door of the snow-bound cabin, two old soldiers talked their days away in Latin. They sat on marble benches overlooking a cypress grove above a still lake in Second Century Italy.

Lucius would look out into the summer haze, and come to attention each time a figure appeared, wondering, the professor knew, if this was the agent of his death.

Then on a morning one May, George Lowell Stoneham was discovered sitting in his cabin with a look of peace on his face. A shrapnel splinter, planted in a young soldier's arm during the Wilderness campaign thirty-five years before, had worked its way loose and found his heart.

Professor Stoneham's daughter and only child, Helen, inherited the Mt. Airey property. Talk at the Thursday Cotillions in the splendid summer ballroom of Baxter's Grande Hotel had long spun around the daughter, "With old Stoneham's eyes and Simon Garde's millions."

For Helen was the first of the Boston girls to marry New York money. And such money and such a New York man! Garde's hands were on all the late nineteenth century levers: steel, railroads, shipping. His origins were obscure. Not quite, a few hinted, Anglo Saxon. The euphemism used around the Aquaphiliacs' Society was "Eastern."

In the great age of buying and building on Mt. Airey, none built better or on a grander scale than Mr. and Mrs. Garde. The old Stoneham property expanded, stretched down to the sea. The new "cottage," Joyous Garde, was sweeping, almost Mediterranean, with its Doric columns and marble terraces, its hundred windows that flamed in the rising sun.

With all this, Helen did not neglect Stoneham Cabin up on the mountain. Over the years, it became quite a rambling affair. The slope on which it was built, the pine grove in which it sat, made its size and shape hard to calculate.

In the earliest years of the century, after the birth of her son, George, it was remarked that Helen Stoneham Garde came up long before the season and stayed well afterwards. And that she was interested in things Chinese. Not the collections of vases and fans that so many clipper-captain ancestors had brought home, but earthenware jugs, wooden sandals, bows and arrows. And she studied the language. Not high Mandarin, apparently, but some guttural peasant dialect.

Relations with her husband were also a subject for discussion. They were rarely seen together. In 1906, the demented millionaire Harry Thaw shot the philandering architect Stanford White on the rooftop of Madison Square Garden in New York. And the men taking part in the Bachelor's Point Grand Regatta that year joked about how Simon Garde had been sitting two tables away. "As easily it might have been some other irate cuckold with a gun and Sanford White might be building our new yacht club right now."

At the 1912 Charity Ball for the Penoquot Landing Fisherfolk Relief Fund in Baxter's Grande Pavilion, the Gardes made a joint entrance. This was an event rare enough to upstage former President Teddy Roosevelt about to campaign as a Bull Moose.

Simon Garde, famously, mysteriously, died when the French liner *Marseilles* was sunk by a U-boat in 1916. Speculation flourished as to where he was bound and the nature of his mission. When his affairs, financial and otherwise, were untangled, his widow was said to be one of the wealthiest women in the nation.

Helen Stoneham Garde, a true child of New England, never took her attention far from the money. Horses were her other interest besides chinoise. She bred them and raced them. And they won. Much of her time was spent on the Mt. Airey estates. Stories of her reclusivity abounded.

The truth, her granddaughter Julia knew, would have stunned even the most avid of the gossips. For around the turn of the century, Lucius had been replaced. A single arrow in the eye had left the old

Rex sprawling on the stone threshold of the shrine. His helmet, his sword, and the matched pair of Colt Naval Revolvers that had been a gift from George Stoneham, lay scattered like toys.

A new Rex, or more accurately a Regina, picked the silver mask out of the dust and put it on. This was Ki Mien from north China, a servant of the goddess of forests and woods, and a huntress of huge ability.

From a few allusions her grandmother dropped, Julia deduced that Helen Garde and the priestess had, over the next two decades, forged a union. Unknown to any mortal on the Island or in the world, they formed what was called in those days a Boston marriage.

In the years that Helen was occupied with Ki Mien, motorcars came to Mt. Airey. Their staunchest supporter was George "Flash" Garde, Simon and Helen's son and only child. "A damned fine looking piece of American beef," as a visiting Englishman remarked.

Whether boy or man, Flash Garde could never drive fast enough. His custom-built Locomobile, all brass and polish and exhaust, was one of the hazards of Olympia Drive. "Racing to the next highball and low lady," it was said at Bachelor's Point. "Such a disappointment to his mother," they sighed at Baxter's.

In fact, his mother seemed unbothered. Perhaps this was because she had, quite early on, arranged his marriage to Cissy Custis, the brightest of the famous Custis sisters. The birth of her granddaughter Julia guaranteed the only succession that really mattered to her.

3.

In 1954, on the evening of the last day of summer, Julia had supper in Old Cottage kitchen with the Eders. Mrs. Eder made the same comforting chicken pie she remembered.

The nursery up at Joyous Garde was vast. On its walls were murals of the cat playing the fiddle and the cow jumping the moon. It contained a puppet theater and a play house big enough to walk around in if you were small enough. But some of Julia's strongest memories of Mt Airey centered on Old Cottage.

The most vivid of all began one high summer day in the early 1920s. Her grandmother, as she sometimes did, had taken Julia out of the care of her English nurse and her French governess.

When it was just the two of them, Helen Stoneham Garde raised her right hand and asked, "Do you swear on the head of Ruggles The One-Eared Rabbit, not to tell anybody what we will see today?"

Time with her grandmother was always a great adventure. Julia held up the stuffed animal, worn featureless with love, and promised. Then they went for a walk.

Julia was in a pinafore and sandals and held Ruggles by his remaining ear. The woman of incalculable wealth wore sensible shoes and a plain skirt and carried a picnic basket. Their walk was a long one for somebody with short legs. But finches sang, fledglings chirped on oak branches. Invisible through the leaves, a woodpecker drilled a maple trunk. Red squirrels and jays spread news of their passage.

Up the side of Mt. Airey, Helen led her grandchild to the silent white pine grove that overlooked deep, still waters. The Cabin itself was all odd angles, gray shingles and stone under a red roof. It was Julia's first visit to the place.

Years later, when she was able to calculate such things, she realized that the dimensions of Stoneham Cabin did not quite pan out. But only a very persistent visitor would note that something was missing, that one room always remained unexplored.

That first time, on a sunny porch, visible from no angle outside the Cabin, Helen Garde set down the basket, unpacked wine and sandwiches, along with milk, and a pudding for Julia. Then she stood behind her granddaughter and put her hands on the child's shoulders.

"Julia, I should like you to meet Alcier, whom we call The Rex."

The man in the doorway was big and square-built with dark skin and curly, black hair. His voice was low, and, like Mademoiselle Martine, he spoke French, though his was different. He wore sandals and a white shirt and trousers. The priest bowed and said, "I am happy to meet the tiny lady."

He was not frightening at all. On the contrary, morning doves fed out of his hand and he admired Ruggles very much. When they had finished lunch, the Rex asked her grandmother if he could show Julia what lay inside.

The two of them passed through a curtain that the child could feel but couldn't see. She found herself in a round room with doors open in all directions. It was more than a small child could encompass. That first time, she was aware only of a cave opening onto a snowy winter morning and an avenue of trees with the moon above them.

Then Alcier faced her across a fire that flickered in the center of the room even on this warm day. He put on a silver mask that covered his face, with openings for his eyes, nostrils and mouth, and said, "Just as your grandmother welcomed me to her house, so, as servant of the gods, I welcome you to the Shrine Of The Twelve Portals."

But even as gods spoke through him, Julia could see that Alcier smiled and that his eyes were kind. So she wasn't a bit afraid.

When it was time to say goodbye, the Rex stood on the porch and bowed slightly. A red-tailed hawk came down and sat on his wrist. Because of Alcier's manners, Julia was never frightened of the Rex. Even later when she had seen him wiping his machete clean.

As a small child, Julia didn't know why her grandmother made her promise not to tell anyone about the hawk and the invisible curtain and the nice black man who lived up in the cabin. But she didn't.

Children who tell adults everything are trying to make them as wise as they. Just as children who ask questions already know why the sky is blue and where the lost kitten has gone. What they need is the confirmation that the odd and frightening magic that has turned adults into giants has not completely addled their brains. That Julia didn't need such reassurance she attributed to her grandmother and to Alcier.

On her next visit, she learned to call the place with the flame, the Still Room. She found out that it was a shrine, a place of the gods, and that Alcier was a priest, though much different than the ones in the Episcopal church. On the second visit she noticed Alcier's slight limp.

Her grandmother never went inside with them. On Julia's next few visits over several summers, she and Alcier sat on stools in the Still Room and looked out through the twelve doors. The Rex patrolled each of these entrances every day. He had a wife and, over the years, several children whom Julia met. Though she never was told exactly where they lived.

Soon, she had learned the name of what lay beyond each portal: jungle, cypress grove, dark forest, tundra, desert, rock-bound island, marsh, river valley, mountain, cave, plains, sandy shore.

At first she was accompanied up the mountain by her grandmother. Then, in the summer she turned twelve, Julia was allowed to go by herself. By that time, she and Alcier had gone through each of the doors and explored what lay beyond.

The hour of the day, the climate, even Julia came to realize, the continent varied beyond each portal. All but one, in those years, had a shrine of some kind. This might be a grove or a cave, or a rocky cavern, with a fire burning and, somewhere nearby, a body of water still as a mirror.

The plains, even then, had become a wasteland of slag heaps and railroad sidings. Julia did not remember ever having seen it otherwise.

If she loved Alcier, and she did, it was not because he spared her the truth in his quiet voice and French from the Green Antilles. Early on he showed her the fascinating scar on his left leg and explained that he was an escaped slave, "Like each Rex past and to be."

He told her how he had been brought over the wide waters when he was younger than she, how he had grown up on a plantation in the Sugar Islands. How he had been a house servant, how he had run away and been brought back in chains with his leg torn open.

Julia already knew how one Rex succeeded another. But on that first summer she visited the cabin alone, she and Alcier had a picnic on the wide, empty beach on the Indochina Sea, and she finally asked how it had happened.

Before he answered, Alcier drew the silver mask out of the satchel he always carried. Julia noticed that he hardly had to guide it. The mask moved by itself to his face. Then he spoke.

"Where I lived, we had a public name for the bringer of wisdom And a private name known only by those to whom She spoke. When I was very young, She sent me dreams. But after I was taken beyond the sea, it was as if I was lost and She couldn't find me.

"Then, after I had escaped and been recaptured and brought back to my owner, She appeared again and told me what to do. When I awoke, I followed Her command.

"With the chains that bound my hands, I broke the neck of one who came to feed me. With that one's knife, I killed him who bore the keys. With the machete he dropped, I made the others flee. My left leg carried me well. My right was weak. I did not run as I once had.

"In the forest, hunters chased me. But the goddess drew me into a mist and they passed by. Beside a stream, a hare came down to drink. I killed her and drank her blood. That morning, hunters went to my left and to my right. I slipped past them as before.

"Then it was past mid-day. I stood in shadows on the edge of a glade. And all was silent and still. No leaf moved. In the sky directly above me, the sun and a hawk stood still. And I knew gods were at work here. I heard no sounds of hunters. For I was at the heart of the forest.

"I saw the lodge made of wood and stone and I knew it was mine for the taking. If I killed the King of this place. I said a prayer to the goddess and let her guide me.

"Not a leaf moved, not a bird sang. Then I saw the silver mask and knew the Rex was looking for me. My heart thumped. I commanded it to be still. The head turned one way then another. But slowly. The Rex was complacent, maybe, expecting to find and kill me easily. Or old and tired.

"My goddess protected me. Made me invisible. Balanced on my good leg and my bad, I stood still as the Rex crossed the glade. I studied the wrinkled throat that hung below the mask. And knew I would have one chance.

Just out of range of my knife, the priest hesitated for an instant. And I lunged. One great stride. I stumbled on my bad leg. But my arm carried true. The knife went into the throat. And I found it was a woman and that I was king in her place.

"The shrine has existed as long as the gods. Along one of the paths some day, will come the one who succeeds me," he told her. "When the gods wish, that one will do away with me."

The Rex could speak of his own death the same way he might about a change of the seasons. But some time after that, on a visit to the Still Room, Julia noticed derricks and steel tanks on the rocky island. When she asked Alcier about the destruction of another shrine, he seemed to wince, shook his head, and said nothing.

4.

At night in Old Cottage years later, Julia looked out the windows into the dark. And saw Mount Airey by daylight. The cabin and the grove were gone. The bare ground they had stood on was cracked and eroded. She told Mrs. Eder that she was going to visit Stoneham Cabin next morning.

Falling asleep, Julia remembered the resort as it had been. As a child, she had learned to swim at Bachelors' Point and heard the story of Mount Airey being spun. Men tamed and in trunks, women liberated in one piece suits, swam together now and talked of the useful Mr. Coolidge and, later, the traitorous Franklin Delano Roosevelt.

When she was fifteen, her father died in an accident. Nothing but the kindest condolences were offered. But Julia, outside an open door, heard someone say, "Ironic, Flash Garde's being cut down by a speeding taxi."

"In front of the Stork Club, though, accompanied by a young lady described as a 'hostess.' He would have wanted it that way." She heard them all laugh.

By then, cocktail hour had replaced afternoon tea at Baxter's. In tennis whites, men sat with their legs crossed, women with their feet planted firmly on the ground. Scandal was no longer whispered. Julia knew that her mother's remarriage less than two months after her father's death would have been fully discussed. As would the decision of this mother she hardly ever saw to stay in Europe.

Julia's grandmother attended her son's funeral and shed not a tear. Her attitude was called stoic by some. Unfeeling by others. No one at Baxter's or Bachelor's Point had the slightest idea that the greatest love of Helen Garde's life had, over their twenty years together, given her hints of these events yet to come.

After her father's death and her mother's remarriage, Julia visited the Rex. From behind the silver mask, Alcier spoke. "The gods find you well. You will wed happily with their blessings," he said. "The divine ones will shield your children."

Much as she adored Alcier, Julia thought of this as fortune teller stuff. She began, in the way of the young, to consider the Rex and the Shrine of the Twelve Portals as being among the toys of childhood.

That fall, she went to Radcliff as her grandmother wished. There, the thousand and one things of a wealthy young woman's life drove thoughts of the gods to the back of her mind. They didn't even re-emerge on a sunny day on Brattle Street in her senior year.

Julia and her friend Grace Shipton were headed for tennis lessons. At the curb, a young man helped a co-ed from Vassar into the seat of an MG Midget. He looked up and smiled what would become a well-known smile. And looked again, surprised. It was the first time he had laid eyes on the woman he would marry.

Before this moment, Julia had experienced a girl's tender thoughts and serious flirtations. Then her eyes met those of the young man in the camel-hair jacket. She didn't notice the boy who watched them, so she didn't see his mischievous smile or feel the arrow. But in a moment of radiance her heart was riven.

When Julia asked Grace who the young man was, something in her voice made the Shipton heiress look at her. "That's Robert Macauley," came the answer. "The son of that lace curtain thug who's governor of New York."

Julia Garde and young Robert Macauley were locked in each other's hearts. All that afternoon she could think of nothing else. Then came the telegram that read, "Sorry to intrude. But I can't live without you."

"Until this happened, I never believed in this," she told him the next afternoon when they were alone and wrapped in each others' arms.

Robert proposed a few days later. "The neighbors will burn shamrocks on your front lawn," he said when Julia accepted. She laughed, but knew that might be true. And didn't care.

Polite society studied Helen Stoneham Garde's face for the anger and outrage she must feel. The heiress to her fortune had met and proposed to marry an Irishman, A CATHOLIC, A DEMOCRAT!

But when Julia approached her grandmother in the study at Joyous Garde and broke the news, Helen betrayed nothing. Her eyes were as blue as the wide Atlantic that lay beyond the French doors. And as unknowable.

"You will make a fine looking couple," she said. "And you will be very happy."

"You knew."

"Indirectly. You will come to understand. The wedding should be small and private. Making it more public would serve no immediate purpose."

"Best political instincts I've encountered in a Republican," the governor of the Empire State remarked on hearing this. "Be seen at mass," he told his son. "Raise the children in the Church. With the Garde money behind you, there'll be no need to muck about with concrete contracts."

"There will be a war and he will be a fighter pilot," Helen told Julia after she had met Robert. Before her granddaughter could ask how she knew, she said impatiently, "All but the fools know a war is coming. And young men who drive sports cars always become pilots."

It was as she said. Robert was in Naval Flight Training at Pensacola a month after Pearl Harbor. The couple's song was "They Can't Take That Away From Me."

Their son, Timothy, was not three and their daughter Helen was just born when Robert Macauley sailed from San Francisco on the aircraft carrier *Constellation*. Julia saw him off, then found herself part of the great, shifting mass of soldiers and sailors home on leave, women returning after saying goodbye to husbands, sons, boyfriends.

On a crowded train, with sailors sleeping in the luggage racks, she and a Filipino nurse cried about their men in the South Pacific. She talked with a woman, barely forty, who had four sons in the army.

Julia felt lost and empty. She reread the *Metamorphoses* and *The Odyssey* and thought a lot about Alcier and the Still Room. It had been two years since she had visited Mount Airey. She felt herself drawn there all that winter.

Early in spring, she left her children in the care of nurses and her grandmother and went by train from New York to Boston and from Boston to Bangor. She arrived in the morning and Mr. Eder met her at the station. They drove past houses with victory gardens and V's in the windows if family members were in the service.

A sentry post had been established on the mainland end of Wenlock Sound Bridge. The Army Signal Corps had taken over Bachelors' Point for the duration of the war.

The bar at Baxter's was an officers' club. On Olympia Drive, some of the great houses had been taken for the duration. Staff cars, jeeps, canvas-topped trucks, stood in the circular drives.

It was just after the thaw. Joyous Garde stood empty. Patches of snow survived on shady corners of the terraces. The statues looked as if they still regretted their lack of clothes.

Julia found a pair of rubber boots that fit and set off immediately for Stoneham Cabin. In summer, Mt. Airey was nature in harness, all bicycle paths and hiking parties. In Mud Time, dry beds ran with icy water, flights of birds decorated a gray sky, lake-sized puddles had appeared, the slopes lay leafless and open.

Julia saw the stranger as she approached the cabin. But this was her land and she did not hesitate. Sallow faced, clean-shaven with the shadow of a beard, he was expecting her. When she stepped onto the porch, he came to attention. She knew that sometime in the recent past he had murdered Alcier.

"Corporal John Smalley, Her Britannic Majesty's London Fusiliers," he said. "Anxious to serve you, my lady."

In the Still Room, when they entered, Julia looked around, saw wreckage in the desert shrine, smashed tanks on the sand. Dead animals lay around the oasis, and she guessed the water was poisoned.

The murderer put on the silver mask and spoke. His voice rang. Julia felt a chill.

"It's by the will of the gods that I'm here today. By way of a nasty scrap in the hills. Caught dead to rights and every one of us to die. Officers down. No great moment. But the sergeant major was gone. A spent round richoted off my Worsley helmet and I was on me back looking up.

"I lay still but I could hear screams and thought it was up and done with and I would dance on hot coals for as long as it took. For cheating and philandering and the cove I stabbed in Cheapside. And I prayed as I'd never done.

"Then He appeared. Old Jehovah as I thought, all fiery eyes and smoke behind his head. Then He spoke and it seems it was Mars himself. I noticed he wore a helmet and carried a flaming sword. He told me I was under His protection and nothing would happen to me.

"Good as His word. No one saw when I rose up and took my Enfield. He lead the way all through the night, talking in my ear. About the shrine and the priest that lives here.

"A runaway slave it always is who kills the old priest and takes over. And I choked at that. Not the killing, but Britains never will be slaves and all.

"Lord Mars told me enlistment in Her Majesty's Army came close enough. New thinking, new blood was what was needed. Led me to a hill shrine before dawn. Left me to my own devices.

"The shrine's that one through that portal behind your ladyship. A grove with the trees all cut short by the wind and a circle of stone and a deep pool. When I was past the circle and beside the pool, the wind's sound was cut off and it was dead still.

"A path led down to the pool and on it was a couple of stones and a twig resting on them. And I knew not to disturb that. So I went to ground. Oiled my Enfield. Waited. Took a day or two. But I was patient. Ate my iron rations and drank water from the pool.

"When he came, it was at dusk and he knew something was up. A formidable old bugger he was. But . . ."

He trailed off. Removed the mask. "You knew him. Since you were a little girl, I hear."

Julia's eyes burned. "He had a wife and children."

"I've kept them safe. He'd put a sum aside for them from shrine offerings and I saw they had that. Got my own bit of bother and strife tucked away. We know in this job we aren't the first. And won't be the last. Living on a loan of time so to speak."

He pointed to the ruined shrines. "The gods have gotten wise that things will not always go their way."

The corporal told her about defense works and traps he was building. Like a tenant telling the landlady about improvements he is making, thought Julia. She knew that was the way it would be between them and that she would always miss her noble Alcier.

Just before she left, Smalley asked, "I wonder if I could see your son, m'lady. Sometime when it's convenient."

Julia said nothing. She visited her grandmother, eighty and erect, living in Taos in a spare and beautiful house. Her companion was a woman from the Pueblo, small, silent and observant.

"Timothy is the whole point of our involvement," said the old woman. She sat at a table covered with breeding charts and photos of colts. "You and I are the precursors."

"He's just a child."

"As were you when you were taken to the shrine. Think of how you loved Alcier. He would have wanted you to do this. And you shall have your rewards. Just as I have."

"And they are?"

"At this point in your life, you would despise them if I told you. In time, they will seem more than sufficient."

Julia knew that she would do as the Rex had asked. But that summer Robert was stationed in Hawaii. So she went out to be with him instead of going to Mount Airey. The next August, she gave birth to Cecilia, her second daughter.

The year after that, Robert was in a naval hospital in California, injured in a crash landing on a carrier flight deck. His shoulder was smashed but healed nicely. A three inch gash ran from his left ear to his jaw. It threw his smile slightly off-kilter.

He seemed distant, even in bed. Tempered like a knife. And daring. As if he too sensed death and destiny and the will of the gods.

When the war was over Robert had a Navy Cross, a trademark smile and a scar worth, as he put it, "Fifty-thousand votes while they still remember."

Over his own father's objections, the young Macauley ran for congress from the West Side of Manhattan. The incumbent, one of the old man's allies, was enmeshed in a corruption scandal. Robert won the primary and the election. His lovely wife and three young children were features of his campaign.

Julia paid a couple of fast visits to the cabin. On one of them the Corporal told her, "I know it's a kid will be my undoing. But it will be a little girl." On another he said, "The gods would take it as a great favor, if you let me speak to your son."

Thus it was that one lovely morning the following summer, Julia left her two little daughters in the huge nursery at Joyous Garde and brought Timothy to Stoneham Cabin. As if it was part of a ritual, she had Mrs. Eder pack lunch.

Julia stuck a carton of the Luckies she knew the Corporal favored into the basket and started up the hill. Her son, age seven and startlingly like the father he rarely saw, darted around, firing a toy gun at imaginary enemies.

The corporal, tanned and wiry, sat on the back porch, smoking and cleaning his rifle. Tim stared at him wide-eyed. "Are you a commando?" he asked after the introductions were made and he'd learned that their guest was English.

"Them's Navy," Smalley said. "And I'm a soldier of the Queen. Or King as it is."

Julia stared down at Mirror Lake. Except when Smalley spoke, she could imagine that Alcier was still there.

Something even more intense than this must have happened to her grandmother after the death of Ki Mien.

"Have you killed anybody?"

"Killing's never a nice thing, lad. Sometimes a necessity. But never nice," Smalley said. "Now what do you say that we ask your mother if I can show you around?"

Later, on their way back to the cottage, Timothy was awestruck.

"He showed me traps he had set! In a jungle! He told me I was going to be a great leader!"

As her grandmother had with her, Julia demanded his silence. Timothy agreed and kept his word. In fact, he rarely mentioned the cabin and the shrine. Julia wondered if Smalley had warned him not to. Then and later, she was struck by how easily her son accepted being the chosen of the gods.

Fashion had passed Mt. Airey by. That summer, the aging bucks at Bachelors' Point drawled on about how Dewey was about to thrash Truman. And how the Rockefellers had donated their estate to the National Parks Service.

"What else now that the Irish have gotten onto the island."

"And not even through the back door."

That summer, Helen Stoneham Garde stayed in New Mexico. But Joyous Garde jumped. "Prominent Democrats from the four corners of the nation come to be bedazzled," as Congressman Macauley murmured to his wife.

Labor leaders smoked cigars in the oak and leather splendor of Simon Garde's study. Glowing young Prairie Populists drank with entrenched Carolina Dixiecrats. The talk swirled around money and influence, around next year's national elections and Joe Kennedy's boy down in Massachusetts.

Above them, young Macauley with his lovely wife stood on the curve of the pink and marble stairs. Julia had grown interested in this game. It reminded her of her grandmother's breeding charts and race horses.

The following summer, Helen Stoneham Garde returned to her estate. Afternoons at Baxter's were drowsy now and dowager-ridden.

"Carried in a litter like royalty."

"Up the mountain to the cabin."

"Returned there to die it seems."

"Her daughter and son-in-law will have everything." Shudders ran around the room.

On an afternoon of warm August sun and a gentle sea breeze, Julia sat opposite her grandmother on the back porch of Stoneham Cabin. "Only the rich can keep fragments of the past alive," Helen told her. "To the uneducated eye, great wealth can be mistaken for magic."

Below them, a party had picnicked next to Mirror Lake a bit earlier. Hikers had passed though. But at the moment, the shore was deserted, the surface undisturbed. The Rex was not in evidence.

Helen's eye remained penetrating, her speech clear. "A peaceful death," she said, "is one of the gifts of the gods."

Julia wished she had thought to ask her grandmother more questions about how their lives had been altered by the shrine. She realized that her own introduction to it at so young an age had occurred because Helen could not stand dealing with the man who had murdered the one closest to her.

The two sat in a long silence. Then the old woman said, "My dearest child, I thought these might be of interest," and indicated a leather folder on the table.

Julia opened it and found several photos. She stared, amazed at the tree-lined Cambridge Street and the young couple agape at their first glimpse of each other. She couldn't take in all the details at once: the deliveryman hopping from his cart, the elderly gent out for a stroll, the boy who walked slightly behind what must have been his parents.

Small, perhaps foreign in his sandals, he alone saw the tall, dark-haired young man, the tall blond young woman, stare at each other in wonder.

"You knew before . . ." Julia said looking up. She didn't dare breathe. Her grandmother still smiled slightly. Her eyes were wide. Beside her stood a figure in a silver mask. Tall and graceful. Not Corporal Smalley. Not at all. He wore only a winged helmet and sandals. Hermes, Lord Mercury, touched Helen with the silver caduceus staff he carried.

Julia caught her breath. Her grandmother slumped slightly. Helen Stoneham Garde's eyes were blank. Her life was over. The figure was gone.

5.

"First day of Autumn," Martha Eder said when Julia came down the Old Cottage stairs the morning after her return. A picnic basket had been packed. Julia had not brought cigarettes for Smalley, had reason to think they weren't necessary.

The air was crisp but the sun was warm enough that all Julia needed was a light jacket. As she set out, Henry Eder interrupted his repair of a window frame. "I can go with you, see if anything needs doing." When she declined, he nodded and went back to his work.

Grief was a private matter to Mainers. Besides, even after three quarters of a century, Julia's family were still "summer folk," and thus unfathomable.

The walk up Mount Airey was magnificent. Julia had rarely seen it this late in the year. Red and gold leaves framed green pine. Activity in the trees and undergrowth was almost frantic. A fox, intent on the hunt, crossed her path.

After her grandmother's death, she had returned to the cabin only on the occasions when she brought Tim. In the last few years, she hadn't been back at all.

She remembered a day when she and Robert sat in the study of their Georgetown mansion and Timothy knocked on the door. Just shy of twelve, he wore his Saint Anthony's Priory uniform of blazer and short pants. In 1951, the American upper class kept its boys in shorts for as long as possible. A subtle means of segregating them from the masses.

Representative Robert Macauley, (D-NY), was maneuvering for a Senate nomination in what promised to be a tough year for Democrats. He looked up from the speech he was reviewing. Julia, busy with a guest list, watched them both.

Timothy said, "What I would like for my birthday this year is a crewcut. Lots of the kids have them. And I want long pants when I'm not in this stupid monkey suit. And this summer I want to be allowed to go up to the cabin on Mount Airey by myself."

Julia caught the amusement and look of calculation in her husband's eyes. Did his kid in short pants gain him more votes from women who thought it was adorable than he lost from men who thought it was snooty?

"In matters like this, we defer to the upper chamber," he said with a quick, lopsided smile and nodded to Julia.

She felt all the pangs of a mother whose child is growing up. But she negotiated briskly. The first demand was a throwaway as she and her son both knew.

"No crewcut. None of the boys at your school have them. The brothers don't approve." The brothers made her Protestant skin crawl. But they were most useful at times like this.

"Long pants outside school? Please!" he asked. "Billy Chervot and his brothers all get to wear blue jeans!" Next year would be Timothy's last with the brothers. Then he'd be at Grafton and out in the world.

"Perhaps. For informal occasions."

"Jeans!"

"We shall see." He would be wearing them, she knew, obviously beloved, worn ones. On a drizzly morning in Maine. His hair would be short. He'd have spent that summer in a crewcut.

Julia had studied every detail of a certain photo. She estimated Tim's age at around fifteen. The shot showed him as he approached Stoneham Cabin. He wore his father's old naval flight jacket, still too big for him, though he had already gotten tall.

"Mount Airey?" the eleven-year-old Tim had asked.

She heard herself saying, "Yes. That should be fine. Check in with Mrs. Eder when you're going. And tell her when you come back. Be sure to let me know if anything up there needs to be done."

Her son left the room smiling. "What's the big deal about that damned cabin?" her husband asked.

Julia shrugged. "*The Wasps of the Eastern United States*," she said and they both laughed. The title of her grandfather's tome was a joke between them. It referred to things no outsider could ever understand or would want to.

Julia returned to her list. She had memorized every detail of the photo of their son. He had tears in his eyes. The sight made her afraid for them all.

Her husband held out a page of notes. "Take a look. I'm extending an olive branch to Mrs. Roosevelt. Her husband and my dad disagreed." He grinned. Franklin Roosevelt, patrician reformer and Timothy Macauley, machine politician, had famously loathed each other.

Julia stared at her husband's handwriting. Whatever the words said would work. The third photo in the leather folder her grandmother had given her showed FDR's widow on a platform with Robert. Julia recognized a victory night.

She could trace a kind of tale with the photos. She met her husband. He triumphed. Their son went for comfort to the Rex. A story was told. Or, as in *The Iliad*, part of one.

That day in the study in Georgetown, she looked at Robert Macauley, in the reading glasses he never wore publicly, and felt

overwhelming tenderness. Julia could call up every detail of the photo of their meeting.

Only the boy in the background looked directly at the couple
who stared into each other's eyes. He smiled. His hand was raised.
Something gold caught the sun. A ring? A tiny bow? Had Robert and
she been hit with Eros' arrow? All she knew was that the love she felt
was very real.

How clever they were, the gods, to give mortals just enough of
a glimpse of their workings to fascinate. But never to let them know
everything.

That summer, her son went up Mount Airey alone. It bothered
Julia as one more sign he was passing out of her control. "The gods
won't want to loose this one m' lady," Smalley had told her.

Over the next few years, Timothy entered puberty, went away to
school, had secrets. His distance increased. When the family spent
time at Joyous Garde, Tim would go to the Cabin often and report to
her in privacy. Mundane matters like "Smalley says the back eaves
need to be reshingled." Or vast, disturbing ones like, "That jungle
portal is impassable now. Smalley says soon ours will be the only
one left."

Then came a lovely day in late August 1954. Sun streamed
through the windows of Joyous Garde, sailboats bounced on the water. In the ballroom, staff moved furniture. A distant phone rang. A
reception was to be held that evening. Senator Macauley would be
flying in from Buffalo that afternoon.

Julia's secretary, her face frozen and wide-eyed, held out a telephone and couldn't speak. Against all advice, trusting in the good
fortune that had carried him so far, her husband had taken off in the
face of a sudden Great Lakes storm. Thunder, lightning and hail had
swept the region. Radio contact with Robert Macauley's one-engine
plane had been lost.

The crash site wasn't found until late that night. The death
wasn't confirmed until the next morning. When Julia looked for him,
Timothy was gone. The day was cloudy with a chill drizzle. She stood
on the porch of Old Cottage a bit later when he returned. His eyes red.
Dressed as he was in the photo.

As they fell into each others' arms, Julia caught a glimpse that was gone in an instant. Her son, as in the photo she had studied so often, approached Stoneham Cabin. This time, she saw his grief turn to surprise and a look of stunned betrayal. Timothy didn't notice.

The two hugged and sobbed in private sorrow before they turned toward Joyous Garde and the round of public mourning. As they did, he said, "You go up there from now on. I never want to go back."

FINALE

Julia approached the grove and cabin on that first morning of fall. She was aware that it lay within her power to destroy this place. Julia had left a sealed letter to be shown to Timothy if she failed to return. Though she knew that was most unlikely to happen.

A young woman, casual in slacks and a blouse, stood on the porch. In one hand she held the silver mask. "I'm Linda Martin," she said. "Here by the will of the gods."

Julia recognized Linda as contemporary and smart. "An escaped slave?" she asked.

"In a modern sense, perhaps." The other woman shrugged and smiled. "A slave of circumstances."

"I've had what seem to be visions," Julia said as she stepped onto the porch. "About my son and about this property."

"Those are my daughter's doing, I'm afraid. Sally is nine." Linda was apologetic yet proud. "I've asked her not to. They aren't prophecy. More like possibility."

"They felt like a promise. And a threat."

"Please forgive her. She has a major crush on your son. Knows everything he has done. Or might ever do. He was very disappointed last month when he was in pain and wanted to talk to the corporal. And found us."

"Please forgive Tim. One's first Rex makes a lasting impression." Julia was surprised at how much she sounded like her grandmother.

The living room of Stoneham Cabin still smelled of pine. The scent reminded Julia of Alcier and her first visit. As before, a door opened where no door had been. She and Linda passed through an invisible veil and the light from the twelve portals mingled and blended in the Still Room.

"Sally, this is Julia Garde Macauley. Timothy's mother."

The child who sat beyond the flame was beautiful. She wore a blue tunic adorned with a silver boy riding a dolphin. She bowed slightly. "Hello, Mrs. Macauley. Please explain to Timothy that the Corporal knew what happened was Fate and not me."

Julia remembered Smalley saying, "It's a child will be my undoing." She smiled and nodded.

Linda held out the mask, which found its way to Sally's face.

"This is something I dreamed about your son."

What Julia saw was outdoors and in winter. It was men mostly. White mostly. Solemn. Formally dressed. A funeral? No. A man in judicial robes held a book. He was older, but Julia recognized an ally of her husband's, a young congressman from Oregon. This was the future.

"A future," said the voice from behind the mask. Julia froze. The child was uncanny.

Another man, seen from behind, had his hand raised as he took the oath of office. An inauguration. Even with his back turned, she knew her son.

"And I've seen this. Like a nightmare." Flames rose. The cabin and the grove burned.

"I don't want that. This is our home." She was a child and afraid.

Later, Linda and Julia sat across a table on the rear porch and sipped wine. The foliage below made Mirror Lake appear to be ringed with fire.

"It seems that the gods stood aside and let my husband die. Now they want Tim."

"Even the gods can't escape Destiny," Linda said. "They struggle to change it by degrees."

She looked deep into her glass. "I have Sally half the year. At the cusps of the four seasons. The rest of the time she is with the Great Mother. Once her abilities were understood, that was as good an arrangement as I could manage. Each time she's changed a little more."

Another mother who must share her child, Julia thought. We have much to talk about. How well the Immortals know how to bind us to their plans. She would always resent that. But she was too deeply involved not to comply. Foreknowledge was an addiction.

A voice sang, clear as mountain air. At first Julia thought the words were in English and that the song came from indoors. Then she realized the language was ancient Greek and that she heard it inside her head.

The song was about Persephone, carried off to the Underworld, about Ganymede abducted by Zeus. The voice had an impossible purity. Hypnotic, heartbreaking, it sang about Time flowing like a stream and children taken by the gods.

"From the Files of the Time Rangers" was published, got some nice reviews, was on SFWA's Nebula Awards short list for Best Novel. After this I went on to write stories about a speculative fiction author living in Greenwich Village, stories about gay Fairies, post-apocalyptic tales involving telepathy. I stopped thinking and writing about Time and the gods and thought it might be for good.

Though I was born there, I haven't lived in Boston since I was eighteen. That was in 1962, over fifty years ago as I write this. But looking for material, I go back to the city and to those years I spent there. For me Boston in the mid-20th century feels like a legend, one only I remember and have to tell before it gets forgotten.

One day I was thinking of ways to tell the story of being a kid in South Boston circa 1950, living with my parents in the D Street Housing Project and going to St. Peter's School. Suddenly the Fool of God came marching into the tale, bringing with him Heaven, Hell and the Singularity.

Writing about the Fool was amusing. In so many ways he sounds like me, reminds me of myself—maybe as I would have been if I hadn't been able to escape the place of my birth and got recruited by one side or the other in the War Between Good and Evil.

A MEMBER OF THE WEDDING OF HEAVEN AND HELL

The Fool of God, on a mission from Heaven, moved up the Timestream passing through portals from one world to the next. In the second century of the Caliphate of Mercy, a period others call the eighth century AD, he emerged from a portal in Alexandria, smiled the slack off-center smile that looked a bit half-witted, and batted the breeze with the crew as he sailed across the Mediterranean on a fast markab to a portal in Marseille that would carry him hundreds of years further Upstream.

Closing in on his destination, the Fool taxied across a St. Petersburg ruled by the mad Czarina Anastasia, sat in a sled wrapped in bearskin rugs as a six horse team bore him to a Buddhist monastery whose portal gave him passage to a world where the monastery buildings housed a station of the Great China Railway. He negotiated centuries and continents to reach a backwater of the Timestream and a certain world in which it was June 1960.

That date was a safe distance Downstream from both the Singularity and the Last Judgment. A wedding was scheduled for 11:30 on a Saturday that its planners had reason to know would be sunny. Late that morning, attendees assembled at the Church of the Holy Redeemer, a well-to-do suburban Roman Catholic parish in the Eastern United States for the marriage of Aiden Brown to Maria Quinn.

All would seem ordinary unless you were one who could see that the two ushers standing in front of the church in morning coats, starched white shirts, and ties with glittering studs, polished shoes and striped pants were minor demons in human form.

The demons' names in this time and place were Bill and Bob. Both were over six feet and brawny but different enough so as not to be identical (which often attracts unnecessary attention). Bob was blond with the beginning of a receding hairline; Bill was darker, with a slightly bent nose.

An older couple, nicely dressed, parked a '60 Pontiac Catalina sedan and approached. The man seemed slightly startled at the sight of the two; the woman just smiled and refused Bob's offer of a helping hand on the church stairs.

When the couple was past, Bill murmured, "I'm starting to wonder when the big guns are going to show."

A family group: mother, father and four kids ranging in age from a girl maybe six to a boy around twelve piled out of a Chevy Nomad station wagon. The others passed by with scarcely a glance. But the little girl stared at them wide-eyed.

When the family was up the stairs, Bill said, "They're from the bride's side is my guess. A few years up the Stream and that kid's going to get recruited by the enemy or us. Nothing we do here is undercover. Hell versus Heaven's a sporting event."

Bob said, "One day they pull you forty years Downstream to this world with variations you never saw before and expect you to blend in like piss on a yellow rug."

"And we do it and we don't ask why," said Bill.

"It's the minor tweaks that get you," Bob said, "the little things—that Denver 2020 where they drove on the left."

"We lived to tell about it, which not everyone there got to do," Bill reminded him.

A red Jaguar convertible pulled into the parking lot and a large figure with wide shoulders, sunglasses and a tuxedo got out.

"Oh, my. It's the Defiler," Bob muttered.

"Major reinforcement on the groom's side," said Bill.

The Defiler didn't so much walk as roll, as if he were on treads to the passenger door. He opened it, bowed slightly, and gave his hand to a lovely dark-haired lady who looked to be in her early thirties. She wore a picture hat, stiletto heels, a little black dress, and a string of pearls.

"And here's the Fiend!" said Bob. The two straightened up and stood, each with his hands clasped at the small of his back.

The couple came towards them with the Defiler on the woman's left and about three paces behind, his face blank, a fighting machine on medium alert. The Fiend looked right at them.

"Door demons, at ease," she murmured when she was a short distance away. "Anything?" she asked Bill.

"Civilians: eighty-four so far," he said softly. "Theirs and ours. About even. The heavenly host—the bride and half a dozen bridesmaids—are inside."

"We got a roof demon on top of the church. And woods demons covering . . ." Bob started to tell her.

Without breaking stride the Fiend looked around and for an instant flames brighter than the sun leaped up wherever she looked. They were on the grass, the walk, the front of the church, on the two door demons who now wore hairless green skin and glowing red eyes.

It lasted only a moment and all was as before, except there was just a hint of sulfur in the air. As the Fiend passed the two, she reached out, and faster than a human eye could follow, slipped her hand halfway into Bob's chest and drew it back.

Guests approaching blinked at the flash of pyrotechnics. Their noses crinkled slightly at the smell. Most thought it was all their imaginations.

When the Fiend, the Defiler, and the wedding guests had gone up the steps, Bill said quietly, "If the Fiend wants to know, She asks."

"She didn't need to do that," said Bob. His words were slurred. "She touched my heart and her hand is sharp and cold like an ice pick."

"Sometimes I think you got called up by the wrong side," Bill muttered. "You're lucky she didn't sic the Defiler on you."

Inside, the organist warmed up by running through a fugue. A bridesmaid poked her head out the door and looked around like she expected someone.

"So far, nothing new from their side," said Bill. "I don't get it."

The Great Fool was more or less in formal clothes when he got off the commuter train in a nearby town and hailed a taxi. He had the driver cruise slowly toward the Church of the Holy Redeemer.

Driving up in the cab, the Fool reached out mentally and scanned the assembly. He recognized the barely human outline of the Defiler, smiled the off center smile, and wondered once again where Satan got his reputation for subtlety. He found the Fiend, realized he recognized her, and frowned.

When the cab pulled up at the church, he was startled and fumbled for his money. The two ushers watched intently as he got out, stocky and kind of dumpy, looking like he hadn't combed his hair. His morning coat seemed too big; the cummerbund was unbuttoned and the tie undone. One shoe was untied.

"Holy shit," mumbled Bob, "this is even bigger than I thought!"

"Door demons!" said the Fool, "underlings of evil! Are your names still Nick and Nock?"

"Not locally," said the Demon called Bill.

The Great Fool looked at Bob and asked, "Nothing to say to me Nicky? You talked a lot back in Denver 2020. And as usual so did I. We discussed my boss and your boss quite freely. You did a lot of screaming. Many souls got saved in Denver. Do you recall that?"

Bob tried to speak, but instead gulped. The Fool said, "I had to travel further Upstream after that. You both know the kinds of security they have in the mid Twenty-first century. One of the things I got asked before they'd let me on a plane was whether my teeth were all my own and I said, 'Do you think I rent them? Of course they're mine—some I grew, some I had installed at my own personal expense.'"

The Fool of God laughed as the demons started to edge back.

"Of course I could have said they were all just a gift from the Creator," said the Fool. He smiled as he spoke, and his teeth flashed brighter than gold in the sunlight.

The two flinched, blinded, and the Fool, moving even faster than the Fiend, put his hands on Bill and Bob's chests. He didn't have to touch them to see their souls, but there was no sense in having that known.

He looked inside and saw the dark knots and bonds with which their hearts, brains and souls were bound to Lucifer.

In a twinkling he plucked a few strings and there was an image in the air of a ray of sunlight piercing dark clouds. Both of them staggered.

"Fine talking to you Chip and Dale," said the Fool of God and slopped up the stairs with his untied shoe flapping.

The one called Bill looked more than a bit dazed. He said, "We need to tell Her," and turned towards the church.

Bob stopped him. "If She wants to know, She'll ask. Just like you said."

*

Inside the door the waiting bridesmaid genuflected, rose, took the Fool's arm and said, "My name is Anna."

"An angel fair in maiden guise," he said.

"You're too kind, sir," Anna replied.

A quick glance showed him the golden knots with which she was bound to the Creator. She was as far below the heavenly variety of angel as a school crossing guard is to the director of Interpol. But the heavenly hosts, the Cherubim, Seraphim, Thrones, Dominations and the rest never stirred out of paradise. They found humans, endowed them with special abilities and sent them to do the work.

Like the Fool, Anna had been recruited from one of the thousands of worlds along the Stream. In the hierarchy to which they both belonged, the Fool thought of himself as a kind of street cop in the mold of various family members.

She led him to a side chapel where there waited what outwardly seemed an ordinary bridal party. The Fool, of course, saw wings and halos amid the flurry of activity as the bridesmaids worked to pull him together. And soon he stood laced, zipped, combed and with a fresh white carnation in his boutonnière.

All in white the bride Maria Quinn—Chief Guardian Angel of this part of this world—watched and said, "I'm honored that you're here. I hope your presence means I have Heaven's blessing."

Silently for once, the Fool drew her aside, and glanced into her soul, caught her memories. She exhibited all the expected signs: a heavenly vision at a very young age, a call from above to become a divine recruit, a fast rise in the heavenly ranks to a supervisory position. To his surprise there was no evidence she'd been tampered with by satanic powers.

"I was called to the Gates of Heaven, which are all light and music and glory beyond envisioning," he said. "That meant an assignment of great importance. I received instructions from beings of an order of grace one can hardly even imagine who told me to come here and see what this was all about—an angel marrying a slave of Satan. I broke all rules and records getting here."

She said, "I insisted that the wedding be in the church. And Aiden agreed."

"That's the devil's name?"

"Aiden Brown is his name. However it may seem to some, what

we're doing is our own idea. We love and understand each other. This is a backwater world. But here the representatives of Heaven and Hell go about their business a lot more openly than in any world I've seen or heard of.

"I love the work," she said, "the occasional miracle, making things a bit easier for the poor and the oppressed for my having been here. During an exorcism I met Aiden who was there to take custody of a demon that had been expelled from the body of a child. Aiden was the enemy but he apologized for this having been done to a kid. The demon in question had gotten out of control.

"What he does isn't that different from what I do. He tries to make things bearable for those in despair, cuts corners, brings a bit of color to their misery."

The Fool thought of heresies and cults and of what happened to those, so sadly misguided, who formulated or joined them.

"Fairly quickly," he said, "you got engaged to a representative of the Dark Powers in this boondocks. You've caused ripples up and down the Time Stream, all the way to Heaven and, I have reason to believe, Hell. I don't think I have to explain to you why this has gotten attention."

"I'd heard tales about the Fool of God," she said, looking him right in the eye. "How you blunder through worlds seeming to talk to no point but always manage to have things come true and right at the end.

"We all know what happens a few generations up the Timestream—humanity disappears. What a few of us are doing here might be an answer to that. I'll accept all the blame if I'm wrong. But I thought you might be more understanding."

The Fool contemplated the amazing twists and turns that people used to justify their wrongful deeds. He thought of the ones similar to Maria Quinn that he'd encountered along the Time Lanes and how he'd never met one he didn't like.

But the Fool also knew it was more than possible he'd have to crush her plans—and maybe her. He remembered his last teacher, an ancient operative of Heaven who lived in a stone house in the mountains on a world from which Satan was totally excluded. The Old Fool as he was known had often told him, "Sometimes we must do a little bad in order to do a great good."

So he smiled and said, "Some people have an interior editor, a stern gentleman or a dour lady, who shuts them down at the first sign of thoughtlessness or indiscretion with the admonition, 'Have a care, you thoughtless cad!'

"Mine's a wispy little fellow who, when he says, 'Don't you think you might tone it down?' gets told by me, 'Stick it where the sun won't shine you sniveling sodomite,' and who then mumbles, 'Very well, as you think best.'

"So you see there's no point in taking me seriously," said the Fool. He had become aware of something going on in the main church and excused himself from the chapel for a moment.

When he stepped out the door time stood almost still around him. The crowd in the church moved so slowly he had to look closely to see it happen. An elderly woman being helped up the aisle was almost stationary. A kid in velvet shorts bouncing up and down with excitement seemed suspended in air. It felt as if he was inside a bowl and his own movements seemed fast and fluid as a fish.

It's known to all that Satan plays tricks with time. Reflecting on that, the Fool became huge and clad in chain mail. The sword he drew shone with a blinding white light as he turned to face the one figure in the church thatmoved as fast as he did.

With a small smile, the Fiend approached him. The fact she hadn't brought that blunt object, the Defiler, let him understand they were under a flag of truce. He allowed his eyes to open wide in surprise and said, "Daina Zukor! It's you who's done all this?"

"Can it, O'Malley," she replied, "and put away the sword and iron pants. You turned a couple of my demons silly on your way in and you knew I was here. I dropped the Lithuanian name when I signed up and left Southie. It's now Diana and I'm Chief Fiend of this sector of the Timestream. I understand misdirection and confusion are your specialties, but we're old friends and with me you can give them a rest."

"Diana then!" The sword and armor faded away. "You've come a long way down a very wrong path from South Boston. The nuns at St Peter's, in their various lives on any iteration of that world, would be so saddened to hear you're playing for the other side."

She shook her head impatiently. "Half the people on Hell's payroll went to school with nuns or brothers. They're like recruiting sergeants."

He was amused. "I remember you well; walking me to school every day. It always seemed to be raining back then."

"Fifty cents a week your mother gave me to walk you to St Pete's and back again," she said. "I was nine and in the fourth grade. Big money and responsibility: it made me feel like an adult."

She flashed an image of Timmy O'Malley, in a certain 1950, wearing a yellow raincoat, boots and hat, all somehow too big or too small for him, holding her hand tight.

He showed her his memory of a tall (to a five-year-old) thin and determined girl crossing what seemed an endless playground towards an impossibly distant church and school.

"Not many people in the D Street Housing Projects were like you and your parents," she said.

"We had a fire in the building where we'd been living. My old man flew for the army in the war and D Street was built for the returning G.I., so that's where we ended up.

"They were failed actors, left-wing Catholics. The local public school wasn't good or wasn't near or maybe wasn't strange enough, so they found St. Peter's. Lots of kids from Lithuania learning English and classes were in both languages. My parents thought that was amusing."

She grinned at her memories. "The nuns loved the way you talked, stories you made up. And you looked so innocent and silly with your shirt tails half out of your pants. Once at recess a kid, Peter Ozols I think his name was, teased you and you kicked him hard in the nuts.

"When the nuns arrived you apologized, cried, begged his forgiveness and got off scot-free. Not long afterwards you were gone. The next time I heard of Timothy O'Malley he was God's Fool and roving enforcer."

He looked the crowd over. "You've got the place rigged for mischief," he said, "Demons three deep around the church, Devils all over the groom's side of the nave. And I see an Imp of the Perverse in velvet shorts."

She followed his gaze. "That's the ring-bearer, a kid with more talent than either of us had at his age. What? You think if you hadn't showed up we'd have run a black mass? We don't do that anymore. Like your side doesn't burn witches now: at least not literally."

From long experience the Fool suspected that some form of mayhem would have taken place if he hadn't arrived. But Satan, as he knew, will always do the unexpected, so the Fool just beamed at his old baby sitter.

He had noticed the slow approach of a young man in formal clothes. On the Fiend's command, this figure was suddenly inside the bubble of still-time she had created. The man bowed slightly to the Fiend, who told the Fool, "You must meet Aiden Brown, the groom."

The Fool thought this one looked deceptively presentable and bright enough in the way of the Devil's people. He pegged him as a Security Devil: a young man who could keep secrets and find out secrets.

Aiden shook hands gingerly and the Fool glanced into him. Like all Devils' souls, his was a bare and barren place with the black bonds of Satan everywhere.

"The bride says you two met in the line of duty," said the Fool, "and decided to go further."

"Sir, I never thought I'd end up wanting to get hitched to an angel, but then I met Maria. I grew up on this world. My family are church people. They aren't all happy with the way I went but they live with it and I respect them.

"Our two sides balance each other out. We need to stop fighting and see if we can't prevent this place getting destroyed."

"Your side provides a balance against truth, against mercy. Do we need that?" the Fool asked, but he smiled as he did.

"Back to your post, Brown," the Fiend said. "We're about to begin." The groom took a few steps and melded into the crowd.

"Bride and groom are well coached," said the Fool.

The Fiend looked disappointed. "Don't you think two childhood friends like us getting assigned here means the ones we work for want us to co-operate? Without people's souls to fight over what's the point of Heaven and Hell? Humanity is all we have.

"I've never seen any place like this. Khrushchev and Eisenhower just signed a mutual non-aggression pact. The Cold War turned a dozen other worlds to ash. Here it's over."

She indicated the church. "My instructions are to make this wedding happen. What are your boss's orders?

"I've never seen Him," the Fool heard himself say. "I've been to the Heavenly Gates but never beyond them. I can't even focus on the ones who summon me. The Cherubim at the gates are these huge glowing presences. Their faces are so far above me I can't see them. They told me to investigate this situation and determine what to do."

He couldn't believe he'd told her this. Where was the interior editor when he needed one?

She seemed sympathetic. "I've never seen my boss either. Devils and fiends, the ones that date back to the beginning of the Great Feud, sit around administering, meditating. Long ago they started hiring people like me to do the dirty work.

"As a kid I envied people who lived in the projects. D Street got bad very fast. Eventually they tore it down. But at the start the heat worked, the windows weren't broken. We lived in a walk up. My old man drank. My mother had war refugee relatives who stayed in our living room. One cousin was a few years older than me and a predator.

"Satan's people were sharp. His emissary was a nurse at the neighborhood clinic. I was ten and ready. I was taught and had all manner of abilities implanted in me. Same story on your side?"

She waited for a response and when the Fool remained silent her smile went away.

"Maybe I was wrong in thinking you'd understand, O'Malley. But the wedding's going forward. Don't get in the way. Doing this is the reason we two were created."

As she spoke flames sprouted from the floor and walls and encircled the Fool.

He recalled governments destroyed, cities devastated for flouting divine will. His reply was a lightning bolt smashing open the roof of the church, a frigid wind bearing a fist of ice that flattened the flames.

In seconds all this was gone. The Fiend turned away, gestured, and the organ sounded: the people moved freely. Perhaps some had caught a hint of brimstone, a fleeting chill.

Minutes later the Fool stepped out of the chapel, prepared to walk up the aisle with Marie on his arm. She'd told him that when he gave her away it would be as Henry Quinn, her supposed uncle. It bothered him that he found this appealing.

The Fool remembered being little Timmy O'Malley in the D Street Project playing on the sidewalk one day with a bunch of other kids. He had a wooden rifle that he'd gotten for Christmas. He was a cowboy or maybe an Indian with his sneaker laces flapping and a runny nose.

Suddenly out of nowhere came the older brother of the kid he'd kicked the week before. He was looking for Tim. The brother was eight, maybe nine, almost an adult to a six-year-old. Tim hated the Projects, the fights, the school where everybody spoke another language.

He didn't think, didn't hesitate. He swung his rifle butt, maybe like someone he'd seen on TV, and caught the brother on the forehead. The kid staggered backwards. Blood trickled from his forehead. He turned and ran down the street howling.

On the corner he passed Timmy's mother, who hadn't seen what happened. She was horrified, grabbed Timmy, and hustled him up to the apartment before some dreadful harm could happen to him. That night she told his father. "It was awful: a little boy with blood streaming down his face."

Never did it occur to her that her kid might have done it and he never told her. When they moved shortly afterwards to a leafy neighborhood where they had a back yard, Timothy saw that incident as a miracle staged just for him.

Then the organ struck up "The Bridal March" from *Lohengrin,* and the Fool started up the aisle. He saw the feathers and halos on members of the congregation, on the bride, bridesmaids, and even the little flower girl. He knew Marie was searching his face for clues as to what would happen.

In fact his instructions were confused. At the Gates of Heaven the Cherubim had told him to investigate thoroughly and to halt the ceremony if he felt it was blasphemous. But then Seraphim (who outranked them) took the Fool aside and told him to let the ceremony proceed if he was sure it wasn't a trick.

Both Cherubim and Seraphim said he was to remain until all was settled. He knew that if he allowed the marriage to come to pass he could be here for years waiting to see if this experiment worked. If he stopped the ceremony he'd have to stay and deal with the consequences.

A long life was one of the perks (or one the curses) of his job. He could well be here until humankind disappeared. Or until it survived.

The beings that had sent him on this mission stood so tall their faces were in the clouds. He wondered what secrets they had concealed; recalled rumors the Creator hadn't been seen even by the highest circles of Heaven for eons. This could mean his mission originated with some cabal among the Heavenly Host.

On the groom's side could be seen a plentitude of horns and glowing red eyes. The Fiend sat with the Defiler on the center aisle. She avoided meeting his eyes, was obviously tense waiting for the possible life or death of this experiment. The Defiler's dead eyes were on him, poised for battle. The Fool could handle whatever threats they posed.

He could turn at that moment and take Marie against her will away from the altar and out of the church. He could level the building. Instead he kept walking.

The bridal party approached the groom, his best man, a fellow Devil in morning clothes, and the sharp-eyed little ring bearer with a forked tail who waited at the foot of the altar. Officiating was a monsignor, a genial time-server with a rich parish who saw none of this and had no idea what was happening.

Old St Peter's in South Boston with its Lithuanian and its English masses was where The Fool first had a statue meet his stare and follow him with its eyes. It was there that he saw angels at the consecration and thought it meant he had a vocation to be a priest.

A few years later, an angel visited him in his sleep and hinted he was meant for bigger things as an agent of heaven. In his teens he began discovering his powers. One day, all he knew about peoples' souls was what the nuns had told him. The next morning, he could look right inside and see them.

He had thought it was a miracle, a revelation. Now he saw it as something implanted, saw himself, the Fiend, Marie, Aiden, angels and door demons as subjects in an experiment.

The Fool remembered the planet where he'd been groomed for his current position. On that world any trace of Satan had been eradicated. The people were pious, simple, and eventually bored.

The Old Fool lived in a large stone house in the mountains. With a beard down to his knees and a taste for orchids, cigars, and chocolate, he was a source of insight once or twice a day and a font of confusion the rest of the time.

He didn't have as many bells and whistles installed in him as did his young pupil. But he once told the Fool, "The works of humankind may become as strong as God or Satan but perhaps not stronger than God and Satan."

Doubtless that world too had been an experiment, one that failed. Technology crept in. By the late 21st century it was a wasteland like a thousand other worlds where the Deity picked up his marbles and summoned the Apocalypse. On the far side of those dead planets was said to be the Singularity, devoid of humanity, God and Satan.

This ceremony today was part of an experiment to see if the Old Fool was right.

Nostalgia is a dangerous game for one like him. But the Fool wondered if versions of his family and himself—a kid in his teens—might be alive on this world and what the Fiend could tell him about them.

It was within his power to bring all this to an end. Instead, the Great Fool moved forward to give the bride away. He recited the words, took Marie's hand and Aiden's in his.

Then he stepped back, and as the ceremony proceeded, as the pair recited their vows, he decided to rain down flowers, fat cigars, and Hershey bars on the congregation as the Mendelssohn played. It would honor his old teacher and ease tensions.

Later there would always be time for devastation and ruin if they turned out to be advisable. Or perhaps he would find a stone house in the mountains somewhere and ride this planet towards survival or destruction.

Someone like me, who writes personal fiction, finds himself returning to the Boston neighborhoods of his childhood and adolescence, to the things he did, and jobs he held when he first lived in Manhattan.

Part Three:
HOME AGAIN

My fiction is heavily informed by my life, and New York is where I've led most of that. This story was written for Ellen Datlow's Blood and Other Cravings *2011 anthology. Themed anthologies these days are a lot more wide open than was the case some years back.*

Instead of one vampire story after another, this volume featured all manner of addictions and compulsion. But I went with blood suckers, mixed it with bits of contemporary Manhattan and memories of troubled times for a story of a very special cyclical fad.

The Sixth Avenue Flea Market was a New York weekend institution from the early 1980s into the 21st century. I bought there and for a period of years, whatever the season, I sold there. Firefly flashlights, dealers who had seen EVERYTHING, club kids wandering into the market in the dawn: all of that is first hand.

Ichordone, the methadone of vampires, is obviously an invention. But the mores and ways of addiction and recovery are not. In the end the writer uses every part of his or her life.

As a side note, the world of same sex partners and their adopted children is part of gay life becoming everyday life. The twist I inserted into it says more about the needs of a storyteller in a themed anthology than it does about a process that has enabled me to meet some of the most wonderful small people I've ever encountered.

BLOOD YESTERDAY, BLOOD TOMORROW

Ai Ling, show Aunt Lilia and everyone else how you can play the Debussy 'Claire de Lune,'" Larry said as his partner Boyd beamed at his side. Lilia Gaines was at the dinner party as a friend of one of the hosts, Larry Stepelli.

She had, in fact, been his roommate in the bad old days. Twenty-five years before she and Larry had entered Ichordone therapy as a couple and left it separately and stayed that way.

The exquisitely dressed Asian girl sat, tiny but fully at ease, at the piano. At one time Lilia had wondered if only well-to-do gay couples should be allowed to raise kids.

Behind Ai Ling, the windows of the West Street duplex looked over the Hudson and the lights of New Jersey on a late June evening. And amazingly, almost like a beautifully rendered piece of automata, the child played the piece with scarcely a flaw.

Amidst the applause of the dozen guests and her fathers, Ai Ling curtseyed and went off with her Nana. Lilia, not for the first time, considered Larry's upward mobility. This dinner party was for some of Boyd's clients, a few people whom Larry sought to impress and one or two like her whom he liked to taunt with his success.

A woman asked Boyd what preschool his daughter attended. One of his clients dropped the names of two Senators and the President in a single sentence.

A young man who had been brought by an old and famous children's book illustrator talked about the novel he was writing, "It's YA and horror lite on what at the moment is a very timely theme," he said.

Larry smiled and said to Lilia, "I walked past Reliquary yesterday and you were closed."

"Major redecoration," she replied. Their connection had once been so close that at times each could still read the other. So they both knew this wasn't so.

He tilted his handsome head with only a subtle touch of gray and raised his left eyebrow a fraction of an inch.

Lilia knew he was going to ask her something about her shop and how long it could survive. She didn't want to discuss the subject just then.

Larry's question went unasked. Right then the young author said, "It's a theme which sometimes gets overworked but never gets stale. The book I'm doing right now is titled, *Never Blood Today.* You know, a variation on, 'Jam tomorrow and jam yesterday but never jam today' from *Alice in Wonderland.* In fact the book is Alice with Vampires! Set in a well-to-do private high school!"

The writer looked at Larry with fascination as he spoke. Boyd frowned. The illustrator who had a show up in Larry's gallery rolled his eyes.

Larry smiled again but just for a moment. For Lilia, the writer's conversation was an unplanned bonus.

A woman in an enviable apricot silk dress with just a hint of sheath about it changed the subject to a reliably safe one: how nicely real estate prices had bottomed out.

Then Boyd suggested they all sit down to dinner. Boyd Lazlo was a corporate lawyer, solid, polite, nice looking, completely opaque. Lilia Gaines knew he didn't much trust her.

Lilia and Larry went back to the time when Warhol walked the earth, Manhattan was seamy and corroded, and an unending stream of young people came there to lose their identities and find newer, more exotic ones. Back then Boyd was still a college kid preparing to go to Yale Law.

These many summers later, Manhattan was gripped by nostalgia for old sordid days, and Lilia had something to show Larry that would evoke them. But it was personal, private, and she hadn't found a moment alone with him.

At the end of the evening he stood at the door saying goodbye to the illustrator. The young writer looked wide-eyed at Larry and even at Lilia. The mystique of old evil: she understood it well.

As Larry wished him farewell, Lilia caught the half wink her old companion gave the kid and was certain Larry was bored.

She remembered him in the Ichordone group therapy standing in tears and swearing that when he walked out of there cured of his habit he would establish a stable relationship and raise children.

Boyd was down the hall at the elevator kissing and shaking hands. Lilia and Larry were alone. Only then did he put his hands on her shoulders and say, "You have a secret; give it up."

"Something I just found," she said, reached into her bag, and handed him a folded linen napkin. You'd have had to know him as well as she did to catch the eyes widening by a millimeter. Stitched into the cloth was what, when Lilia first saw it years before, had looked like a small gold crown, a coronet. Curving below the coronet in script were the words "Myrna's Place." The same words were above it upside down.

Before anything more could be said, Boyd came back looking a bit concerned and as if he needed to speak to Larry alone. So Lilia thanked both of them for dinner and took her leave. She noticed that Larry had made the napkin disappear.

Years ago when New York was the wilder, darker place, Larry and Lilia's apartment was on a marginal street on the Lower East Side, and they pursued careers while watching for their chance. He acted in underground films with Madonna before the name meant anything and took photos; she sold dresses she'd designed to East Village Boutiques.

Patti Smith and Robert Mapplethorpe was the model for all the young couples like them: the poker faced serious girl with hair framing her face and the flashy bisexual guy. They were in the crowd at the Pyramid Club, Studio 54, and the Factory. Drugs and alcohol were their playthings. Love did enter into it, of course, and even sex when their stars crossed paths.

Since they needed money, they also had an informal business selling antiques and weird collectibles at the flea market on Sixth Avenue in the Twenties.

In those days that stretch of Manhattan was a place of rundown five story buildings and wide parking lots—fallow land waiting for a developer. On weekends, first one parking lot, then a second, then a third, then more blossomed with tables set up in the open air, tents pitched before dawn.

It became a destination where New Yorkers spent their weekend afternoons sifting through the trash and the gems. Warhol, the pale prince, bought much of his fabled cookie jar collection there.

During the week, Larry and Lilia haunted the auction rooms on Fourth Avenue and Broadway south of Union Square, swooped down on forlorn vases and candy dishes, old toys, unwanted lots of parasols and packets of photos of doughboys and chorus girls, turn of the century nude swimming scenes, elephants wearing bonnets and top hats.

Since it kind of was their livelihood, they both tried to be reasonably straight and sober at the moment Sunday morning stopped being Saturday night. While it was still dark they'd go up to Sixth Avenue with their treasures in shopping carts, rent a few square feet of space and a couple of tables and set up their booth.

In the predawn, out of town antique dealers, edgy interior decorators, compulsive collectors, all bearing flashlights, would circulate among the vans unloading furniture and the tables being carried to their places by the flea market porters.

Beams of light would scan the dark and suddenly, four, five, a dozen of them would circle a booth where strange, interesting, perhaps even valuable stuff was being set up.

Lilia and Larry wanted that attention. Then came the very drowsy weekday auction when they found a lot consisting of several cartons of distressed goods: everything from matchbooks and champagne flutes, to mirrors and table cloths all with the words "Myrna's Place" in an oval and the gold design that looked like a small crown, a coronet.

The name meant nothing to them. They guessed Myrna's was some kind of uptown operation—a speakeasy, a bordello, a bohemian salon—they didn't quite know.

Old, hard-bitten market dealers called themselves "Fleas."

Larry said, "Fleas call the trash they sell Stuff."

"And this looks like Stuff," Lilia replied.

"And plenty of it," they said at the same moment, which happened with them back then. They bid their last fifty dollars and got the lot.

That Sunday morning they rented their usual space and a couple of tables. Other recent finds included a tackily furnished tin dollhouse, a set of blue and white china bowls, a few slightly decayed leather jackets, several antique corsets, a box of men's assorted arm garters, and a golf bag and clubs bought at an apartment sale. They had dysfunctional old cameras and a cracked glass jar full of marbles. Prominently displayed was a selection of Myrna's Place stuff.

The couple in the booth across from theirs seemed to loot a different place each week. That Sunday it was an old hunting lodge. They had a moose head, skis, snow shoes and blunt, heavy ice skates, Adirondack chairs, and gun racks.

Larry and Lilia set up in the pre-dawn dark as flashlights darted about the lot. Then one fell on them. A flat faced woman with rimless glasses and eyes that showed nothing turned her beam on the golf clubs.

She shrugged when she saw them up close. But as she turned to walk away, her light caught a nicely draped tablecloth from Myrna's Place. "Thirty dollars for the lot," she said indicating all the Myrna items.

Larry and Lilia hesitated. Thirty dollars would pay the day's rent for the stall. Then another light found the table. A middle aged man with the thin, drawn look of a veteran of many Manhattan scenes was examining Myrna's wine glasses. "Five dollars each," Lilia told him and he didn't back off.

To the woman who had offered thirty for the entire lot, Larry said, "Thirty for the tablecloth."

The woman ground them down to twenty. The thin, drawn man bought four wine glasses for fifteen dollars and continued examining the merchandise.

Lilia and Larry's booth attracted the pre-dawn flashlights. It was like being attacked by giant fireflies. Nobody was interested in anything else. It was all Myrna's Place. Old Fleas paused and looked their way.

As dawn began to slide in between the buildings, the thin, drawn man found a small ivory box.

"Myrna Lavaliere, who and where are you now?" he asked, and opened the lid. It was full of business cards bearing the usual double Myrna's Place and coronet logo. Below that was an address on the Upper East Side, a Butterfield 8 telephone number and the motto, "Halfway between Park Avenue and Heaven."

"More like far from Heaven and down the street from Hell," the man said. "You kids have any idea what you have here?"

Larry and Lilia shrugged. Other customers wanted their attention.

"Wickedness always sells," the man told them. "And after the war in the late 1940s, rumor had it this place was wicked. Myrna's was a townhouse where you went in human and came out quite otherwise."

A tall woman with a black lace kerchief tied around her long neck and wearing sunglasses in the dawn light had stopped examining a pair of Myrna's Place candlesticks and paused to listen.

She gave a short, contemptuous laugh and said in an unplacable accent, "Oh please, spare these not-terribly-innocent children all the sour grape stories spread by all the ones who couldn't get inside the front door of Myrna's. What happened there happened before and will happen again. If you know anything about these phenomena at all you know that."

She faced him and raised the glasses off her eyes for a moment. Neither Larry nor Lilia could see her face. But apparently her stare was enough to cause the man to first back away, then scuttle off.

"Fifty gets you the candlesticks," Larry told her. They were getting bold.

"I just wanted to make sure these weren't as good as the pair I have. But I will let others know about you. I think the time is right."

Then the wizened pack rats and sleek interior decorators were all at the booth hissing at each other as they pawed through the items. Lilia and Larry tried to spot people they thought might actually have gone to Myrna's.

As morning sunlight began to hit the Sixth Avenue Market, club kids coming from Danceteria in '50s drag found Larry and Lilia's stall. Dolled up boys in pompadours, girls in satin evening gowns who looked like inner tension was all that held them together, stopped on their way downtown. They seemed fascinated, whispered and giggled, but didn't buy much: a handkerchief, a cigarette holder.

But the stock of Myrna's Place items was almost cleaned out when a lone Death Punk girl, her eye shadow and black hair with green highlights looking sad in the growing light, appeared. She pawed through the remaining items, dug in her pockets, and gave Larry three dollars and seventeen cents, all she had with her, for a stained coaster.

Around then Lilia realized that if she held any of the items at a certain angle, the Myrna's Place design looked like an upper and lower lip and the coronet was sharp, gold teeth. Once she saw that and pointed it out to Larry they couldn't see them any other way.

They weren't naive. In the demimonde they inhabited, gossip lately concerned ones called the Nightwalkers. About then they began wondering about Myrna's Place.

2.

Thirty years later on the morning after the dinner party, Larry called Lilia on her cell phone several times. But she was on an errand that took her uptown and onto the tram to Roosevelt Island. Though this situation hadn't occurred recently, Lilia remembered how to play Larry when she had something that he wanted.

Roosevelt Island lies in the East River between Manhattan and Queens. On that small spot in the midst of a great city is a little river town of apartment houses. Along the main street, the buildings project out over the sidewalks, providing a covered way.

In one period of Lilia's life the sun was unbearable and had to be avoided. Now walking under cover, she was glad the habit had remained and helped her avoid skin cancer.

Lilia remembered the others who took the cure when she and Larry did: the old man with wild white hair and gleaming eyes who required three times as much Ichordone as anyone else in the program and wore a muzzle like a dog because he tried to bite; the mousy woman who had been turned into a vampire when she saw Bela Lugosi as Dracula on TV twenty years before.

Generations ago, Roosevelt Island was called Welfare Island. It was where hospitals for contagious diseases were located. Their ruins still dot the place. Hospitals are still located there, most of them quite ordinary.

But in one there is a ward for patients with Polymorphous Light Eruption: (allergy to the sun) and Haemophagia: (strange reactions to blood), and several other exotic diseases. Behind the hospital are cottages.

In one of those sat the person Lilia had come to see. She was in a wheelchair, wrapped in blankets and looking out the window at the sunlight and water. The woman had seemed ancient to Lilia that morning years before at the Flea Market when she examined the candlesticks and told the man to spare her his sour grapes stories. Now Myrna Lavaliere was a mummy—nothing more than skin and bones and a voice.

"When one is old the smell of rot—one is falling apart—is omnipresent. Men are the worst but none are immune. "Each time you come here you are awe-struck by my age and corruption. I don't blame you. I am well over a hundred. My addiction first to blood and then to Ichordone prolonged my life but look at the result.

"Up in the hospital they'd have me in restraints with my head immobilized because they're afraid I'd bite them." She laughed noiselessly and showed Lilia her toothless gums.

"All I want," she said, "is to die in this room with a bit of privacy, not up in that cadaver warehouse." She indicated the main hospital building. "Like everything else in this country, it requires money."

In earlier meetings, she had told Lilia how much longer she had to live, how much that would cost, and how many treasures from Myrna's Place and other clubs she had stashed in storage lockers.

Lilia had told her of a plan she had. Today she told her what was required to implement it. "I need more bait for the market," she said.

Their eyes met and they understood one another. A nurse's aide was called and she brought Lilia a package of collectibles like the one she'd been given the week before.

3.

Lilia waited until she was back at her shop before answering one of Larry's calls.

Immediately he asked, "Where did you find it?" She heard voices echoing behind him in Stepelli, his large gallery space in West Chelsea.

She told him a tale of the Garage, that last sad remnant of the once sprawling Sixth Avenue Flea Markets, and the napkin she found the Sunday before when she ducked in there to get out of the rain.

"Was there anything else from Myrna's Place?" he asked.

"This is all I found," she said. "But the dealer said there was quite a flurry when she opened. Young people apparently."

"Where did she get it? Does she have any more?"

"Yes," Lilia told him, and gave no hint of her amusement. "She got it from a woman who got it from a man who may have more. I have a lead on her source."

None of this was entirely true, but in his eagerness that escaped him.

It was Friday afternoon. They made plans to visit the Garage early Sunday morning.

Her shop, Reliquary: once so very trendy and notorious, later a charmingly creepy hold-over, a bit of stylish nostalgia, now hung by a thread. The landlord, unable to find another tenant, had let Lilia slide on the rent from month to month. His patience was running out.

That afternoon as Lilia went on various errands, she remembered the Saturday night and Sunday morning after Larry and her first triumph.

The second week they brought all their good Myrna's Place stuff: the flasks, the scarves, the elephant foot umbrella stand. They were surrounded from the moment they set foot in the flea market. All the flashlights were around them. Customers from the previous week were back and others as well.

The dealers who looted a house each week had a daycare center's worth of children's chairs, toys. They paused to watch the commotion across the aisle.

Larry and Lilia discovered that the first Death Punk girl had been a harbinger. Out of the night, smelling of cigarettes and amyl nitrate came club boys and girls in black from head to pointed toe shoes. There were the retro and extreme retro kids, dressed as twenties flappers, Edwardian roués and whores. One young man with a cravat and a face painted almost white carried a small, antique medical bag and was called Doctor Jekyll.

They bought small souvenirs—a tea cup or a doily. When asked what was so fascinating about Myrna's Place, they shrugged and said this was Nightwalker stuff, the new thing.

Then, in the pre dawn, the club kids, awe-struck, watched as half a dozen figures flitted toward them like bats, like shadows. Lilia heard the Flea across the way call out to someone, "Dracula and company just showed up!"

The newcomers all seemed tall, elongated. They wavered in the first light. Many of them actually wore capes. They were thin and their smiles were a brief flash of teeth.

As they moved through the kids around Larry and Lilia's tables, one of them reached over and, almost to fast to see, pulled down the collar of a girl's jacket and first kissed then nipped her neck. The club girl shivered with ecstasy.

Lilia was uneasy, but Larry was star struck. Here was true glamour, the very heart of the most exclusive club back rooms. The sky was getting light. The newcomers surveyed the booth, nodded, put on sunglasses, exchanged glances and smiled. These people were impressed with him.

Raised cloaks hid what happened from the casual customers. In an eye-flash, Larry's leather jacket and shirt were pulled off his shoulders. The smiles and fine sharp teeth looked like the ones on the Myrna's Place logo.

Larry's eyes went wide. A tiny trickle of blood ran down his chest. He stared after them as they left the market and didn't even notice Lilia pulling his clothes back in place.

Other customers appeared. Larry and Lilia were Flea celebrities and had a good day—even the dollhouse sold.

Larry was bedazzled. Lilia knew he always gravitated to the key clique and always managed to get himself accepted. Now he'd found a group so special it was legend, and they loved him.

That week Larry was distant and distracted. He got on her nerves. She got on his. The next Sunday morning they brought to market all the remaining Myrna's Place material and everything else they had for sale.

In the predawn the flashlights found them and so did the woman with the neck scarf and sunglasses. The club kids stared at her reverently. She glanced at Larry and almost smiled. She gave Lilia a slip of paper with some names.

"In one's old age, collections, however beloved, become a burden. These are ones who are ready to give up theirs."

As she turned to go, the young Nightwalkers appeared. They bowed their heads and parted for her. "Myrna," Lilia heard them murmur, "Myrna Lavaliere." The woman nodded and disappeared into the last of the night.

When the Nightwalkers exposed Larry's neck, Lilia told them not to because it had made him stupid. But he pointed at her and capes were raised, Lilia's arms were pinned, her blouse opened. Before she could even cry out, she felt teeth and a nick on the side of her neck.

Lilia turned to see who had done this, but the effort made her head spin. Lilia knew a few things about drugs. None felt like this: it was like acid cut with heroin. She and Larry were in trances for the rest of that day and most of the next.

When they recovered, they took the list of names and telephone numbers the one the Nightwalkers called Myrna had given them. The people on the list were old and fragile, looking like they might break. But their eyes were sharp, and sometimes their teeth. They all had memorabilia they were ready to get rid of. One or two liked to bite, but they were mostly harmless.

4.

Late on a summer night thirty years later, Lilia met Larry in front of Reliquary on West Broadway at the trashy end of Soho. Tense, knowing things had to go just right; she noticed that he wore the napkin with the "Myrna's Place" logo displayed like a handkerchief in his jacket pocket. She did wonder where he had told Boyd he was going.

Cabs cruised and groups of young people searched for after hours clubs. On weekends near the solstice, Saturday darkness comes later and Sunday morning is very early. There's almost no place left for the night.

Larry looked at the sign, the darkened windows and shabby aura of the store. "Some amazing times here," he remarked and shook his head.

Once it had been different: "*Cool Reliquary!*" the ads in *The Village Voice* had said. "*Not Your Mommy's Kind of Boutique—Not Your Daddy's Either*" had been the title of the article in *New York Magazine* just after the shop opened in the early '80s.

Suitable designer styles were offered: capes in a variety of lengths, parasols to keep the sun out of the eyes, shirts and blouses that displayed best half open and exposing the throat and neck.

Then there was the tchotchke, relics from what turned out to have been an endless succession of mysterious clubs and salons. Fra Diablo just off Union Square had attracted rumor and curiosity in the 1870s, the Bat Bar flourished just after the turn of the century. Club Indigo in Harlem in the late '20s had introduced white patrons to an impeccable African American staff and entertainment which could only be talked about in whispers.

"All those venues and every one of them produced artifacts," Larry said. "Certain individuals liked to have stuff like that around. Other people in the know would be aware of their interests without a word being spoken."

The two talked over old times as they walked toward Sixth Avenue while looking for a cab. They remembered the time the Nightwalkers first showed up at the Mudd Club, the way columnists in the *The Village Voice* hinted at a craze that was not quite drugs or sex. *The New Yorker* had said, "Some call it a very old European tradition."

Everyone wanted artifacts, to take back to Westchester, to Chicago, to Paris, to Rome, a sign they'd had at least a brush with the tingly and strange. Reliquary was where they got them.

"Daylight was something to be endured," Larry said. "We lived at night."

Lilia remembered those times like she'd seen them through the wrong end of binoculars. But she wasn't going to contradict him or mention the crash that followed the boom.

For her it began when her dentist noticed the way her teeth had grown and ordered her out of his office. Then on one of Lilia's rare visits to the Philadelphia suburbs, her mother mentioned the pallor. "Are those hickeys?" she had asked, catching sight of the bite marks on Lilia's neck.

She remembered the day the newspaper and magazine articles suddenly turned sour. "BLOOD CRAZED!" the tabloids screamed. "CONTAGIOUS DISEASE DISGUISED AS HIP CULT" the magazines cried.

Rich kids' families pulled them into elite and expensive therapy. Everyone else ended up in city hospitals and day clinics. Ichordone, horrible and soul-deadening, was the methadone of vampirism. She wondered if Larry had managed to forget about that, guessing he had, and saw no reason to remind him.

At Sixth Avenue they found a cab and rode uptown through the Village and the old Ladies Mile. Groups hung about the corners, stood in front of the desecrated church which had been a nightclub. For a moment, on a side street, Lilia thought she saw a figure in a cape. She felt Larry tense and knew he'd seen it too.

"It's always been cycles, hasn't it," he murmured. She said nothing. "Every twenty-five, thirty years: one is overdue," he said, and she nodded.

The cab turned on Twenty-Fifth Street and stopped at the Garage. This last stronghold of the Flea Market was set in the middle of the block and went right through to Twenty-Fourth. The official opening was 8 AM but dealers were already setting up. Their vans rolled up and down the garage ramps, and visitors were slipping in along with them.

A thin young woman and buff boy, both in black, went down the ramp to the lower level. Lilia let Larry take the lead and follow them down. She wondered if all this was going to work.

The place had none of the mystery of the pre-dawn flea market. It smelled of exhaust and bad coffee and was lighted, so there was no need for flashlights. Older buyers watched dealers unpack their stock.

The couple in black drifted toward the back of the selling floor and a little knot of young people just out of the bars and clubs in a far corner.

Larry headed in that direction without looking to see if Lilia was with him. She was a step or two behind, following him back into a world they'd once known.

She knew what he was going to find: place cards with celebrity names: Cole Porter, Winston Guest, and Dorothy Parker from Club Indigo. Delicate fans decorated with cats baring their teeth from the Golden Palace, which had flourished down in Chinatown once upon a time. And, of course, salted into the mix were a few items from Myrna's Place. This was the contents of the parcel Lilia had been given on Roosevelt Island a couple of days before.

She watched the way Larry took in not only the items for sale but the ones who had come to look at them. A few more kids stopped by. This was a gathering spot, like their booth had been thirty years before.

They looked at Larry and his napkin with its crest of lips and teeth displayed. He asked the dealer where she had gotten the stuff and if she had any more.

The dealer was Eastern European and had trouble with English on certain occasions. She said a woman had sold them and hadn't left a name. No she didn't have any more. She was good at this and didn't once glance Lilia's way.

The onlookers stirred. Lilia turned and saw figures in sunglasses moving in the shadows cast by pillars and vans. Nightwalkers had arrived. A new, less formal generation in shorts and flip-flops: though Lilia noticed that several still wore capes.

Other dealers and their customers paused and shook their heads. Lilia's spine crawled. She wondered if all this was worth it. Then she saw something which again confirmed that fate was with her.

The young writer of the Alice and the Vampires book was seemingly borne along as a kind of trophy by the Nightwalkers. His eyes were wide and he looked dazed. His shirt was open and several small puncture wounds ringed his neck and throat.

Larry's eyes widened and Lilia knew he'd once again found his exclusive clique. Clearly it was open to the young and pretty but perhaps also to the well-to-do.

He reached for his wallet, asked the dealer how much she wanted for the lot of vampire tchotchke. He didn't flinch at the gouger price Lilia had told her to charge. The crowd seemed disturbed by this interloper.

Lilia whispered, "I know the location of a treasure trove of similar stuff."

Larry nodded and distributed the items among the club kids and Nightwalkers alike. They became interested in this stranger. Then the young writer recognized Larry, got free of his handlers, hugged him and nipped his neck a little.

Lilia handed out faded cards for Reliquary while promising, "Memorabilia *and* fashion. Come see us during the week."

As she did she thought about T-shirts—hip, enigmatic ones. She knew distressed fashions that could be turned over for very little money and she believed capes could be brought back one more time. Larry clearly was fascinated, so the money was there.

The crowd broke up, headed to the exits. Larry and Lilia followed them but when they reached the street all of them—club kids and Nightwalkers alike—had disappeared.

He seemed a little lost as they went toward a spot Lilia knew would be open at this hour. She wondered if he was remembering the Ichordone, the withdrawal, the dental clinics where teeth got filed down, the group therapy where a dozen other recovering vampires talked about their mothers.

"Don't worry, we'll get the audience back," Lilia said. There was a bit of blood on Larry's neck. When she pointed this out he dabbed it with the Myrna's Place napkin. And when she told Larry how much she'd need to get Reliquary up and going again, he nodded.

Lilia was certain she wasn't going to get hooked again. Larry probably would. For a moment she remembered his little adopted girl and hesitated.

Then she recalled the moment thirty years before in the flea market when she'd tried to keep the Nightwalkers away from him and he'd shut her up by siccing them on her.

So instead of little Ai Ling, Lilia thought of Boyd who might dump Larry but would make sure his daughter was well taken care of. She took Larry's arm and led him to the spot where they could discuss the money.

Another themed anthology story: in this case, Kathy Sedia's Bewere the Night. *Werewolves could be the subject, but the anthology was about transformation: werecleaning ladies and Trotskyites made appearances in other stories. I ditched the fangs, the fur, the waking up naked in the alley wondering what had happened.*

Instead I went for actors. As I've said, I have a certain background there. My parents were in the theater when I was small. Later, my mother wrote for a Boston TV show called Swan Boat, *and my father had a small part in a* Devil's Disciple *production much like the narrator's parents. The leafy, hilly Ashmont neighborhood was where we lived in the early '50s. After South Boston, it seemed almost rural.*

Josie Gannon, the narrator, is not me in at least as many ways as she/he is. I'm not an actor nor a hermaphrodite.

Otherness and magic—basic theater ingredients—are what I've tried to evoke here. Josie Gannon and Thad Ransome are different even without their extra-human talents.

Sam Shepard, playwright and actor, makes an off-stage appearance in the story. In fact, Thad Ransom, wereactor, has about him some of my early memories of the very young Shepard, years before the Pulitzer Prizes and movie roles, when he was a drummer for the Holy Modal Rounders and an object of wonder and desire on St Mark's Place.

The reader will notice that a minor character's name is Mary Robinette Kowal. This story was offered for Tuckerization (a character would be named after the highest bidder) as part of a charity fundraiser. The excellent writer MRK won and I'm happy to have her name associated with the story.

A SONG TO THE MOON

This is the early 19th century part of Manhattan. Normally on such a night in a quiet cul-de-sac in the West Village you'd be able to see the full Dog Day moon hanging right over the low buildings.

But tonight outside the Cherry Lane, that tiny old theater, banks of klieg lights blot it out. You'd hardly think those still in town would be willing to come out of their air-conditioned apartments. However, a crowd chokes curving, ancient Commerce Street on this muggy night in a torrid August.

We didn't get intense publicity, but with a cult that's not necessary. All it took were brief notices in Time Out, a bit in the *The Village Voice*, mention on internet sites, especially L-ROD the Luna-Related-Obsessive-Disorder blog. The message was: Thad Ransom live!

Just that slogan, this place and time. The crowd started to line up in the afternoon. The theater only seats one hundred and eighty-three and those first in line were let inside an hour ago.

Many others, old theater devotees and a lot of young people, are still in the street waiting for a glimpse of a legend, a touch of lunar magic.

People with a certain edge who have been in the city since mythic times remember a very young Ransom at a tiny cafe on Cornelia Street in an unknown writer's first play on a night very much like this one. He was tranformed before them, his eyes got huge, his face awestruck as he described the crash of an airplane.

For others, Thad Ransom is a screen icon, famous for moments like the one where the camera slides past a crowd of onlookers in the *Kindness of Wolves*.

For a few seconds a face caught by the lens sharpens into a muzzle, the eyes gleam, the viewer tries to catch another glimpse and can't. It's the first sight of a serial killer.

Theories abound as to what tricks were used to produce that effect. But insiders know the scene was intentionally filmed at a certain moment on a certain night. And many believe that live on nights like this is the only way to see our kind perform.

Cops, emergency medics, and bartenders will tell you that a full moon brings out the beast. But all they have is anecdotes. Ransom is the proof, as am I in my way.

I should be inside, but I feel the tension they call Moon Itch stirring inside me and need to be out here tonight. So I stand in the doorway of the old apartment house across the street from the Cherry Lane. In tight black slacks and a black turtleneck, wearing light make-up, I'm ready to perform. A ritual is about to take place and I am the priest and also the priestess.

New Yorkers are ever on the watch for celebrities, and some have noticed me. "Josie Gannon" I hear them murmur as they stare like I'm the Sybil or a shaman.

My book *The Why of Were* makes me an L-ROD expert, gets me on TV as a talking head when Lunar-Related-Obssessive-Disorder gets discussed. And Ransom aficionados know I'm embedded in his story. When we were both new in this city, I was the androgynous roommate.

Edia, his first New York girlfriend, died of an overdose and can't be here tonight. Random and Selka, his first wife, parted under unfortunate circumstances. He stabbed her on a certain night of the month. It wasn't a really serious wound and she didn't press charges. But she also won't be showing up.

Wife Two hasn't been heard from lately. On parting she said, "It's waking up every day figuring out how long it is till the next full moon and wondering who he's going to be when it happens."

Before and after each of them I was best girl, therapist and pillow boy. I think of myself as a shaman: a woman with the strength of a man and a man with the insight of a woman. But after all these years I wonder if this is love, obsession or the absense of an alternative. At times it feels like he and I are the only true examples of a breed.

Channeling our ability or affliction is the skill. A shiver goes through me and I let my face shift from older woman to young boy, from girl to old man. For all their fascination, the fans are afraid to approach me, and that, I think, is only right.

Some members of the crowd and I share a tension, a discomfort in our skin as the time slips close to midnight. A face here and there flickers, a body appears to be fluid.

The Moon Itch, real or imagined, is almost palpable. Many are impatient; some think this is a last chance to see Thad Ransom, the great shape shifter.

Then from a sound system in the theater lobby comes a crystal clear soprano: Dvorak's water nymph Rusalka laments to the silver night goddess her hopeless love for a mortal. Our show tonight is called *A Song to the Moon.*

On cue, hand drums are heard around the corner and the crowd turns. A voice proclaims, "You know who I am. I'm the thunder at twilight and the cry at the gates."

And there amid a phalanx of young, black-clad players is Thad Ransom, six-foot-four with a shock of white hair, half man, half mythic creature, all actor. At this moment the voice is Barrymore's, the eyes could belong to an intelligent coyote. But the haminess is all his. Ransom's managed to become a man notorious for being notorious.

A camera and a boom microphone follow him. Another camera is inside the open door of the theater. He is the subject of a documentary which explains the venue, the lights and the hour.

As I step forward the young players see me, reach out, and get me through the crowd. Some of our company are actors, a couple are musicians. Some are just shape shifter wannabees, but tonight there are gleaming eyes and bared teeth in the group.

I notice that especially in Tomlinson, called Tommy, the company bad boy and favorite, the one who reminds everyone of the young Ransom. Tommy's bouncing on his toes.

A couple of punks in the crowd bark, someone howls, and Tomlinson answers with a long howl of his own. I'm used to danger, but I wince at how the crowd plays with moon-driven actors.

A young actress, Mary Kowal, puts her army around Tommy. Ransom kisses me on the cheek and sweeps me with him. He turns at the lobby door and says to the crowd, "I am the fear every factory owner feels when he finds himself awake in bed in the hours after midnight."

Great stuff: 1940 Broadway socialism. This being the crowd that it is, many besides me recognize the lines from the Kaufmann and Hart comedy *Sat On A Wall.*

In act one, the daughter of a dull, rich family brings home a Greenwich Village artist named Pierce Falkland. His specialty is huge murals of heroic workers and farmers. In the second act, Falkland paints his greatest work on the living room wall and turns their world upside down.

A young John Garfield played it originally on Broadway. Clark Gable, of course, did the movie with a lot less socialism and a lot more kissing.

On the night of a full blue moon almost forty years ago, young Ransom as Falkland blew the minds of the second string critics sent to view a revival of that rickety comedy in this very theater. "Pure Animal Power!" one of them wrote.

Tonight for a few moments the white hair and the years are wiped off his face and he is the young stage radical. Ransom and I have planned and discussed tonight's show for months. But this is unreheased and spontaneous. With such an actor at such an hour it's impossible to predict what will happen.

The crowd, the people looking down from apartment windows applaud. A few howl. At times I wish the Food and Drug Administration would speed up the approval of drug therapy for Luna-Related-Obsessive-Disorder, not for the actors but for the fans.

A camera tracks us as Ransom and I go through the lobby and down the center aisle of the Cherry Lane. The curtain is up, revealing an unadorned stage. The house lights remain on for this performance.

The audience turns to watch us. Our players stop in the standing room at the back of the house.

After this we'll play larger venues—big old theaters, concert halls, open meadows in parks. The Cherry Lane is a choice both sentimental and artistic; an evocation of Ransom's past, a chance to capture a performance in an intimate setting.

Ransom turns his back to the audience and stands motionless, facing the rear wall. The cultists all lean forward in their seats. Behind them our players are a shifting background of black clothes and moving faces.

I sit on a stool stage center. When the music stops, I lean forward and slip into a favorite dual roll as man of learning and priestess of the moon.

"As I speak the clocks have moved past midnight."

Someone down front gives a little yip and someone in back answers. I ignore this.

"In the wild, the hunt for food is all consuming," I tell them. "Some of us have bits of that obsession, especially on a night like this. In the hunt, the ability to choose your physical form is a huge advantage and some of us retain traces of that.

"We are a society addicted to turning problems into excuses and letting cable TV news define our character.

"They whisper that we are a menace. But in my entire career I have seen just five full lupus transformations, and all of them were in hospitals, jails or both."

As I speak, the audience murmurs. I feel my body mass shift, my face crinkle. Without a mirror or monitor I know that my face is half man of learning/half woman of magic.

Ransom turns slowly, faces the audience, steps forward. "My father," he says softly, "would have looked the way I usually do if he'd lived as long as I have and gave up crewcuts." This part he has rehearsed.

"Thaddeus Taylor Ransom preached hellfire in the fields. He'd done a bit of college, University of Nebraska, before he went off to war. Got wounded and frostbitten in the Battle of the Bulge. Won a Silver Star, two purple hearts, maybe lost a few things.

"But my father believed that God in that very time gave him what Dad called his visions and the voice to tell us about them."

Ransom's delivery is slow and steady, growing hypnotic just like his father's must have been. "He could describe the sun at midnight and the red eye of Satan. His family was Presbyterian, but that church wouldn't hold him when he returned. Instead, he discovered The Children of the Fire, an apocalyptic sect. In your moment of spiritual need the Children were there with the comfort of a guaranteed fiery death.

"My father became a preacher. He was a charismatic, a hands-on healer." When Thad reaches this point his face has become stark with burning eyes as its main feature. "He preached on Sundays. And sometimes in church it could seem like he was burning the world down.

"Often, though, he saved the most intense moments for his family. That was my mother and two sisters and me."

Here Ransom's voice rises. "And at certain times, nights like this one, he would gather us in the living room and run something like this, 'The Lord's Great Eyes, God the Father's great eyes are upon us. His fiery gaze is upon us. It burns into your chest, into your heart, into your soul!'

"One of those nights, he woke me up, just me. I must have been ten, maybe eleven, dragged me out in my pajamas to a pasture where there was a pond and baptized me under the moonlight. I'd been baptized years before in daylight and in church.

"But this time he had a pair of torches he'd made with rolled paper and tar. He submerged me in the water, pulled me out by the scruff of the neck and held the torches so close they singed my hair."

"THE UNION OF WATER AND FIRE IN ONE BODY," Ransom yells. His eyes are huge as plates. "MY SON WILL NEVER REST EASY IN YOUR SERVICE, GOD OF FIRE."

And at that moment Ransom is as big and as terrible as that father was to that little kid. I can hear the audience gasp, see their fear.

Then the voice softens; the eyes get a little sad, a bit pensive, become no larger than anyone's. "He collapsed in the pulpit one ordinary Sunday morning six or seven years later and died in the ambulance on the way to the hospital. Over time a bullet fragment had worked its way into his heart.

"Six months later, my mother married a member of the congregation, a man who owned a Buick dealership. My sisters were regular kids. Maybe I was the old man's only legacy.

"When I was eighteen, I left town for state college. I ended up in the Drama Department. They say acting and preaching are related skills. At the end of sophomore year, needing more space between my family and me, I left home and ended up in New York."

He sits on a stool. The audience nods: Ransom's upbringing was extreme but lots of them came here from situations into which they didn't fit. And more than a few get a bit turned inside out by the light of the moon.

I look up and smile. "My launching on the lunar path was a bit less dramatic," I tell them.

"It was on a fine, warm night when I was maybe four. My Irish grandmother was taking clothes down from the line on the roof of the apartment building in Boston where she lived.

"Grandmother hadn't really decided who or what I was—never

did I think. They'd named me Joseph but were already calling me Josie. It's a slippery name that over the years has come to be as much a girl's as a boy's.

"She pointed up at the moon and recited that ancient appeal to the goddess of the night sky. It was invented for protection against the creatures that mean us harm and walk in the silver light:

> 'I see the moon and the moon sees me
> God bless the moon and God bless me'

"Was it also a prayer for those beings who are its worst captives, the women and the men ensnared in the lunar cycle? Could my grandmother sense that in me?

"It was part of the folklore of every nationality long before it became Lunar Related Obsessive Disorder and got discussed on TV and the internet.

"But if it's a disease, where is the virus? If it's a mental disorder where are the conclusive studies? And if the moon's role is a delusion, why are there nights like these?"

I hear my voice at a distance. My face moves on its own. The lunar priest and the woman of science flicker there and a camera catches them.

As I finish, Ransom is prowling the stage. "I came to this city the usual way," he says, "knowing nobody and nothing and almost immediately fell in with the perfect wrong crowd. A girl I met took me to an acting class at the New School."

We are into an old routine, one I can almost watch myself do. "I saw him the first time sitting in that acting studio all legs and hostility," I say. "Afterwards we talked and walked. It was late in the lunar cycle on a summer night with nothing in the sky but the Dog Star. Even without the moon, he was intense. His eyes never blinked. He ended up crashing in the same pad I was staying at."

"I'd never met anyone like Josie," says Ransom. "But I figured this must be how people were in the big city. Josie explained a few things about my life. I realized there was nobody else like Josie—except me in lots of ways.

"I don't know if going to Central Park in the dead of night a couple of weeks later was his idea or her idea."

Laughter follows. "It was yours," I say. "For several reasons, I expected life to include some danger. And I thought anyone we encountered would find you as scary as I did. So I went along."

Remembering that night, I begin to relive it. I can smell the grass, feel the night breeze. As I return to that night I can feel myself change on stage and see Ransom become young again.

"The wonder of that place at midnight is you can forget the city," he says. "Our senses sharpened. We moved in shadows, dodged police patrols, and walked to the north end of the park. The Harlem Mere at 2 A.M. had the Harvest Moon shining on the water. There was a waterfall and lone cars with their lights on high-beam speeding along the drives: the only other sound was the wind rustling in the trees."

"Our heads touched the sky—without acid," I add. And I am there. "We recited Shakespeare 'Oh, swear not by the moon, the fickle moon, the inconstant moon . . .' We sang, "Oh Moon of Alabama."

Acapella we sing a few choruses about finding the next whiskey bar, the next pretty boy. For us the Cherry Lane stage disappears.

Ransom says, "Our senses grew more accute. We realized that a certain rustling in the bushes was not the wind and that it was following us. There was a moment of silence like someone or something was going to attack."

"I told him, 'NOW WE HOWL!'" And just as on that night, our eyes narrow, our jaws jut forward. We move downstage screaming. Our company lining the back of the theater joins in.

I feel the audience gasp and pull back in their seats as we two come forward wild-eyed. I hope the cameras got every bit of it. I remember to hold my hand up. The noise stops.

"It was kids up to no good—like us," Ransom says. "We chased them howling first, then laughing. Next day I remembered it like a dream and had to talk about it to keep the details from slipping away.

"But maybe a week later, this guy stopped me on Bleecker Street and said my eyes were insane. He was Sam Shepard, and his first play was going to be up that weekend at Caffe Chino on Cornelia Street. He wanted me in it. That was my first time in front of a paying audience."

As Ransom speaks, his face relaxes, but not all the way.

"My initiation was a lot less dramatic than Thad's," I say. "You can grow up in a city and stay very unaware of nature. But when I was eight, we lived in a leafy part of Boston. There were hills and big old mansions that were now, many of them, divided up into apartments, into duplexes. But the yards were large and unfenced; the hills looked out on ocean and sky.

"Old Yankees in the neighborhood worked in their gardens by moonlight. They lived in houses they'd grown up in, planted vegetables and talked at night on their porches. They drove model A's, had coal furnaces, and got ice delivered by a man with a horse and cart just as it had happened when they were young.

"They followed ritual: Memorial Day and Fourth of July and Harvest Moon and at Halloween they had pumpkins with candles inside them on their porches.

"Instinctively, I understood the power of a certain grain in the blood."

That old neighborhood decades ago is where I am. I feel smaller. The face of the kid Joseph/Josie wide-eyed but guarded is my face as I speak.

"My parents often seemed very young. They had been actors, people of the theater who settled down, but not entirely. My mother wrote for a local TV show *Boston Common*. On five mornings a week it was songs, the news, dramatic pieces (her specialty) a segment for kids.

"Sometimes she took me with her when she brought scripts over to the station. Old friends she'd acted with worked on the show. They greeted each other with kisses. She'd be flushed with excitement. I never thought to see if it was the full moon.

"My parents always wanted me on the show and I always said no. Maybe some part of me understood where I was going and wanted to delay the trip as long as I could. When *Boston Common* got cancelled after a few years, my mother was devastated, lost.

"By then I had other concerns. At that time boys swam, showered, and took group physical exams naked. As a small child I'd just seemed undeveloped and got teased. With the onset of puberty it grew obvious that I had a cock and a cunt as well. I was taunted, kicked, taken to doctors.

"Drug treatment was suggested, surgery. I didn't want to change and my parents, who knew a little about being different, didn't insist. They moved to another part of the city, enrolled me at a school where I got excused from gym and swimming class.

The secret scared me, but left me feeling superior to others. Danger and lust got intertwined.

"My parents still dabbled, did readings, took small parts in plays. My father was in a production of Shaw's *The Devil's Disciple* done in late spring outdoors in the Public Gardens.

"I went with a couple of fellow outcasts from our high school drama department. The full Flower Moon rose over the trees. By then I knew all the names and phases and was aware of what was up with my parents. I felt my body grow fluid and knew what I was meant to do.

"The next year I was a page boy in *Henry the Fifth*, not a big stretch. Shortly afterwards I was Yum Yum in *The Mikado*. We opened the night of Green Corn Moon and I was sensational.

"Sex was a tense game. I had so many ways of disappointing partners. My freshman year of college I got picked up at a party by one of the boys who'd tormented me back in the old neighborhood. He didn't recognize me. I showed him what I had. His eyes widened in recognition.

"Then I showed him this," and on the stage of the Cherry Lane my face is the Gorgon Medusa's. It's my way of telling the audience we're past the pleasant introductions. They recoil but don't turn to stone.

Ransom has disappeared from the stage. I stand motionless, getting back my face and body. Drums beat out in the lobby and then in the house. Ransom comes down the center aisle, his hair in golden ringlets; his face gleams. Behind him the chorus twirl, buck, roll their eyes back in their heads. They chant:

> "Dance now
> dance again
> when Bacchus
> mighty Bacchus
> leads us"

They are the wild maenads, the women, some played here by guys, who have followed Dionysius all the way from Asia to ancient Thebes. Several have leather drums on which they maintain heartbeats that will go on as long as the performance does. Two others hold aloft on sticks a light-reflecting silver disk: the full moon.

Euripides' *the Bacchae*: maybe everyone sees herself in every great play. But those who follow the silver goddess are close to this one. Order-Pentheus the righteous young king of Thebes—confronts Chaos—Dionysius god of wine and frenzy.

The chorus sings and dances:

> "With my drum that
> the god made for me
> dancing for him
> with my leather drum"

All are supposed to be wild-eyed. But tonight some are barely under control. Intentionally, we are playing with fire. Tommy is the worst, twirling, smacking into others on the crowded stage. He's the company pet. Ransom lets him get away with too much. I catch Tommy's attention, stare right into him. He subsides.

At Lincoln Center many years ago there was the legendary production in which young Ransom played both Pentheus and Bacchus. Tonight he stands at the back of the stage and announces:

> "I am Bacchus. I am Dionysius
> I am a god the son of Zeus"

His eyes are wide and blazing as he goes on to speak of his anger at the city and its ruling family—relatives who have disowned him—and his plans for vengeance.

In Greek drama, actors take multiple roles. With my back to the audience I wear a crown and am Pentheus; young, arrogant, full of hubris, speaking to what he thinks is a lunatic, ordering him imprisoned.

> "Lock him up in the stable
> If you like to dance, dance there"

And all the time the chorus goes on chanting quietly, the drums beat. The silver disc shines on the stage.

Minutes later, Ransom, young and severe, wears the crown and is Pentheus, his face rigid and imperious. Tommy is a messenger describing the packs of maddened Bacchantes which include Pentheus' own mother and aunts, destroying villages, tearing wild beasts and cattle apart:

> "Ribs, hooves, flying asunder"

Pentheus demands to see this for himself. Now I am Dionysius all golden hair and glowing face. I dress him in woman's robes and lead him up the mountain while the chorus around us snaps their teeth like mad dogs. The night, the drums begin to take me. My eyes loose focus.

> "Make the drums roar
> and the hounds of madness
> bay at the moon"

Then we are all supposed to exit except for Mary Kowal, who remains onstage. Tomlinson passing by suddenly turns and bites her on the shoulder. She cries out, shoves him away. This is not acting and I hear the audience gasp. For a heartbeat everyone on stage stops. For a moment it seems that we might all start tearing at each other.

I know Ransom is being dead in the wings. He lies stretched out on the floor, mouth gaping, an expression of horror on his face. I've seen it many times.

It's up to me. I grab Tomlinson, look right into his wild, staring eyes with all the authority of a priestess and the madness of an actor with forty-five years on the New York stage.

"Don't waste this last chance, Tommy," I whisper. His eyes focus and the troupe leads him off. Onstage Mary Kowal as a messenger describes how the Bacchae, maddened, fell upon Pentheus. Agave, his own mother, tore her son's head from his body believing he was a lion.

In the wings we form up in a tight group, pick up dead Pentheus and emerge onto the stage. And now I am Agave marching back into Thebes. In triumph I hold my son Pentheus' bloody head by his mane of hair, his jaw flapping open. Foaming at the mouth I sing:

> "I caught him myself
> This savage beast
> Without weapons or net"

And the chorus chants:

> "And the drums
> Let the drums
> Praise Bacchus
> For this deed"

Slowly Agave understands what she's done. I stare with a face like a mask of horror. The drums cease. Suddenly the lights go down. One spot remains, shining on the silver disc above us. I stand shaking, catching my breath.

The players who carried Ransom and blocked sight of his body while I held up his head put him down and escort him off silently.

My Moon Itch has begun to ebb. The lights come back up. I am alone on the stage.

There is applause. But I shake my head. This isn't over.

"Euripides wrote," I say, "when people had begun to forget the time when woman and god and man and beast weren't as separated and distinct as they are now. But his was a time when all humans male and female were tied by nature to the cycle of the earth, were servants to the phases of the moon.

"They still understood what seems a terrible alien disease to us now and that sometimes it was best to let that beast run."

Again there is applause. Ransom and company are behind me on the stage. It goes on for a while. We take our bows after which we're supposed to make our exit up the center aisle. Instead, Ransom holds up his hands.

He looks drained, old. He puts his arm around Tomlinson's shoulder and around Mary Kowal's. "There's a story theater people tell about a great actor playing a great part. He comes off stage to tumultuous applause and storms to his dressing room in a black mood. 'You were stupendous,' they say, 'why are you so unhappy?'

"'I was incandescent,' is his answer, 'AND I DON'T KNOW WHY.'"

Ransom shakes his head, says in rich actor tones, "Ah, the mystery of ART! But what if you do know why your performance is terrific and the reason why isn't you? What if you're the drum and not the drummer, the brush and not the painter? What if you're a tool intended to give everyone a glimpse of ourselves as we are by nature?

"Descended from hunters of flesh, born to a hunter of souls, I've become a hunter of applause. I'm as surprised as you by some of what happened here. But each night the earth will take a small bite out of the silver goddess. In a week's time it will be sliced away and Josie and I and young Mr Tomlinson and even Mary Robinette Kowal will be very ordinary actors indeed. Try to remember that when the moon is full," he tells Tommy. "You'll not get nearly as many second chances as I was given."

I've heard him say much of this on many different occasions. But it's one of the reason why, when he holds out his arm, I take it and walk with him up the aisle. A camera backs up before us.

People rise, applauding, and he smiles his way into the narrow lobby and out onto Commerce Street.

Outside all is quiet. By arrangement with the block association, the klieg lights are off. The crowd is largely dispersed. The moon has disappeared behind the houses. Cameras follow us to the curb, then stop.

A driver opens the back door of a limo. We kiss the kids goodbye, promise we'll see them all tomorrow, make sure Mary will have the shoulder looked at, and escape before the fans can get to us. The cameras don't follow any further. We'll see them tomorrow also.

Ransom and I settle into the back seat and I give the directions home. Yes. We are roommates again—un folie aux deux.

The energy of the moon has flowed out of us. The wolf sleeps after it has fed. I sink into the seat. "I hope they got the footage they wanted," I say.

Next month we do this at the Chandler in L.A. In October under the Hunter's Moon it's the Colonial in Boston. We're booked two years in advance. The documentary, the long farewell tour—we're showing them how it's done.

"Tomlinson was out of control, tonight," Ransom says. He sounds tired and old. "Much as I like him, I'm afraid Tommy's got to go."

"He reminds me of you at his age," I say. "And he gave you the chance to make that speech."

"What he did was unprofessional."

"Hmmm. Remember the binge you went on after you walked out on Edia?

"I remember waking up from a week-long blackout."

"And discovering you'd signed on to play Cyrano De Bergerac in a former tin can factory in Jersey City."

"The nose was great. You said so yourself."

"They'll find a medical cure for Tommy's problem. We'll be the last of our kind."

But Ransom's asleep and I take his hand. When I first saw him I knew he was dangerous. But it's what I was used to. It's easy to entice and easy to anger when you offer the mixed bag that I did. Now we are as you see us.

On my iPod, Dvorak's Water Nymph sings to the moon of her troubles. I think of her as a creature caught between worlds—like me as a child. I want to tell her that I've seen over 800 moons both silver and blue come and go. And I look forward to seeing some more.

One last story from a themed anthology, again edited by Kathy Sedia. This time it's Bloody Fabulous: *the world of Fashion with a weird urban fantasy twist. My story is stand-alone but one that continues the tale of Lilia, the POV character in my "Blood Yesterday, Blood Tomorrow." We follow the return of the Nightwalkers as a cultural and fashion phenomenon.*

Write Speculative Fiction and all you've ever learned or imagined gets used. My first few years in New York, I worked as a copywriter and eventually as a fashion copywriter. This was in the vast, teaming Garment District, a couple of square miles on Manhattan's West Side where clothes were designed, manufactured and sold.

Modern Manhattan is built on the ruins of old ways of life, old neighborhoods, and old businesses. Years later, the factories and sweatshops, those streets where only fur coats or buttons were made and sold have disappeared. Fashion design alone remains: mind without matter, ideas divorced from the physical consequence. I hope I caught some of that.

SAVAGE DESIGN

Early one evening last September Lilia Gaines pulled open the metal gates of Reliquary on West Broadway at the shoddy Canal Street end of Manhattan's Soho. As she did, she murmured to herself:

"In the city with sleep disorders styles get old fast. But old styles never disappear. They lay waiting for a kiss or a love bite . . ."

She trailed off. Lilia's copywriting skills had never been a big strength and she found herself groping for a punch line.

A really young couple appeared wearing knock-off Louis Vuitton sunglasses and looking like they might be at the start of a long Nightwalker romp. His jacket collar was turned up; she had a wicked, amused smile.

Lilia could remember being like them, a brand new walker in the dark with eyes just a bit sensitive to sunlight. They waited while she unlocked the door, came inside with her, and headed for the relics table at the rear.

In the last few months, this kind of eager customer had started reappearing. Twenty-five and thirty years ago, Reliquary was open all night, closing only when full daylight fell on the storefront and the customers fled.

"Reliquary—Boutique Fashion—So New and SO Undead!" was the slogan in those glory days. Then as now one could find capes in a variety of lengths, elegant black parasols to keep the sun at bay, tops designed for easy exposure of the neck and throat. Some of the stock was a bit shopworn.

There had been good years when Nightwalkers were THE fresh thing. Then there were the lean years when vampires were afraid to show themselves, and Reliquary became a dusty antique store while Lilia worked part time jobs and held on tight to her rent controlled apartment on East Houston Street.

This evening, Lilia watched the boy select a red silk handkerchief displaying a black bat, the long-ago emblem of Bloodsucker Night at the gay disco The Saint. The girl slipped on a pendant with the logo of the Gate of Night, that brief legend of a blood bar on Park Avenue South three decades back. Reliquary had always specialized in memorabilia of past Undead revivals.

Another customer, a man in running clothes and shades, entered and went over to a rack of capes. A woman stepped inside and glanced around, found a repro of a poster for *Fun and Gore*, a scandalous 1930s Greenwich Village "Transylvanian Review."

As the young couple approached the register, the girl pulled the boy's jacket and shirt off his shoulders. She smiled at Lilia as though offering her a piece of expensive white fudge.

This was very young love. Their teeth still looked normal; the small bites on his neck had barely penetrated the skin. Fangs and puncture wounds still lay in their future.

The boy's smile was blank. He knotted the kerchief over the bites but left one showing. Lilia guessed that his first blood buzz had been last night and that he'd be bitten again very shortly.

The girl looked at the photo behind Lilia, raised her sunglasses and said, "That's you!"

The kid was sharp; Lilia nodded. The picture was from the 1980 Mudd Club Undead and Kicking Party where Lilia and Larry had introduced Downtown Manhattan to Nightwalking.

She was front and center along with Larry Stepelli, the bisexual boyfriend who designed all her clothes. In black with faces white as bone, they stood out among the graffiti artists, stray freaks, and Warhol Factory stars.

Lilia knew she should warn these kids where blood sucking was going to lead. She remembered her own addiction and the horrors of Ichordone Therapy. But too many years of marginal living left her unwilling to risk endangering the chance she saw coming.

Instead she gave them a double discount because they would tell their friends about the place. Then she told the girl that she was hiring sales help and took her name. It was Scarlet Jones (an invention, Lilia assumed). The boy was just plain Bret—too paranoid to leave a last name or so blood-dizzy he couldn't remember it.

The phone rang as the kids left and someone with a heavy European accent asked for directions to the store. Lilia felt the good years coming back.

"Staff called in sick?" Even before raising her eyes, Lilia recognized from long ago the throaty, sly voice that somehow made every comment sound dirty but also chilling.

The one called Katya must have come in as the kids left. Well over six feet tall, she stood near the door in a jacket and slacks of fierce gray suede and high heel ankle boots of raw leather.

"Other's shoes are man-made," it was said in certain circles, "but Katya's are made out of men." Maybe it was her imagination, but Lilia could almost see the outlines of ears and fingers in the heels.

"Just me alone, tonight," she said, though that's the way it had been for a long time. "To what do I owe this honor?" It had been at least twenty years since she'd gotten anything but a fraction of a nod and an amused stare from this woman. And it was a rare occasion when their paths had crossed.

Katya glanced at the Mudd Club photo and frowned. Lilia knew she'd caught sight of her young self, a supporting player in Lilia and Larry's big moment. Katya was off to one side with Felice, who had mood swings, and Paulo, who worked part-time as a professional boy. In that intense instant, all five of them were kids without a dime trying to break into the Fashion Trade.

Katya glanced around, and Lilia saw her registering the somewhat tired capes on display, the costume jewelry necklaces with what on second glance turned out to be drop-of-blood motifs.

"Happened to be in the neighborhood," Katya said. "Some intriguing things are to be seen in these quiet little nooks. It's the essence of our business, isn't it, keeping an eye on what is being worn on the streets?"

Katya turned to go as a male couple came in. "I'll tell Paulo and Felice about all this," she said. "I know they'll want to see you too."

The time when they were new in the city and broke was well past. Now Larry was the domestic partner of a rich lawyer. Katya, Felice and Paulo ran Savage Design, which had been a power in New York fashion for as long as that scene's short memory ran.

People in the business went in such fear of the trio that they called them The Kindly Ones and prayed for their help. Before any enterprise was launched, it was considered wise to offer them tribute. The Kindly Ones were THE arbiters and always hungry for something new and perverse or at least hot and retro.

Of their little group, only Lilia had failed to make it. Katya's visit could mean a break for her, one last desperate chance.

Through the window, she watched Katya take in this dark sliver of the neighborhood. A small, elegant hotel a block and a half north marked the start of trendy Soho.

Next to Reliquary was a shop that sold spray paint and other graffiti supplies. The storefronts across the street were dark and empty; the building upstairs was a tenement. This gritty little block was a bit of pre-gentrified New York preserved in a new century.

Next Monday morning, Lilia sat in the conference room of Savage Design sipping coffee. She couldn't decide whether she was more ashamed or bitter when she compared her current life to those of the Kindly Ones.

The Kindly Ones' initial expressions when she arrived left Lilia with no doubt that they found her an amusing curiosity. She kept silent and studied the walls, which were decorated with photos of last spring's coup.

An emblematic black and white photo taken at what might have been dawn, but was more likely dusk, showed a blonde figure wearing an ostentatiously plain dark dress and the slightest smile of triumph.

All was shades of gray except for the handbag. That was in the red and orange tones of an October bonfire. *A Satanic Possession of One's Own!* was the caption.

Around the room, ads displayed belts, scarves, wraps. A photo was headlined, *For the One Willing to Exchange a Flawed Soul for Perfection.*

Satan's Bag, read the caption on the *Harper's Bazaar* double page spread, *Designer Fashion from inside the Fiery Gates!*

Paulo noticed her interest. He still had the face and body of a kid. But now he had the eyes of an old, bored lizard. He wore a short pants suit of navy blue cheviot wool. A yo-yo spun constantly on his right hand.

"Last Spring's triumph," said an ancient voice from inside him. "As of yet nobody knows what to do about next year." His yo-yo slept at the end of its string, looped the loop as he spoke.

Years before, his allowance from a mysterious sugar daddy who insisted he dress like an English schoolboy was often all that kept them in their daily cappuccino and crème brulee.

"The year hasn't even begun," said Felice, whose face today was the mask of tragedy, "and it's already dreary, tired, lacking a defining moment." She was whip thin and dressed in black.

Her mouth appeared to curve even further down. Her eye sockets seemed hollow. It was whispered in the fashion trade that in moments of emotional stress she cried tears of blood.

Katya yawned and said, "Nothing like the designer suicide followed by the show of his work at the Met last year."

"Brilliant timing, yes," said Paolo as the yo-yo spun through the intricate hop-the-fence trick, "but significant because it was one of a kind. If something similar happened now, would anyone be interested?"

Katya said, "We're being rude to our guest. Lilia, darling, understand that we all change over time. With us, Paulo's Sugar Daddy decided it was easier to become a permanent live-in guest and share Paulo's youth at first hand. Felice got tired of trying to suppress her feelings and allowed them to come forth for everyone to see. I went from thinking men were useless to finding a use for them. Perhaps you never wanted to reach that kind of resolution."

She put her feet with the sling-backs like no others up on the table. "Everyone talks as if we had dark powers. But Savage Design is quite a simple straightforward business. Paulo handles the finances, Felice does the promotion, and I'm the scout."

Then she asked, "How's Larry?"

Lilia's answer was careful. "Still hooked up with the rich lawyer. They adopted an Asian child, and are talking about getting married now that it's legal."

She left out the fact Larry and she were talking again and that he'd provided money to keep Reliquary open. Lilia wondered how much they knew about her business or if this was just idle curiosity mixed with bitchiness.

Paulo said, "I understand he's breaking up with that lawyer."

Lilia hadn't heard that.

"I brought Lilia here," Katya told the others, "because her shop is still in business and showing signs of life. I've seen a glimmer on the street that could go semi-major. A Nightwalker revival," she said. Paulo's ancient eyes closed. Felice looked away.

"Round and round we go," Paulo said. "Remember the Boom when everyone was high on blood and being a vampire was utterly hip? Recall the Bust a few years later? Nobody became Dracula and immortal. Everyone was a blood junkie and went into therapy or jail."

"Yes, Katya said, "we've all been there and back. But in one afternoon in Tribeca and Soho I saw a couple of dozen people under twenty-five wearing Blood Sucker artifacts."

"Cyclical but inevitable," murmured Felice, but her mouth was now a straight line.

"Before a look can be revived it must die!" said Paulo thoughtfully. "Or at least be presumed dead!"

"Then there's the boutique itself," said Katya as if Lilia wasn't present. "Reliquary is so passé it's almost tantalizing. And it's on a block that's this kind of time bubble from the old, bad Manhattan of thirty years back. The sort of place people who weren't actually there get nostalgic about—all grit, grunge and decay!"

At the word grunge, Paulo's reptile eyes lit up with old memories and he used both hands to make the yo-yo do "Buddha's Revenge."

"Delicious decay," Felice murmured. The others looked away before her face slipped into the mask of comedy pose. It was said, with reason, that none who saw the laughing mask lived to tell about it.

They discussed what could be done with Reliquary. Lilia stayed very still and alert, determined not to let this opportunity pass her by.

"*Reliquary—Open Dusk to Dawn*" read the store's new webpage headline: "*Costumes and Accessories For Long After Twilight,*" it promised.

A dozen customers were in her store at 3:30 AM and Lilia stood behind the counter keeping an eye out for shoplifters, watching Scarlet Jones greet friends. Lilia knew all about history—especially fashion history—repeating itself the first time as farce, the second as camp.

She noticed that Scarlet's teeth were changing, getting sharper. Her boyfriend, Bret, worked in the stockroom and looked paler and dizzier each time Lilia saw him.

The story was unfolding much faster this time than the last.

Thirty years back the cult grew little by little. Word was spread in print, *"Something REALLY Old Is Very New Again!"* a New York *Post* gossip columnist had said. *"They Walk By Night—Creepy and DELICIOUS!"* read the *Women's Wear Daily* headline as things got underway.

Suddenly Reliquary's door opened and the room stirred. Magnetic, wonderfully turned out in an antique black cape and dark red top, seemingly untouched by age, Larry Stepelli entered with an entourage of models, minor celebrities and star bloggers—all young and male.

Thirty years before, Lilia would have been the one beside him. The flamboyant bisexual guy and plain, serious girl was the perfect pairing of that moment. They were in the vanguard of the trip into the night.

Now they were distant friends and the arrangement was financial. A few months before, she'd sensed Larry's boredom. The rich boyfriend, their adorable adopted child, the art gallery in Chelsea, weren't doing it for him.

So she'd turned him on to the Nightwalker revival she was trying to create. It only took a couple of reminders of their initial encounters with the dark mysteries. His curiosity and desire kicked in. Larry advanced money to pay off the back rent and restock the store.

He walked over and they made kissing gestures. "You must have heard?" he said.

"About your break-up? Sorry."

"Inevitable. I imagine it will all be very civilized. I'll get a settlement and visiting rights with Ai Ling." He looked around. "Business has really picked up."

Lilia said, "Yes. I was even summoned to Seventh Avenue by the Kindly Ones."

"My, MY!"

"Remember when telephone gossip was the fastest news on the planet? Now what any kid posts online, the world knows before the next day dawns."

Larry smiled and turned away. She watched him help a pale young man select a ring with a tiny broken crucifix on it.

Lilia remembered the last Nightwalker scene turning sour. *"BLOODY HELL"* screamed a *Post* headline. *"Nightwalkers in Rehab,"* was a three part series in the *The Village Voice*. But it was years between those first hints and the morning everyone woke up with hideous addictions to blood and biting.

This time the turnaround would be quick. And Lilia knew she had to ride the wave or go under for good.

A few nights later, the Savage Design trio, complete with personal assistants, photographers, a video crew and a special secret, arrived at Lilia's shop.

Paulo, in soccer shorts and jersey, repeatedly kicked a ball against the hydrant in front of Reliquary. The kid's legs did a fast dance step as he stopped the rebound each time then slammed the ball again. Seemingly independent of this, the lizard eyes took in the store and its surroundings.

Felice nodded to Lilia as she went through Reliquary with her face carefully kept in neutral and examined everything while murmuring notes to herself on a hand-held recorder.

"Nothing needs to be changed," she said to the production assistant who followed her. "Treat each dusty corner and gauche display as an asset. Pretend you're an explorer stumbling on a mysterious if tacky Transylvanian castle."

Then she said into the recorder, "Time is more precious than blood on this particular project. It's all a matter of *death* and DEATH."

A team of trimmers lighted and dressed Reliquary's front windows. Katya appeared outside shortly afterwards, towering in dark, rough leather platform shoes with dizzyingly high heels that seemed to be watching when you stared. She herded a couple of long-necked professional models and half a dozen Nightwalker kids whom she'd discovered around the city.

The photography crew did shots of them posing on the sidewalk. "They'll be in here shortly," Katya assured Lilia when she popped into the shop. She also insisted on using Scarlet Jones and Bret in the promotional shots.

"We'll have them behind the counter like they run the place, darling. They exhibit the proper mix of inexperience and incipient damnation."

It went without saying that Lilia herself would stay out of camera range—her's was not the look or age range being aimed for. As the crew began setting up inside, the male model said something to

Katya that Lilia couldn't hear. In reply, Katya looked down at him and pointed to her shoes. The guy wilted.

Scarlet Jones and Bret wore sunglasses as they basked in the photographer's lights. Felice had them change into white silk tops that rested off their shoulders. Lilia noticed that the bites on their necks were deeper and thought these new blouses looked somehow familiar.

Felice turned to her and said, "Of course you recognize the original Herrault design from the last Nightwalker go-round. Maison Herrault itself OK'd these knock-offs.

"I was afraid we'd have to go to Indonesia for production. Time delay on a fad like this can be fatal. But Hurrah for the Recession! Suddenly there are sweatshops in the Bronx—fast, cheap, and with passable quality."

Lilia looked away lest Felice smile. But she heard the other say, "Reliquary will get a six week exclusivity period, after which they'll be sold at other specialty shops throughout North America and world markets. Then," her mouth turned downward, "Blooming-dales, Macy's, and by next summer, Target." She and the young man adjusting Scarlet and Bret's clothes both shuddered.

"Here's a little surprise," said Katya, "someone you'll remember from the 'good' old days."

Paulo somewhat gingerly ushered in a tiny, ancient woman. As she entered, this woman briskly flicked a cigarette butt on the sidewalk while reaching into the formless smock she wore to draw out and light another one.

Lilia looked on amazed. This was the legendary Marguerite, "The Seamstress Extraordinary," as she'd been called back in the old Garment District. It was said that Marguerite could, without measuring, without even looking, cut a sleeve or a pant leg to exactly the length needed.

That afternoon Marguerite smoked one Galois after another. Requests that she stop were met with shrugs, coughs and mumbles in barely recognizable English, "A vice like any other!"

"Amazed?" Paulo murmured to Lilia.

"That she's not dead," Lilia said.

"Not in the usual sense anyway," he replied. "She's become a sort of curator for Herrault. His emissary in this world."

In the old days, Marguerite was employed at the prestigious Maison Herrault's New York branch and lent out to old friends of the late designer. She would always be brought along on fashion shoots in cases of an emergency.

One had arisen in Reliquary just before she appeared. The lapel of the top Bret wore wouldn't lay open at the angle the photographer wanted. Marguerite reached up for Bret's ear, pulled his head down to her eye level, and with a needle, thread, and scissors from inside her smock, made three stitches and fixed the lapel in place.

Decades before as a naïve young intern, Lilia had first encountered Marguerite. It was in a room slightly larger than a closet at the Studio Building where all fashion photography was done back in that day.

There, with fabric fragments thick on the floor, Marguerite stitched buttons onto a waistband while she squinted at the airshaft outside the window and sipped from a small glass of what young Lilia supposed was red wine.

She had been told to take a pair of women's flared slacks and have Marguerite turn them into culottes. This was an emergency, a great crisis—the shoot was to feature culottes but the garment in question did not yet exist.

Marguerite was present for just such moments. She had looked at Lilia with disgust and disapproval as if she was about to send her back to the kitchen with the demand that she be properly braised.

Then, with scarcely a glance at the design sketch Lilia gave her, Marguerite had snipped off one leg, with a second slice snipped the other and cuffed both with a few stitches. She muttered "voila," blew smoke in Lilia's face and shoved the garment at her.

Recalling this, Lilia watched Marguerite finger the tops Scarlet and Bret wore. "Instant prêt a porter!" the old woman muttered to herself. "For such a venue anything more than off-the-rack would not do."

Herrault had been a contemporary of Chanel, protégé of Schiaparelli, lover of Mainbocher, rival of Dior. His 'Sang Chaud' Collection, the master's last great triumph, had defined the look of the prior Nightwalker craze.

His slacks, jackets, skirts and gowns draped the wearer almost rigidly. But his tops were open, flowing. "The throat too is an erogenous zone," he famously said, "I believe the ultimate one." His firm, Maison Herrault, carried on his cult.

Behind Lilia, Katya whispered, "We're doing it backwards this time. First come these knockoffs with a certain flair."

"Herrault's name will never be officially connected with any of this," said Felice. "But the look will be pushed in places like *Our Daily Shmata*. Images being shot today will turn up in every online post about the dark new trend."

"Next spring, Maison Herrault will put out a line that incorporates this 'street fashion,'" said Paulo. "We aim for a quick kill and exit."

The kid's body, restless, started dribbling the heavy soccer ball on the floor. Even Marguerite noticed and winced.

Lilia concentrated on the six weeks in which these tops would be hers alone to sell.

Late the next day, Lilia began seeing images of the shoot on websites like "Stuff I Saw Last Night." One favorite was a shot of Reliquary taken at dusk from across the street. Felice's copy ran with it: *Nightwalkers are all dark glamour, forbidden fashion.*

In the photo, a young guy dressed casually and walking on the sidewalk was caught by surprise and held by the gaze of a woman whose dark clothes seemed to blend into the shadows in which she stood. The silk scarf around her elegant neck flowed over her shoulders as if blown in a night breeze.

The lighted shop windows behind them displayed pairs of manikins echoing the live models' poses. One had the sexes of Nightwalker and potential recruit reversed; in the other both were the same sex.

She scrolled past shots of the interior with Scarlet, Bret and company caught in moments of beauty and mystery. Interspersed with this was more copy:

> *They're the newest thing!*
> *They're exclusive, an ultimate in-group.*
> *You rarely see an unattractive Child of the Night!*
> *And you never meet a dull one!*

Those words came back to Lilia after dark on an evening in the short days of November. A young *Vogue* editor, favored by the Kindly Ones and aiming to steal a prime place in the February book, was shooting a secret preview of Maison Herrault's Fall/Winter collection. Marguerite was on hand.

The Children of the Night were trendy again but Lilia, feeling frumpy and old, was shoved once more into a corner of her own shop. She wore a leather choker under her turtleneck sweater.

The leather held evidence of a few token love bites and at least one deep and sincere chomp customers had sent her way in the last few days. Lilia remembered the soft glow a bite could give both vampire and victim. But she was not going to get hooked like last time.

She was not alone in her corner. Larry had come in as the *Vogue* crew was setting up. Immediately the ethereal young guy with whom he entered was seized by the editor. "Wherever did you find him! Surely he'll want to be part of this!" The young man went with the editor and never once glanced back.

Larry, looking frazzled and worn, told Lilia, "There's going to be a divorce settlement, but not as big as I'd thought. He threatens to bring up vampires as regards visiting rights with Ai-Ling."

"You've been down before," Lilia found herself saying, bucking him up just as in the old days. "Like I was until recently," she added, to let him know she hadn't forgotten his decades of neglect.

He winced and said, "There's stuff I regret."

"Me too. Nightwalker life was wild fun at first. Then came the pain of kicking the blood habit."

"Ichordone therapy," he said. "Methadone for vampires. It was torture. I came out of that cured and brainwashed into thinking all I wanted was to find a rich mate, have a nice life, and raise children."

"You made it clear the future wouldn't include me," she said.

"I wish I was as sure of anything now as I was of EVERYTHING right then," he said. It was as close to an apology as he was likely to give.

Lilia noted with some relish his unsuccessful attempts to catch the eye of the guy he'd come with. But she felt a pang of regret when Larry gave up, said good night, and exited.

Under the lights, Marguerite, cigarette dangling from the corner of her mouth, subdued a recalcitrant ruffle with a swift succession of scissor snips.

Lilia remembered the second episode of their long ago encounter in the Studio Building. A terrible mistake had occurred! The flared slacks had been turned into culottes. BUT the former slacks themselves were needed for a shot that HAD to be done.

The photographer and the art director were afraid to face the

Seamstress Extraordinary, so Lilia was sent again. When she appeared and stuttered through her request, Marguerite had glared at her while fingering the scissors. She pointed at the slacks legs on the floor. Lilia stooped and handed them to her.

Marguerite slugged the last contents of the glass down, picked up a threaded needle. Again, without looking, the ageless woman stitched a leg together once, twice, perhaps six times.

The juncture was almost invisible to the eye and certainly could be to the camera. She handed the slacks back to Lilia. "But the other leg," said the girl.

"En silhouette," said the woman, sank back on a stool and closed her eyes. "One side only," she added.

"I can't take it back like this!"

In a move like a snake, the woman grabbed Lilia's left hand. With scissors she cut the girl's index finger, squeezed out bubbles of blood, and avidly lapped them all off. She repeated this a few times, then picked up the slacks and again with no more than six stitches created a seamless whole. Lilia, in tears, picked up the garment with her unbloodied hand and fled.

For the rest of that day she floated in a world where light blurred her vision into color patterns, where hysterical photographers and art directors existed in a distant place and nothing touched her.

Only later when she and Larry entered the world of the Nightwalkers did Lilia understand that what she'd felt had been just a small corner of the wonder of the Bite. At that point she also had not faced the horrid downside of withdrawal.

At Reliquary the night of the *Vogue* shoot, Lilia didn't notice Marguerite beside her until the old woman grabbed her hair and pulled her head down. With a tiny shears she snipped the leather choker on Lilia's neck and bit her long and deep.

"This is not a game for tourists and amateurs," she hissed as Lilia floated in a blood high. "You will not stand apart and be amused at the workings of my world."

Late that February, all was celebratory in the Savage Design conference room. Maison Herrault had triumphed in New York and Paris. The *Vogue* layout, all dark elegance and pale skin, was displayed on the walls.

Marguerite and the Kindly Ones were very pleased with their shares of the proceeds. Lilia sat as far away from everyone as possible. She floated on the remnants of the prior night's blood buzz and gazed at the artwork through sunglasses.

Under the photos were blocks of Felice's copy. One was: *Fashion is a cyclical phenomenon—the newest sensation withers but never dies.*

Another was: *An amazing top found in a vintage thrift store, a haircut seen in the old photo: we are fascinated and want more. A look, a style starts again.*

Paulo had a yo-yo in each hand. His left was slack, his right performed Shoot the Moon. "We found the boomlet and played it perfectly," he said. "By spring it will be nasty and we'll be nowhere nearby."

He turned to Marguerite. "It's always an inspiration to work with Maison Herrault."

Marguerite said, "An old vice gives comfort like any old habit." She got up slowly and went to the door. "Until next time."

The Kindly Ones rose, made little waves with their fingers, but kept their distance as the ancient woman exited.

"Remember us to M. Herrault," Felice said.

"In whatever corner of hell he occupies," Paulo added when Marguerite was gone. "Undying but at what cost?" The ancient voice wondered.

"Something to consider as old age closes in," said Katya.

They all looked relieved to turn and see Lilia also on her feet and clearly leaving. "Nice working with you," Paulo said in parting. "Maybe again someday."

Lilia glanced back to see Katya put her feet in glistening new ankle boots up on the table. They all picked up copies of a proposal.

Paulo's right hand kept on with Shoot the Moon, while his left began doing "Skyrocket to Mars." The yo-yos orbited around one another as he said, "Here's a related investment opportunity we might look at."

Reliquary was jumping, if that word could be used to describe the cold, covert way Nightwalkers shop for clothes and stalk each other for blood. In the crowded store, each one stared and got stared at from behind dark glasses.

Two cash registers were working. At one, Scarlet Jones wore a blood red scarf from Maison Herrault around her neck. Her face immobile, her skin dead white, fang tips visible though her mouth was closed, she racked up sales without seeming aware she was doing so. Bret more or less bagged the purchases.

Just as attractions the two were worth far more than they were paid and even a good deal more than they stole. Lilia calculated that around the start of the summer this would no longer be true.

By then Reliquary and the Vampire Revival would be edging their way into the limbo reserved for old fads, and she'd have accumulated a nest egg.

Already the store's customers were largely from New Jersey and outer boroughs. Complaints from the neighbors about the crowds were making her landlord nervous. Building and fire inspectors had put in their appearances, and an unmarked car with plainclothes cops sometimes parked across the street.

Lilia sat on a stool and watched it all through a mild haze. The trick, she told herself, was to keep the nips and bites small and the haze manageable. She remembered the bone-wracking horrors of withdrawal too well to want a repeat.

Just then Larry came in the door looking sloppy and vulnerable. He scanned the customers, all of whom ignored him.

Lilia and he had begun hanging around, talking over old times at CBGB's and the Mudd Club. She'd bitten him once or twice—playfully with a bit of vengeance thrown in. Her teeth were hardly fangs.

She wanted to make sure he didn't blow the money he got in the divorce settlement. While the Kindly Ones had said their goodbyes to Marguerite that last time at Savage Design, Lilia had managed to get a couple of glimpses of the investment proposal on their table.

They were involved in the development of a Betty Ford style clinic for vampires on an estate up the Hudson. Kids like Scarlet, Bret and many others had families able to pay for their recoveries.

Lilia intended to invest Larry's money. If that worked out, she might invest some of her own savings. He crossed the shop towards her and she watched his throat.

Certainly one of my best known stories, "If Angels Fight" won the World Fantasy Award for best novella of 2007, was on the Nebula Awards short list, and got reprinted in five Year's Best volumes—this last was a record which I believe still stands.

Parts are set in contemporary and bygone New York, in the Washington suburbs and even in Canada. But I believe it's the segments around Codman Square, in Dorchester, in Boston in the 1950s that seal the deal.

So much of this was pieces of memory I'd carted around with me. The perilous ledge around the District Courthouse, the rescue of the little kid on the Neponset River ice, the gradual alienation of the gay narrator, the overgrown vacant lot that was Fitzie's, Melville Avenue with its politicians' houses: all of that was used (repurposed I suppose we'd say now). The encounter with the young JFK sat unused for decades. Only years later did I consider the amount of nagging that Rose Kennedy, the ultimate Irish mother, must have expended to get her son to visit his aunt on her birthday.

Now I'm amazed it took me so long to find a use for this snippet.

Politics is the lifeblood of this story as it is with others of mine ("The Mask of the Rex" earlier in this book is one). It was there and then I learned it, not taught but in the air, possibly in the water, certainly in the bars. All very Irish and surviving now mostly in tellings like this one.

IF ANGELS FIGHT

1.

Outside the window, the blue water of the Atlantic danced in the sunlight of an early morning in October. They're short, quiet trains, the ones that roll through Connecticut just after dawn. I sipped bad tea, dozed off occasionally, and awoke with a start.

Over the last forty years, I've ridden the northbound train from New York to Boston hundreds of times. I've done it alone, with friends and lovers, going home for the holidays, setting out on vacations, on my way to funerals.

That morning, I was with one who was once in some ways my best friend and certainly my oldest. Though we had rarely met in decades, it seemed that a connection endured. Our mission was vital and we rode the train by default: a terrorist threat had closed traffic at Logan Airport in Boston the night before.

I'd left messages canceling an appointment, letting the guy I was going out with know I'd be out of town briefly for a family crisis. No need to say it was another, more fascinating, family disrupting my life, not mine.

The old friend caught my discomfort at what we were doing and was amused.

A bit of Shakespeare occurred to me when I thought of him:

Not all the water in the rough rude sea
Can wash the balm off from an anointed king

He was quiet for a while after hearing those lines. It was getting towards twenty-four hours since I'd slept. I must have dozed because suddenly I was in a dark place with two tiny slits of light high above. I found hand and foot holds and crawled up the interior wall of a stone tower. As I got to the slits of light, a voice said, "New Haven. This stop New Haven."

2.

Carol Bannon had called me less than two weeks before. "I'm going to be down in New York the day after tomorrow," she said. "I wondered if we could get together." I took this to mean that she and her family wanted to get some kind of fix on the present location and current state of her eldest brother, my old friend Mark.

Over the years when this had happened it was Marie Bannon, Mark and Carol's mother, who contacted me. Those times I'd discovered channels through which she could reach her straying son. This time, I didn't make any inquiries before meeting Carol, but I did check to see if certain parties still had the same phone numbers and habits that I remembered.

Thinking about Marky Bannon, I too wondered where he was. He's always somewhere on my mind. When I see a photo of some great event, a reception, or celebrity trial, a concert or inauguration— I scan the faces, wondering if he's present.

I'm retired these days, with time to spend. But over the years, keeping tabs on the Bannons was an easy minor hobby. The mother is still alive, though not very active now. The father was a longtime Speaker of the Massachusetts House and a candidate for governor who died some years back. An intersection in Dorchester and an entrance to the Boston Harbor tunnel are still named for him.

Carol, the eldest daughter, got elected to the City Council at the age of twenty-eight. Fourteen years later she gave up a safe U.S. House seat to run the Commerce Department for Clinton. Later she served on the 9/11 commission and is a perennial cable TV talking head. She's married to Jerry Simone, who has a stake in Google. Her brother Joe is a leading campaign consultant in DC. Keeping up the idealistic end of things, her little sister Eileen is a member of Doctors Without Borders. My old friend Mark is the tragic secret without which no Irish family would be complete.

Carol asked me to meet her for tea uptown in the Astor Court of the St. Regis Hotel. I got there a moment after four. The Astor Court has a blinding array of starched white table cloths and gold chandeliers under a ceiling mural of soft, floating clouds.

Maybe her choice of meeting places was intentionally campy. Or maybe because I don't drink anymore she had hit upon this as an amusing spot to bring me.

Carol and I always got along. Even aged ten and eleven I was different enough from the other boys that I was nice to my friends' little sisters.

Carol has kept her hair chestnut but allowed herself fine gray wings. Her skin and teeth are terrific. The Bannons were what was called dark Irish when we were growing up in Boston in the 1950s. That meant they weren't so white that they automatically burst into flames on their first afternoon at the beach.

They're a handsome family. The mother is still beautiful in her eighties. Marie Bannon had been on the stage a bit before she married. She had that light and charm, that ability to convince you that her smile was for you alone that led young men and old to drop everything and do her bidding. Mike Bannon, the father, had been a union organizer before he went nights to law school, then got into politics. He had rugged good looks, blue eyes that would look right into you, and a fine smile that he could turn on and off and didn't often waste on kids.

"When the mood's upon him, he can charm a dog off a meat wagon," I remember a friend of my father's remarking. It was a time and place where politicians and race horses alike were scrutinized and handicapped.

The Bannon children had inherited the parents' looks and, in the way of politicians' kids, were socially poised. Except for Mark, who could look lost and confused one minute, oddly intense the next with eyes suddenly just like his father's.

Carol rose to kiss me as I approached the table. It seemed kind of like a Philip Marlowe moment: I imagined myself as a private eye, tough and amused, called in by the rich dame for help in a personal matter.

When I first knew Carol Bannon, she wore pigtails and cried because her big brother wouldn't take her along when we went to the playground. Recently there's been speculation everywhere that a distinguished Massachusetts senator is about to retire before his term ends. Carol Bannon is the odds-on favorite to be appointed to succeed him.

Then, once she's in the Senate, given that it's the Democratic Party we're talking about, who's to say they won't go crazy again and run one more Bay State politician for President in the wild hope that they've got another JFK?

Carol said, "My mother asked me to remember her to you."

I asked Carol to give her mother my compliments. Then we each said how good the other looked and made light talk about the choices of teas and the drop-dead faux Englishness of the place. We reminisced about Boston and the old neighborhood.

"Remember how everyone called that big overgrown vacant lot, Fitzie's?" I asked. The nickname had come from its being the site where the Fitzgerald mansion, the home of Honey Fitz, the old mayor of Boston once stood. His daughter, Rose, was mother to the Kennedy brothers.

"There was a marble floor in the middle of the trash and weeds," I said, "and everybody was sure the place was haunted."

"The whole neighborhood was haunted," she said. "There was that little old couple who lived down Melville Avenue from us. They knew my parents. He was this gossipy elf. He had held office back in the old days, and everyone called him The Hon Hen, short for 'the Honorable Henry.' She was a daughter of Honey Fitz. They were aunt and uncle of the Kennedy's."

Melville Avenue was and is a street where the houses are set back on lawns and the garages are converted horse barns. When we were young, doctors and prosperous lawyers lived there along with prominent saloon owners and politicians like Michael Bannon and his family.

Suddenly at our table in the Astor Court, the pots and plates, the Lapsing and scones, the marmalade, the clotted cream and salmon finger sandwiches, appeared. We were silent for a little while and I thought about how politics had seemed a common occupation for kids' parents in Irish Boston. Politicians' houses tended to be big and semi-public with much coming and going and loud talk.

Life at the Bannons' was much more exciting than at my house. Mark had his own room and didn't have to share with his little broth-

er. He had a ten-year-old's luxuries: electronic football, enough soldiers to fight Gettysburg if you didn't mind that the Confederates
were mostly Indians, and not one but two electric train engines which
made wrecks a positive pleasure. Mark's eyes would come alive
when the cars flew off the tracks in a rainbow of sparks.

"What are you smiling at?" Carol asked.

And I cut to the chase and said, "Your brother. I remember the
way he liked to leave his room. That tree branch right outside his
window: he could reach out, grab hold of it, scramble hand over hand
to the trunk."

I remembered how the branches swayed and sighed and how
scared I was every time I had to follow him.

"In high school," Carol said, "at night he'd sneak out when he
was supposed to be in bed and scramble back inside much later. I
knew, and our mother, but no one else. One night the bough broke as
he tried to get back in the window. He fell all the way to the ground,
smashing through more branches on the way.

"My father was down in the study plotting malfeasance with
Governor Furcolo. They and everyone else came out to see what had
happened. We found Mark lying on the ground laughing like a lunatic. He had a fractured arm and a few scratches. Even I wondered if
he'd fallen on his head."

For a moment I watched for some sign that she knew I'd been
right behind her brother when he fell. I'd gotten down the tree fast
and faded into the night when I saw lights come on inside the house.
It had been a long, scary night, and before he laughed Mark had started to sob.

Now that we were talking about her brother, Carol was able to
say, almost casually, "My mother has her good days and her bad days.
But for thirty years she's hinted to me that she had a kind of contact
with him. I didn't tell her that wasn't possible because it obviously
meant a lot to her."

She was maintaining a safe zone, preserving her need not to
know. I frowned and fiddled with a sliver of cucumber on buttered
brown bread.

Carol put on a full court press. "Mom wants to see Mark again
and she thinks it needs to be soon. She told me you knew people and
could arrange things. It would make her so happy if you could do
whatever that was again."

I too kept my distance. "I ran some errands for your mother a couple of times that seemed to satisfy her. The last time was fourteen years ago and at my age I'm not sure I can even remember what I did."

Carol gave a rueful little smile. "You were my favorite of all my brother's friends. You'd talk to me about my dollhouse. It took me years to figure out why that was. When I was nine and ten years old I used to imagine you taking me out on dates."

She reached across the table and touched my wrist. "If there's any truth to any of what Mom says, I could use Mark's help too. You follow the news.

"I'm not going to tell you the current administration wrecked the world all by themselves or that if we get back in it will be the second coming of Franklin Roosevelt and Abe Lincoln all rolled into one.

"I am telling you I think this is end game. We either pull ourselves together in the next couple of years or we become Disneyworld."

I didn't tell her I thought we had already pretty much reached the stage of the U.S. as theme park.

"It's not possible that Mark's alive," she said evenly. "But his family needs him. None of us inherited our father's gut instincts, his political animal side. It may be a mother's fantasy, but ours says Mark did."

I didn't wonder aloud if the one who had been Marky Bannon still existed in any manifestation we'd recognize.

Then Carol handed me a very beautiful check from a consulting firm her husband owned. I told her I'd do whatever I could. Someone had said about Carol, "She's very smart and she knows all the rules of the game. But I'm not sure the game these days has anything to do with the rules."

3.

After our little tea, I thought about the old Irish American city of my childhood and how ridiculous it was for Carol Bannon to claim no knowledge of Mark Bannon. It reminded me of the famous Bulger brothers of South Boston.

You remember them: William Bulger was first the President of the State Senate and then the President of the University of

Massachusetts. Whitey Bulger was head of the Irish mob, a murderer and an FBI informant gone bad. Whitey was on the lam for years. Bill always claimed, even under oath, that he never had any contact with his brother.

That had always seemed preposterous to me. The Bulgers' mother was alive. And a proper Irish mother will always know what each of her children are doing no matter how they hide. And she'll bombard the others with that information no matter how much they don't want to know. I couldn't imagine Mrs. Bannon not doing that.

What kept the media away from the story was that Mark had—in all the normal uses of the terms—died, been waked and memorialized some thirty-five years ago.

I remembered how in the Bannon family the father adored Carol and her sister Eileen. He was even a tiny bit in awe of little Joe who, at the age of six, already knew the name and political party of the governor of each state in the union. But Michael Bannon could look very tired when his eyes fell on Mark.

The ways of Irish fathers with their sons were mysterious and often distant. Mark was his mother's favorite. But he was, I heard it whispered, dull normal, a step above retarded.

I remembered the way the Bannons' big house could be full of people I didn't know and how all the phones—the Bannons were the only family I knew with more than one phone in their house—could be ringing at once.

Mike Bannon had a study on the first floor. One time when Mark and I went past, I heard him in there saying, "We got the quorum. Now who's handling the seconding speech?" We went up to Mark's room and found two guys there. One sat on the bed with a portable typewriter on his lap, pecking away. The other stood by the window and said, ". . . real estate tax that's fair for all."

"For everybody," said the guy with the typewriter, "Sounds better." Then they noticed we were there and gave us a couple of bucks to go away.

Another time, Mark and I came back from the playground to find his father out on the front porch talking to the press who stood on the front lawn. This, I think, was when he was elected Speaker of the Lower House of the Great and General Court of the Commonwealth of Massachusetts, as the state legislature was called.

It was for moments like these that Speaker Bannon had been created. He smiled and photographers' flashes went off. Then he glanced in his son's direction, the penetrating eyes dimmed, the smile faded. Remembering this, I wondered what he saw.

After it was over, when his father and the press had departed, Mark went right on staring intently at the spot where it had happened. I remember thinking that he looked kind of like his father at that moment.

One afternoon around then the two of us sat on the rug in the TV room and watched a movie about mountain climbers scaling the Himalayas. Tiny black and white figures clung to ropes, made their way single file across glaciers, huddled in shallow crevices as high winds blew past.

It wasn't long afterwards that Mark, suddenly intense, led me and a couple of other kids along a six inch ledge that ran around the courthouse in Codman Square.

The ledge was a couple of feet off the ground at the front of the building. We sidled along, stumbling once in a while, looking in the windows at the courtroom where a trial was in session. We turned the corner and edged our way along the side of the building. Here we faced the judge behind his raised desk. At first he didn't notice. Then Mark smiled and waved.

The judge summoned a bailiff, pointed to us. Mark sidled faster and we followed him around to the back of the building. At the rear of the courthouse was a sunken driveway that led to a garage. The ledge was a good sixteen feet above the cement. My hands began to sweat but I was smart enough not to look down.

The bailiff appeared, told us to halt and go back. The last kid in line, eight years old where the rest of us were ten, froze where he was and started to cry.

Suddenly the summer sunshine went gray and I was inching my way along an icy ledge hundreds of feet up a sheer cliff.

After a moment that vision was gone. Cops showed up, parked their car right under us to cut the distance we might fall. A crowd, mostly kids, gathered to watch the fire department bring us down a ladder. When we were down, I turned to Mark and saw that his concentration had faded.

"My guardian angel brought us out here," he whispered.

The consequences were not severe. Mark was a privileged character and that extended to his confederates. When the cops drove us up to his house, Mrs. Bannon came out and invited us all inside. Soon the kitchen was full of cops drinking spiked coffee like it was St. Patrick's Day, and our mothers all came by to pick us up and laugh about the incident with Mrs. Bannon.

Late that same summer, I think, an afternoon almost at the end of vacation, the two of us turned onto Melville Avenue and saw Cadillacs double parked in front of the Hon Hen's house. A movie camera was set up on the lawn. A photographer stood on the porch. We hurried down the street.

As we got there, the front door flew open and several guys came out laughing. The camera started to film, the photographer snapped pictures. Young Senator Kennedy was on the porch. He turned back to kiss his aunt and shake hands with his uncle.

He was thin with reddish brown hair and didn't seem entirely adult. He winked as he walked past us and the cameras clicked away. A man in a suit got out of a car and opened the door, the young senator said, "OK, that's done."

As they drove off, the Hon Hen waved us up onto the porch, brought out dishes of ice cream. It was his wife's birthday and their nephew had paid his respects.

A couple of weeks later, after school started, a story with plenty of pictures appeared in the magazine section of the Globe: a day in the life of Senator Kennedy. Mark and I were in the one of him leaving his aunt's birthday. Our nun, Sister Mary Claire, put the picture up on the bulletin board.

The rest of the nuns came by to see. The other kids resented us for a few days. The Cullen brothers, a mean and sullen pair, motherless and raised by a drunken father, hated us for ever after.

I saw the picture again a few years ago. Kennedy's wearing a full campaign smile, I'm looking at the great man, open mouthed. Mark stares at the camera so intently that he seems ready to jump right off the page.

4.

The first stop on my search for Mark Bannon's current whereabouts was right in my neighborhood. It's been said about Greenwich Village that here time is all twisted out of shape like an abstract metal sculpture: past, present and future intertwine.

Looking for that mix, the first place I went was Fiddler's Green way east on Bleecker Street. Springsteen sang at Fiddler's and Madonna waited tables before she became Madonna. By night it's a tourist landmark and a student magnet, but during the day it's a little dive for office workers playing hooky and old village types in search of somewhere dark and quiet.

As I'd hoped, "Daddy Frank" Parnelli, with eyes like a drunken hawk's and sparse white hair cropped like a drill sergeant's, sipped a beer in his usual spot at the end of the bar. Once the legend was that he was where you went when you wanted yesterday's mistake erased or needed more than just a hunch about tomorrow's market.

Whether any of that was ever true, now none of it is. The only thing he knows these days is his own story, and parts of that he can't tell to most people. I was an exception.

We hadn't talked in a couple of years, but when he saw me he grimaced and asked, "Now what?" like I pestered him every day.

"Seemed like you might be here and I thought I'd stop by and say hello."

"Real kind of you to remember an old sadist."

I'm not that much younger than he is, but over the years, I've learned a thing or two about topping from Daddy Frank. Like never giving a bottom an even break. I ordered a club soda and pointed for the bartender to fill Daddy Frank's empty shot glass with whatever rye he'd been drinking.

Daddy stared at it like he was disgusted, then took a sip and another. He looked out the window. Across the street, a taxi let out an enormously fat woman with a tiny dog. Right in front of Fiddler's, a crowd of smiling Japanese tourists snapped pictures of each other.

A bearded computer student sat about halfway down the bar from us with a gin and tonic and read what looked like a thousand page book. A middle-aged man and his wife studied the signed photos on the walls while quietly singing scraps of songs to each other.

Turning back to me with what might once have been an enigmatic smile, Daddy Frank said, "You're looking for Mark Bannon."

"Yes."

"I have no fucking idea where he is," he said. "Never knew him before he appeared in my life. Never saw him again when he was through with me."

I waited, knowing this was going to take a while. When he started talking, the story wasn't one that I knew.

"Years ago, in Sixty-nine, maybe Seventy, its like, two in the afternoon on Saturday, a few weeks before Christmas. I'm in a bar way west on Fourteenth Street near the meat packing district. McNally's maybe or the Emerald Gardens, one of them they used to have over there that all looked alike. They had this bartender with one arm, I remember. He'd lost the other one on the docks."

"Making mixed drinks must have been tough," I said.

"Anyone asked for one, he came at them with a baseball bat. Anyway, the time I'm telling you about, I'd earned some money that morning bringing discipline to someone who hadn't been brought up right. I was living with a bitch in Murray Hill. But she had money and I saw no reason to share.

"I'm sitting there and this guy comes in wearing an overcoat with the collar pulled up. He's younger than me but he looks all washed out like he's been on a long complicated bender. No one I recognized, but people there kind of knew him."

I understood what was being described and memory supplied a face for the stranger.

"He sits down next to me. Has this piece he wants to unload, a cheap 32. It has three bullets in it. He wants ten bucks. Needs the money to get home to his family. I look down and see I still have five bucks left."

I said, "A less stand up guy might have wondered what happened to the other three bullets."

"I saw it as an opportunity. As I look back I see, maybe, it was a test. I offer the five and the stranger sells me the piece. So now I have a gun and no money. All of a sudden the stranger comes alive, smiles at me and I feel a lot different. With a purpose, you know?

"With the buzz I had, I didn't even wonder why this was. All I knew was I needed to put the piece to use. That was when I thought of Klein's. The place I was staying was over on the East Side and it was on my way home. You remember Klein's Department Store?"

"Sure on Union Square. KLEIN'S ON THE SQUARE was the motto and they had a big neon sign of a right angle ruler out front."

"Great fucking bargains. Back when I was six and my mother wanted to dress me like a little asshole, that's where she could do it cheap. As a kid I worked there as a stock boy. I knew they kept all the receipts, whatever they took in, up on the top floor, and that they closed at six on Saturdays."

As he talked, I remembered the blowsy old Union Square, saw the tacky Christmas lights, the crowds of women toting shopping bags, and young Frank Parnelli cutting his way through them on his way to Klein's.

"It's so simple I do it without thinking. I go up to the top floor like I have some kind of business. It's an old-fashioned store way back when people used cash. Security is one old guy wearing glasses. I go in the refund line and when I get up to the counter, I pull out the gun. The refunds ladies all soil their panties.

"I clean the place out. Thousands of bucks in a shopping bag and I didn't even have to go out of my way. I run down the stairs and nobody stops me. It's dark outside and I blend in with the crowd. As I walk down Fourteenth, the guy from the bar who sold me the gun is walking beside me.

"Before he looked beat. Now it's like the life has been sucked out of him and he's the living dead. But you know what? I have a locker at Grammercy Gym near Third Ave. I go in there so I can change from my leathers into a warm up jacket and a baseball cap. Like it's the most natural thing, I give the guy a bunch of bills. He goes off to his family. I don't ever see him again.

"I'm still drunk and amazed. That night I'm on a plane. Next day I'm in L.A. Both of those things for the first time. After that I'm not in this world half the time. Not this world like I thought it was anyway. And somewhere in those first days, I realized I wasn't alone inside my own head. A certain Mark Bannon was in there too."

I looked down the bar. The student was drinking his gin, turning his pages. The couple had stopped singing and were sitting near the window. The bartender was on his cell phone. I signaled and he refilled Frank's glass.

"It was a wild ride for a few years," Daddy Frank said. "We hitched up with Red Ruth, who ran us both ragged. She got us into politics in the Caribbean: Honduras, Nicaragua, stuff I still can't talk about, Ruth and me and Bannon.

"Then she got tired of us, I got tired of having Mark Bannon on the brain, and he got tired of me being me. It happens."

He leaned his elbow on the bar and had one hand over his eyes. "What is it? His mother looking for him again? I met her that first time when she had you find him. She's a great lady."

"Something like that," I said. "Anyone else ask you about Mark Bannon recently?"

"A couple of weeks ago someone came around asking questions. He said he has like a news show on the computer. Paul Revere is his name? Something like that. He came on like he knew something. But a lot smarter guys than him have tried to mix it up with me."

"No one else has asked?"

He shook his head.

"Anything you want me to tell Marky if I should see him?"

Without taking his hand away from his eyes, Daddy Frank raised the other, brought the glass to his lips and drained it. "Tell him it's been thirty years and more and I was glad when he left but I've been nothing but a bag of muscles and bones ever since."

5.

As evening falls in the South Village, the barkers come out. On opposite corners of the cross streets they stand with their spiels and handbills.

"Come hear the brightest song writers in New York," said an angry young man handing me a flyer.

A woman with snakes and flowers running up and down her arms and legs insisted, "You have just hit the tattoo jackpot!"

"Sir you look as if you could use a good . . . laugh," said a small African American queen outside a comedy club.

I noticed people giving the little sidelong glances that New Yorkers use when they spot a celebrity. But when I looked there was no one I recognized. That happens to me a lot these days.

Thinking about Mark Bannon and Frank Parnelli, I wondered if he just saw Frank as a vehicle with a tougher body and a better set of reflexes than his own? Did he look back with fondness when they parted company? Was it the kind of nostalgia you might have for a favorite horse or your first great car?

It was my luck to have known Mark when he was younger and his "guardian angel" was less skilled than it became. One Saturday when we were fourteen or so, going to different high schools and drifting apart, he and I were in a hockey free-for-all down on the Neponset River.

It was one of those silver and black winter Saturday afternoons when nothing was planned. A pack of kids from our neighborhood was looking for ice to play on. Nobody was ever supposed to swim or skate on that water, so that's where a dozen of us headed.

We grabbed a stretch of open ice a mile or so from where the Neponset opens onto the Nantasket Roads, the stretch of water that connects Boston Harbor to the Atlantic Ocean. Our game involved shoving a battered puck around and plenty of body checks. Mark was on my team but seemed disconnected like he was most of the time.

The ice was thick out in the middle of the river but old and scarred and rutted by skates and tides. Along the shore where it was thin, the ice had been broken up at some points.

Once I looked around and saw that some kids eight or nine years old were out on the ice in their shoes jumping up and down, smashing through it and jumping away laughing when they did. There was a whir of skates behind me and I got knocked flat.

I was the smallest guy my age in the game. Ice chips went up the legs of my jeans and burned my skin. When I got my feet under me again, the little kids were yelling. One of them was in deep water holding onto the ice which kept breaking as he grabbed it.

Our game stopped and everyone stood staring. Then Mark came alive. He started forward and beckoned me, one of the few times he'd noticed me that afternoon. As I followed him, I thought I heard the words "Chain-Of-Life." It was a rescue maneuver that, maybe, Boy Scouts practiced but I'd never seen done.

Without willing it, I suddenly threw myself flat and was on my stomach on the ice. Mark was down on the ice behind me and had hold of my ankles. He yelled at the other guys for two of them to grab his ankles and four guys to grab theirs. I was the point of a pyramid.

Somehow I grabbed a hockey stick in my gloved hands. My body slithered forward on the ice and my arms held the stick out toward the little kid. Someone else was moving my body.

The ice here was thin. There was water on top of it. The kid grabbed the stick. I felt the ice moving under me, hands pulled my legs.

I gripped the stick. At first the kid split the ice as I pulled him along. I wanted to let go and get away before the splitting ice engulfed me too.

But I couldn't. I had no control over my hands. Then the little kid reached firm ice. Mark pulled my legs and I pulled the kid. His stomach bounced up onto the ice and then his legs. Other guys grabbed my end of the stick, pulled the kid past me.

I stood and Mark was standing also. The little boy was being led away, soaked and crying, water sloshing in his boots. Suddenly I felt the cold—the ice inside my pants and up the sleeves of my sweater—and realized what I'd done.

Mark Bannon held me up, pounded my back. "We did it! You and me!" he said. His eyes were alive and he looked like he was possessed. "I felt how scared you were when the ice started to break." And I knew this was Mark's angel talking.

The other guys clustered around us yelling about what we'd done. I looked up at the gray sky, at a freighter in the distance sailing up the Roads towards Boston Harbor. It was all black and white like television, and my legs buckled under me.

Shortly afterwards as evening closed in, the cops appeared and ordered everybody off the ice. That night, a little feverish, I dreamed and cried out in my sleep about ice and TV.

No adult knew what had happened, but every kid did. Monday at school, ones who never spoke to me asked about it. I told them even though it felt like it had happened to someone else. And that feeling, I think, was what the memory of his years with Mark Bannon must have been like for Daddy Frank.

6.

As soon as Frank Parnelli started talking about Paul Revere, I knew who he meant and wasn't surprised. I called Desmond Eliot and he wasn't surprised to hear from me either. Back when I first knew Des Eliot, he and Carol Bannon went to Harvard/Radcliffe and were dating each other. Now he operates the political blog, *Midnight Ride: Spreading the Alarm.*

A few days later, I sat facing Eliot in his home office in suburban Maryland. I guess he could work in his pajamas if he wanted to. But, in fact, he was dressed and shaved and ready to ride.

He was listening to someone on the phone and typing on a keyboard in his lap. Behind him were a computer and a TV with the sound turned off. The screen showed a runway in Jordan where the smoking ruins of a passenger plane were still being hosed down with chemicals. Then a Republican senator with Presidential ambitions looked very serious as he spoke to reporters in Washington.

A brisk Asian woman, who had introduced herself as June, came into the office, collected the outgoing mail, and departed. A fax hummed in the corner. Outside, it was a sunny day and the trees had just begun to turn.

"Yes, I saw the dust up at the press conference this morning," he said into the phone. "The White House, basically, is claiming the Democrats planted a spy in the Republican National Committee. If I thought anyone on the DNC had the brains and chutzpa to do that I'd be cheering."

At that moment Des was a relatively happy man. *Midnight Ride* is, as he puts it, "A tool of the disloyal opposition," and right now things are going relatively badly for the administration.

He hung up and told me, "Lately every day is a feast. This must be how the right wing felt when Clinton was up to his ass in blue dresses and cigars." As he spoke he typed on a keyboard, probably the very words he was uttering.

He stopped typing, put his feet up on a coffee table and looked out over his half frame glasses. His contacts with the Bannons go way back. It bothers him that mine go back further.

"You come all the way down here to ask me about Mark Bannon," he said. "My guess is it's not for some personal memoir like you're telling me. I think the family is looking for him and thinks I may have spotted him like I did with Svetlanov."

I shook my head like I didn't understand.

"Surely you remember. It was twenty years ago. No, a bit more. Deep in the Reagan years. Glasnost and Perestroika weren't even rumors. The Soviet Union was the Evil Empire. I was in Washington, writing for *The Nation*, consulting at a couple of think tanks, going out with Lucia, an Italian sculptress. Later on I was married to her for about six months.

"There was a Goya show at the Corcoran that Lucia wanted to see. We'd just come out of one of the galleries and there was this guy I was sure I'd never seen before, tall, prematurely gray.

"There was something very familiar about him. Not his looks, but something. When he'd talk to the woman he was with whatever I thought I'd recognized didn't show. Then he looked my way and it was there again. As I tried to place him, he seemed like he was trying to remember me.

"Then I realized it was his eyes. At moments they had the same uncanny look that Mark Bannon's could get when I first knew him. Of course by then Mark had been dead for about thirteen years.

"Lucia knew who this was: a Russian art dealer named Georgi Svetlanov, the subject of rumors and legends. Each person I asked about him had a different story: he was a smuggler, a Soviet agent, a forger, a freedom fighter."

Eliot said, "It stuck with me enough that I mentioned it the next time I talked to Carol. She was planning a run for congress and I was helping. Carol didn't seem that interested.

"She must have written the name down, though. I kept watch on Svetlanov. Even aside from the Bannon connection he was interesting. Mrs. Bannon must have thought so too. He visited her a few times that I know of."

Marie Bannon had gotten in touch with me and mentioned this Russian man someone had told her about. She had the name and I did some research, found out his itinerary. At a major opening at the Shifrazi Gallery in Soho, I walked up to a big steely-haired man who seemingly had nothing familiar about him at all.

"Mark Bannon," I said quietly but distinctly.

At first the only reaction was Svetlanov looking at me like I was a bug. He sneered and began to turn away. Then he turned back and the angel moved behind his eyes. He looked at me hard, trying to place me.

I handed him my card. "Mark Bannon, your mother's looking for you," I said. "That's her number on the back." Suddenly eyes that were very familiar looked right into mine.

Des told me, "I saw Svetlanov after that in the flesh and on TV. He was in the background at Riga with Reagan and Gorbachev. I did quite a bit of research and discovered Frank Parnelli among other things. My guess is that Mark Bannon's . . . spirit or subconscious or whatever it is—was elsewhere by 1992 when Svetlanov died in an auto accident. Was I right?"

In some ways I sympathized with Eliot. I'd wondered about that too. And lying is bad. You get tripped by a lie more often than by the truth.

But I looked him in the face and said, "Mark wasn't signaling anybody from deep inside the skull of some Russian, my friend. You were at the wake, the funeral, the burial. Only those without a drop of Celtic blood believe there's any magic in the Irish."

He said, "The first time I noticed you was at that memorial service. Everyone else stood up and tiptoed around the mystery and disaster that had been his life. Then it was your turn and you quoted Shakespeare. Said he was a ruined king. You knew he wasn't really dead."

"Des, it was 1971. Joplin, Hendrix. Everyone was dying young. I was stoned, I was an aspiring theater person and very full of myself. I'd intended to recite Dylan Thomas' 'Do Not Go Gentle,' but another drunken Mick beat me to that.

"So I reared back and gave them *Richard the Second,* which I'd had to learn in college. Great stuff:

'Not all the water in the rough rude sea
Can wash the balm off from an anointed king;
The breath of worldly men cannot depose
The deputy elected by the Lord'

"As I remember," I said, "The contingent of nuns who taught Mark and me in school was seated down front. When I reached the lines:

'. . . if angels fight,
Weak men must fall . . .'

"They looked very pleased about the angels fighting. Booze and bravura is all it was," I said.

Partly that was true. I'd always loved the speech, maybe because King Richard and I share a name. But also it seemed so right for Mark. In the play, a king about to loose his life and all he owns on earth invokes royal myth as his last hope.

"When I was dating Carol I heard the legends," Des told me. "She and her sister talked about how the family had gotten him into some country club school in New Jersey. He was expelled in his third week for turning the whole place on and staging an orgy that got the college president fired.

"They said how he'd disappear for weeks and Carol swore that once when he came stumbling home, he'd mumbled to her months before it happened that King and Bobby Kennedy were going to be shot.

"Finally, I was at the Bannons with Carol when the prodigal

returned and it was a disappointment. He seemed mildly retarded, a burnout at age twenty-five. I didn't even think he was aware I existed.

"I was wrong about that. Mark didn't have a license or a car anymore. The second or third day he was back, Carol was busy. I was sitting on the sun porch, reading. He came out, smiled this sudden, magnetic smile just like his old man's and asked if that was my Ford two door at the end of the driveway.

"Without his even asking, I found myself giving him a lift. A few days later, I woke up at a commune in the Green Mountains in New Hampshire with no clear idea of how I'd gotten there. Mark was gone, and all the communards could tell me was, 'He enters and leaves as he wishes.'

"When I got back to Boston, Carol was pissed. We made up, but in a lot of ways it was never the same. Not even a year or two later when Mike Bannon ran for governor and I worked my ass off on the campaign.

"Mark was back home all the time then, drinking, taking drugs, distracting the family, especially his father, at a critical time. His eyes were empty and no matter how long everyone waited, they stayed that way. After the election he died, maybe as a suicide. But over the years I've come to think that didn't end the story."

It crossed my mind that Eliot knew too much. I said, "You saw them lower him into the ground."

"It's Carol who's looking this time isn't it?" he asked. "She's almost there as a national candidate. Just a little too straight and narrow. Something extra needs to go in the mix. Please tell me that's going to happen."

A guy in his fifties looking for a miracle is a sad sight. One also sporting a college kid's crush is sadder still.

"Just to humor you, I'll say you're right," I told him. "What would you tell me my next step should be?"

The smile came off his face. "I have no leads," he said. "No source who would talk to me knows anything."

"But some wouldn't talk to you," I said.

"The only one who matters won't. She refuses to acknowledge my existence. It's time you went to see Ruth Vega."

7.

I was present on the night the angel really flew. It was in the summer of '59 when they bulldozed the big overgrown lot where the Fitzgerald mansion had once stood. Honey Fitz's place had burned down just twenty years before. But to kids my age, Fitzie's was legendary ground, a piece of untamed wilderness that had existed since time out of mind.

I was finishing my sophomore year in high school when they cleared the land. The big old trees that must have stood on the front lawn, the overgrown apple orchard in the back, were chopped down and their stumps dug up.

The scraggly new trees, the bushes where we hid smeared in war paint on endless summer afternoons waiting for hapless smaller kids to pass by and get massacred, the half flight of stone stairs that ended in midair, the marble floor with moss growing through the cracks, all disappeared.

In their place a half dozen cellars were dug and houses were built. We lost the wild playground but we'd already outgrown it. For that one summer we had half finished houses to hide out in.

Marky and I got sent to different high schools outside the neighborhood and had drifted apart. Neither of us did well academically and we both ended up in the same summer school. So we did hang out one more time. Nights especially we sat with a few guys our age on unfinished wood floors with stolen beer and cigarettes and talked very large about what we'd seen and done out in the wide world.

That's what four of us were up to in a raw wood living room by the light of the moon and distant street lamps. Suddenly a flashlight shone in our faces and someone yelled, "Hands over your heads. Up against the wall."

For a moment, I thought it was the cops and knew they'd back off once they found out Marky was among us. In fact it was much worse: the Cullen brothers and a couple of their friends were there. In the dim light I saw a switchblade.

We were foul mouthed little twerps with delusions of delinquency. These were the real thing: psycho boys raised by psycho parents. A kid named Johnny Kilty was the one of us nearest the door.

Teddy—the younger, bigger, more rabid Cullen brother—pulled Johnny's T-shirt over his head, punched him twice in the stomach and emptied his pockets.

Larry, the older, smarter, scarier Cullen, had the knife and was staring right at Marky. "Hey, look who we got!" he said in his toneless voice. "Hands on your head, faggot. This will be fucking hilarious."

Time paused as Mark Bannon stared back slack jawed. Then his eyes lit up and he smiled like he saw something amazing.

As that happened, my shirt got pulled over my head. My watch was taken off my wrist. Then I heard Larry Cullen say without inflection, "This is no good. Give them their stuff back. We're leaving."

The ones who held me let go; I pulled my T-shirt back on.

"What the fuck are you talking about?" Teddy asked.

"I gotta hurt you before you hear me?" Larry asked in dead tones. "Move before I kick your ass."

They were gone as suddenly as they appeared, though I could hear Teddy protesting as they went through the construction site and down the street. "Have you gone bird shit stupid?" he asked. I didn't hear Larry's reply.

We gathered our possessions. The other guys suddenly wanted very badly to be home with their parents. Only I understood that Mark had saved us. When I looked, he was staring vacantly. He followed us out of the house and onto the sidewalk.

"I need to go home," he whispered to me like a little kid who's lost. "My angel's gone," he said.

It was short of midnight though well past my curfew when I walked Marky home. But outside of noise and light from the bars in Codman Square, the streets were quiet and traffic was sparse. I tried to talk, but Marky shook his head. His shoes seemed to drag on the pavement. He was a lot bigger than me, but I was leading him.

Lights were on at his place when we got there and cars were parked in the driveway. "I need to go in the window," he mumbled and we went around back. He slipped as he started to climb the tree and it seemed like a bad idea. But up he went and I was right behind him.

When the bough broke with a crack, he fell smashing through other branches and I scrambled back down the trunk. The lights came on but I got away before his family and the governor of the

Commonwealth came out to find him on the ground laughing hysterically.

The next day, I was in big trouble at home. But I managed to go visit Mark. On the way, I passed Larry Cullen walking away from the Bannons' house. He crossed the street to avoid me.

Mark was in bed with a broken wrist and a bandage on his leg. The light was on in his eyes and he wore the same wild smile he'd had when he saw Larry Cullen. We both knew what had happened but neither had words to describe it. After that, Mark and I tended to avoid each other.

Then my family moved away from the neighborhood and I forgot about the Bannons pretty much on purpose. So it was a surprise years later when I came home for Christmas that my mother said Mark Bannon wanted to speak to me.

"His mother called and asked about you," she said. "I've heard that Mark is in an awful way. They say Mike Bannon's taken that harder than loosing the governorship."

My father looked up from the paper and said, "Something took it out of Bannon. He sleepwalked through the campaign. And when it started he was the favorite."

Curiosity, if nothing else, led me to visit Mark. My parents now lived in the suburbs and I lived in New York. But the Bannons were still on Melville Avenue.

Mrs. Bannon was so sad when she smiled and greeted me that I would have done anything she asked.

When I saw Mark, one of the things he said was, "My angel's gone and he's not coming back." I thought of the lost, scared kid I'd led home from Fitzie's that night. I realized I was the only one, except maybe his mother, that he could tell any of this to.

I visited him a few times when I'd be up seeing my family. Mostly he was stoned on pills and booze and without the angel he seemed lobotomized. Sometimes we just watched television like we had as kids.

He told me about being dragged through strange and scary places in the world. "I guess he wasn't an angel. Or not a good one." Doctors had him on tranquilizers. Sometimes he slurred so badly I couldn't understand him.

Mike Bannon, out of office, was on committees and commissions and was a partner in a law firm. But he was home in his study a lot and the house was very quiet. Once as I was leaving, he called me in, asked me to sit down, offered me a drink.

He wondered how his son was doing. I said he seemed OK. We both knew this wasn't so. Bannon's face appeared loose, sagging.

He looked at me and his eyes flashed for a moment. "Most of us God gives certain . . . skills. They're so much a part of us we use them by instinct. We make the right move at the right moment and it's so smooth it's like someone else doing it.

"Marky had troubles but he also had moments like that. Someone told me the other day you and he saved a life down on the river when you were boys because he acted so fast. He's lost it now, that instinct. It's gone out like a light." It seemed he was trying to explain something to himself and I didn't know how to help him.

Mark died of an overdose, maybe an intentional one, and they asked me to speak at the memorial service. A few years later, Big Mike Bannon died. Someone in tribute said, "A superb political animal. Watching him in his prime rounding up a majority in the lower chamber was like seeing a cheetah run, an eagle soar . . ."

". . . a rattlesnake strike," my father added.

8.

A couple of days after my meeting with Des Eliot, I flew to Quebec. A minor border security kerfuffle between the U.S. and Canada produced delays at both Newark International and Jean Lesage International.

It gave me a chance to think about the first time I'd gone on one of these quests. Shortly after her husband's death, Mrs. Bannon had asked me to find Mark's angel.

A few things he'd told me when I'd visited, a hint or two his mother had picked up, allowed me to track one Frank Parnelli to the third floor of a walk-up in Washington Heights.

I knocked on the door, the eyehole opened, and a woman inside asked, "Who is it?"

"I'm looking for Ruth Vega."

"She's not here."

"I'm looking for Mark Bannon."

"Who?"

"Or for Frank Parnelli."

The eyehole opened again. I heard whispers inside. "This will be the man we had known would come," someone said, and the door opened.

Inside were statues and pictures and books everywhere: a black and white photo of Leon Trotsky, a woman's bowling trophy, and what looked like a complete set of Anna Freud's *The Psychoanalytic Study of The Child.*

A tiny old woman with bright red hair and a hint of amusement in her expression stood in the middle of the room looking at me. "McCluskey, where have you been?"

"That's not McCluskey, mother," said a much larger middle-aged woman in a tired voice.

"McCluskey from the Central Workers Council! Where's your cigar?" Suddenly she looked wise. "You're not smoking because of my big sister Sally, here. She hates them. I like a man who smokes a cigar. You were the one told me Woodrow Wilson was going to be president when I was a little kid. When it happened I thought you could foretell the future. Like I do."

"Why don't you sit down," the other woman said to me. "My niece is the one you're looking for. My mother's a little confused about past and present. Among other things."

"So McCluskey," said the old woman, "Who's it going to be next election? Roosevelt again, that old fascist?" I wondered whether she meant Teddy or FDR.

"I know who the Republicans are putting up," she said. It was 1975 and Gerald Ford was still drawing laughs by falling down stairs. I tried to look interested.

"That actor," she said. "Don Ameche. He'll beat the pants off President Carter. At that moment I'd never heard of Carter. "No not Ameche, the other one."

"Reagan?" I asked. I knew about him. Some years before he'd become governor of California, much to everyone's amusement.

"Yes, that's the one. See. Just the same way you told me about Wilson, you've told me about Reagan getting elected president."

"Would you like some tea while you wait?" asked the daughter, looking both bored and irritated.

We talked about a lot of things that afternoon. What I remembered some years later, of course, was the prediction about Reagan.

With the Vega family there were always hints of the paranormal along with a healthy dose of doubletalk.

At that moment the door of the walkup opened and a striking couple came in. He was a thug who had obviously done some boxing, with a nicely broken nose and a good suit. She was tall and in her late twenties with long legs in tight black pants, long red hair drawn back, a lot of cool distance in her green eyes.

At first glance the pair looked like a celebrity and her bodyguard. But the way Ruth Vega watched Frank Parnelli told me that somehow she was looking after him.

Parnelli stared at me. And a few years after I'd seen Marky Bannon's body lowered into the ground, I caught a glimpse of him in a stranger's eyes.

That was what I remembered when I was east of Quebec walking uphill from the Vibeau Island Ferry dock.

Des knew where Ruth was though he'd never actually dared to approach her. I believed if she wanted to stop me from seeing her, she would already have done it.

At a guess, Vibeau Island looked like an old fishing village that had become a summer vacation spot at some point in the mid-twentieth century and was now an exurb. Up here it was chilly even in the early afternoon.

I saw the woman with red hair standing at the end of a fishing pier. From a distance I thought Ruth Vega was feeding the ducks. Then I saw what she threw blow out onto the Saint Lawrence and realized she was tearing up papers and tossing them into the wind. On first glance, I would have said she looked remarkably as she had thirty years before.

I waited until I was close to ask, "What's wrong Ms Vega, your shredder broken?"

"McCluskey from the Central Workers Council," she said, and when she did, I saw her grandmother's face in hers. "I remember that first time we met, thinking that Mark's mother had chosen her operative well. You found her son and were very discreet about it."

We walked back to her house. It was a cottage with good sight lines in all directions and two large black schnauzers snarling in a pen.

"That first time was easy," I replied. "He remembered his family and wanted to be found. The second time was a few years later and that was much harder."

Ruth nodded. We sat in her living room. She had a little wine, I had some tea. The décor had a stark beauty, nothing unnecessary: a gun case, a computer, a Cy Twombly over the fireplace.

"The next time Mrs. Bannon sent me out to find her son, it was because she and he had lost touch. Frank Parnelli when I found him was a minor Village character. Mark no longer looked out from behind his eyes. He had no idea where you were. Your grandmother was a confused old woman wandering around her apartment in a nightgown.

"I had to go back to Mrs. Bannon and tell her I'd failed. It wasn't until a couple of years later that Svetlanov turned up."

"Mark and I were in love for a time," Ruth said. "He suggested jokingly once or twice that he leave Parnelli and come to me. I didn't want that, and in truth he was afraid of someone he wouldn't be able to control.

"Finally being around Parnelli grew thin and I stopped seeing them. Not long afterwards Mark abandoned Parnelli and we both left New York for different destinations. A few years later, I was living in the Yucatan and he showed up again. This time with an old acquaintance of mine.

"When I lived with grandmother as a kid, she was in her prime and all kinds of people were around. Political operatives, prophetesses, you name it. One was called Decker, this young guy with dark eyes and long dark hair like classical violinists wore. For a while he came around with some project on which he wanted my grandmother's advice. I thought he was very sexy. I was ten.

"Then he wasn't around the apartment. But I saw him: coming out of a bank, on the street walking past me with some woman. Once on a school trip to the United Nations Building, I saw him on the subway in a naval cadet's uniform.

"I got home that evening and my grandmother said, 'Have you seen that man Decker recently?' When I said yes, she told me to go do my homework and made a single very short phone call. Decker stopped appearing in my life.

"Until one night in Mexico, a knock came on my door and there he stood looking not a day older than when I'd seen him last. For a brief moment, there was a flicker in his eyes and I knew Mark was there but not in control.

"Decker could touch and twist another's mind with his. My grandmother, though, had taught me the chant against intrusive thoughts. Uncle Dano had taught me how to draw, aim and fire without even thinking about it.

"Killing is a stupid way to solve problems. But sometimes it's the only one. After Decker died, I played host to Mark for about an hour before I found someone else for him to ride. He was like a spark, pure instinct unfettered by a soul. That's changed somewhat."

When it was time for my ferry back to the city, Ruth rose and walked down to the dock with me.

"I saw his sister on TV the other night when they announced she would be appointed to the Senate. I take it she's the one who's looking for him?"

I nodded and she said, "Before too long idiot senators will be trying to lodge civil liberty complaints after martial law has been declared and the security squads are on their way to the capital to throw them in jail. Without Mark she'll be one of them."

Before I went up the gangplank, she hugged me and said, "You think you're looking for him but he's actually waiting for you."

After a few days back in New York, memories of Vibeau Island began to seem preposterous. Then I walked down my block late one night. It was crowded with tourists and college kids, barkers and bouncers. I saw people give the averted celebrity glance.

Then I spotted a black man with a round face and a shaven head. I did recognize him: an overnight hip hop millionaire. He sat in the back of a stretch limo with the door open. Our eyes met. His widened then dulled, and he sank back in his seat.

At that moment, I saw gray winter sky and felt the damp cold of the ice covered Neponset. *On old familiar ground,* said a voice inside me, and I knew Mark was back.

9.

Some hours later, passengers found seats as our train pulled out of New Haven.

"Ruth said you were waiting for me," I told Mark silently.

And Red Ruth is never wrong.

"She told me about Decker."

I thought I had selected him. But he had selected me. Once inside him I was trapped. He was a spider. I couldn't control him. Couldn't escape. I led him to Ruth as I was told.

He showed me an image of Ruth pointing an automatic pistol, firing at close range.

I leaped to her as he died. She was more relentless than Decker in some ways. I had to promise to make my existence worthwhile. To make the world better.

"If angels fight, weak men must fall."

Not exactly an angel. Ego? Id? Fragment? Parasite?

I thought of how his father had something like an angel himself. *His body, soul and mind were a single entity. Mine weren't.*

I saw his memory of Mike Bannon smiling and waving in the curved front windows of his house at well-wishers on the snowy front lawn. Bannon senior never questioned his own skills or wondered what would have happened if they'd been trapped in a brain that was mildly damaged. Then he saw it happen to his son.

When I thought that, I found myself in the dark tower again with two tiny slits of light high above. I found hand and foot holds and crawled up the interior stone walls. This time, I looked through the slits of light and saw they were the eyeholes of a mask. In front of me were Mike and Marie Bannon looking very young and startled by the sudden light in the eyes of their troublingly quiet little boy.

When the train approached Boston, the one inside me said, *Let's see the old neighborhood.*

We took a taxi from Back Bay and drove out to Dorchester. We saw the school we'd gone to and the courthouse and place where I'd lived and the houses that stood where Fitzie's had once been.

My first great escape.

That night so long ago came back. Larry Cullen, seen through the eyeholes of a mask, stood with his thin psycho smile. In a flash I saw Mark Bannon slack-jawed and felt Cullen's cold fear as the angel took hold of his mind and looked out through his eyes.

Cullen's life was all horror and hate. His father was a monster. It should have taught me something. Instead I felt like I'd broken out of jail. After each time away from my own body it was harder to go back.

Melville Avenue looked pretty much the way it always did. Mrs. Bannon still lived in the family house. We got out of the car and the one inside me said, *When all this is over, it won't be forgotten that you brought me back to my family.*

In the days since then, as politics has become more dangerous, Carol Bannon has grown bolder and wilier. And I wonder what form the remembering will take.

Mrs. Bannon's caregiver opened the door. We were expected. Carol stood at the top of the stairs very much in command. I thought of her father.

"My mother's waiting to see you," she said. I understood that I would spend a few minutes with Mrs. Bannon and then depart. Carol looked right into my eyes and kissed me. Her eyes flashed and she smiled.

In that instant the one inside my head departed. The wonderful sharpness went out of the morning and I felt a touch of the desolation that Mark Bannon and all the others must have felt when the angel deserted them.

COPYRIGHTS

ABOUT THE AUTHOR

Richard Bowes has lived in Manhattan for nearly 50 years. He has written fashion copy, worked at a library information desk, and sold antique toys in flea markets. He's also won a bunch of awards and has published six novels, seventy short stories and four story collections, including this volume you currently hold. You can learn more at his website Rickbowes.com

OTHER TITLES FROM FAIRWOOD/DARKWOOD PRESS

CPSIA information can be obtained at www.ICGtesting.com
Printed in the USA
BVOW08s2148051013

332971BV00002B/8/P